Ghosts of Midnights Past

JESSICA ARDEN

Ebook ISBN: 978-1-946188-02-1

Print ISBN: 978-1-946188-03-8

Published by Wayfarer

CONTENTS

CHAPTER 1

NEW YEAR'S EVE

EARLY AFTERNOON

Wendy Deveaux'd had her fill of spirits for the year. *Maybe for a whole lifetime*, she thought as she guided her last group of tour patrons down St. Peter Street through the throngs of revelers getting an early start on the New Year's festivities. But when your family's in the ghost tour business, spirits are sort of an occupational hazard.

Most of her tour groups were fine, but this afternoon she just couldn't with these people. First, a woman pulled a feint faint outside Hotel Provincial after proclaiming that in a past life she'd seen grisly horrors at the hospital previously on the site. She'd recovered quickly enough after the salt-and-pepper-haired gentlemen she'd been making eyes at since LaFitte's Blacksmith Shop helped her up and offered her the rest of his hurricane. On top of that, Wendy'd also had the joy of not one but three smartasses with bodies of twenty-year olds and senses of humor of twelve-year-old boys. If she heard one more Scooby Doo joke, she was going to do something that would really make them say, "Zoinks." And if anyone else told her she should see that new holiday movie *Wings of Love*, she was going to lose it.

But they were finally at the last stop. Five more minutes and she was free. She swerved around a group of college-aged girls in sparkly dresses and gathered the group around. Smartass number one made a snide comment and told Wendy to smile. Her urge to punch him in the face was curbed only by a desire not to sully their Yelp rating. She clenched and unclenched her fists. You can do anything for five minutes, Alec used to say. Listen to an awful band, try something new, fall in love.

The unexpected thought of him sent a wistful ache into her chest and stirred up a cocktail of uncomfortable emotions. It snuck up on her like this sometimes. Before her thoughts could wander into areas she'd blocked off with mental caution tape, she shook it off and launched into her final ghostly anecdote about another tragic love story.

Minutes later, after a goodbye and a silent good riddance, Wendy breathed a sigh of relief and forced her aching feet into Deveauxs' Historical Haunts' gift shop. She could use some spirits of the alcoholic variety to celebrate the end of two weeks of triple shifts, but that would have to wait. Her feet might stage a protest if she tried to walk to her car outside the French Quarter before resting for a bit.

Still trying to stave off further thoughts of Alec, she picked up a Voodoo doll key chain that had fallen on the floor. For all the crowds filling the streets talking about New Year's resolutions and drinking themselves to a happy new year, her shop was surprisingly empty save for a few people milling around. The stagnant air of patchouli and sage and dust hit her as she slipped inside—the scent at once comforting and stifling. She ambled down the aisle filled with gris-gris bags, various crystals, and books on French Quarter scandals, and felt her relieved smile fade into a frown. This shop was where her days had begun and ended for as long as she could remember. Everyone else seemed to be making New

Year's resolutions and moving along with life, but Wendy was still here. Mostly running the business end of things now that the doctors had ordered her dad to slow down after his bypass surgery, but still in the same place she'd always been.

She stopped to straighten the stand of brochures and business cards on the front counter that separated the store from the offices. Her mood lifted slightly at the sight of the logo and graphics—her own handiwork on display.

Perched on a stool near the register, Wendy's cousin Julie sighed and tapped a pen to her lips.

Wendy's shoulders relaxed a little more at the sight of her best friend and partner in ghost touring. "Ah, the only person I don't want to stab right now. How's the dissertation coming?"

Julie brushed back a curtain of wavy dark brown hair and looked up from her notebook.

"Ugh, don't ask. Slowly," she said, but her expression brightened as she looked up at Wendy. Though Wendy had inherited her mom's fiery auburn hair and fair skin, the Deveaux cousins looked so much alike they were often mistaken for sisters, especially when smirking. They had the same defiant curve to their hips, smart mouths and fondness for tall boots. But while Julie's footwear and demeanor said *come hither*, Wendy's stompy version warned to proceed with caution.

"Which do you think's a better title?" Julie asked. "Double Homicide, Double Cross, Double Espresso, or Anne Taylor Pantsuit is the New Orange is the New Black: Sophia Durocher's Life In Prison?"

"Definitely the second one." Wendy snorted and grabbed a bottle of water from the fridge behind the counter. "Maybe it wouldn't take so long if you didn't insist on writing everything out longhand."

"Hey, if it was good enough for Dickens and Voltaire, it's good enough for me."

Julie's fiancé Griffin emerged from the stockroom and sauntered up to the counter, his green eyes glinting. "Plus, you can't rush perfection." He set his tool bag down and slipped an arm around Julie's waist. She nuzzled into him.

Wendy rolled her eyes. "I think they can hear my groan in outer space."

But even though she protested, she let a wisp of amusement break through her resting scowl face. Despite her initial reservations about Griffin and her usual dislike of people in general, she had to admit he'd grown on her in the last few years. Sort of. A little.

"What were you doing in the stockroom, anyway?"

"Your dad asked me to fix the shelf that broke."

Wendy frowned. "I was going to do that." Eventually.

"He thought you could use a hand."

Julie set down her pen. "He also said something about how you need to get out of here sometimes. Maybe it was falling asleep in the mashed potatoes that tipped him off."

"Just because I care about our family business succeeding—" Wendy started.

"You *are* starting to get that eau de patchouli." Julie smelled the air and smirked at her.

Wendy sniffed and folded her arms across her chest, doing a mental calculation of how many hours she'd spent at the shop or doing tours the last three weeks. She'd done all the corporate event tours, all of Norman's tour shifts, and the payroll so Paige could have four days off at Christmas. Her aching calves reminded her she'd walked so much with extra tour shifts, she could probably do the Appalachian Trail without breaking a sweat. Except for the no shower and no restaurant thing. That would be a definite no-go. But still, yeah, she'd been here a lot lately.

"I almost forgot," Julie said, breaking Wendy out of her haze. "Norman and his new girlfriend dropped something off for you." A mischievous smile played at the corners of Julie's mouth, making Wendy's eyes narrow.

Julie reached behind the cash register and produced a forbidding-looking potted plant.

Wendy raised an eyebrow and lifted one of the waxy green mouths that looked like it wanted to bite anything in its path. The corners of her mouth curved upward. She could relate. Perched inside the pot were a craft store pear and a grey plastic bird.

"Aww, a man-eating plant. It looks just like you," Griffin said.

Wendy shot him a glare. "And I was just starting not to hate you."

Julie passed her a card. "This came with it."

Inside, her employee Norman's barely legible handwriting corrected the pre-packaged message.

On the first day of Christmas, my true love third favorite employee gave to me a partridge bird of indeterminate species in a pear tree.

Wendy shook her head, a smile cracking through her fatigue, and she flipped the card open to read the message.

Hey boss,

Thanks for covering my tour shifts all twelve days of Christmas so I could go do this insane thing. Delia says thank you too, by the way. It turns out she's just as cool in person as in the game. And equally hot (and I say that in the most respectful way).

Thanks for pushing me out the door even though it was last minute and not telling me I was crazy. You're the grumpy big sister I never had.

-Norman

Wendy's cold, dead heart swelled a bit. Not that she'd admit it to anyone.

"What's this about?" Julie prodded a plastic cockroach that Wendy had missed inside the flowerpot. Wendy shrugged and shook her head.

"It's Norman. Who knows?"

He was an acquired taste, that was for sure, but Wendy had a soft spot for fellow misfits.

"So I guess things worked out with him and his lady love," Julie said.

"Guess so." Wendy turned back to the pot.

"Good for him," Julie said. "May we all be so bold."

Though it was just an offhand comment, Wendy's eyebrows drew together. The sentiment caused an unexpected stir of discomfort. What would her life be like now if she'd taken a chance and made a different choice?

Until today, she'd successfully pushed off thoughts of Alec for most of the week—probably because she'd been too blissfully busy for her brain to dwell on anything but work, shower, repeat—but even though she'd trained herself to shut down the sentimentality, she couldn't stop a few memories from surfacing now. She remembered the way it felt to wake up next to him, with his sleep mussed hair and the salt and cedar smell of his skin. The notes they'd hidden for each other with the most ridiculous platitudes they could find, like *Failure is the condiment that gives success its flavor*. The way he would run the gauntlet of her sarcasm to get to what was really underneath. The look in his eyes when she said she wanted to move to Vancouver with him after his assignment here ended. The sound of his voice when she couldn't make herself get on the plane, couldn't leave here after all.

Each thought twisted a knife inside her. There was no use dwelling on this. Stupid sentimental New Year's bullshit. So much of it from her tourists must have rubbed off on her. New Year's resolution—*Stop moping around and deal with the choices you've made.*

Swallowing around the lump in her throat, Wendy gathered up her Venus flytrap. "We still on for our *Doctor Who* marathon in a few hours?" she asked Julie. It was their New Year's pre-game tradition to watch a few Christmas specials and drink spiked eggnog before going out.

"You know it." Julie searched her cousin's face and her features clouded with concern.

Wendy tried to rearrange whatever was showing up on her face, with limited success.

"Sure you don't want to go to Miss Peacock's with us after?" Griffin asked. God, even he was being nice to her. She must look awful.

"Come on. Heavy metal mariachis. How can you say no to that?" Julie said.

Wendy sighed. "Oh, I'll find a way."

Once safely in her office, Wendy positioned her new plant on her desk. She collapsed into her chair and rolled her aching shoulders, still trying to shake this pensive state that had so rudely set itself upon her.

Her life was good. Of course it was. She had all of her family close by. She'd been here to step in and run things for her dad after his surgery. Since she'd started booking events and had streamlined some of their systems, their profits had been steadily increasing. Her parents didn't have to worry about medical costs anymore now that she'd taken on a bigger role. That alone was worth it. A small price to pay for not choosing what she wanted.

She pushed a stack of paperwork aside and stretched until her stompy boots clattered onto the desk. She wriggled into her seat and breathed out a sigh. Finally, some time to relax.

But none of the tension flooded from her shoulders. Apparently, her back and spine didn't get the message either.

Wendy muttered a string of expletives and followed the buzzing sound of a fly to where it landed in the mouth of her new carnivorous plant. Maybe Griffin was right—there were four words she never thought she'd say—that it was a rather fitting gift. If anyone dared to get too close, even if Wendy tried to fight against her instinctive reaction, she closed up and they got the business end of her acerbic wit and lifetime of baggage she'd acquired thanks to those awful girls in high school. She scooted closer and watched in morbid fascination as the fly wandered around the pinkish plant mouth. The thing was a minefield of tiny translucent hair triggers. One wrong step, and...Wendy's shoulders tensed even further at the impending doom playing out before her. But seconds ticked by and nothing happened. Huh.

Maybe this was some kind of vegetarian flytrap, an evolved sort that had figured out a way to circumvent its baser instincts.

Maybe she could figure out a way to do the same.

But just as she entertained the notion, the jaws snapped shut. Despite its frantic buzzing, the poor fly was trapped.

It got what was coming to it for chancing an encounter with a prickly plant.

A few minutes later, once Wendy had distracted herself with a cup of tea, Griffin poked his head around the doorframe.

"What?" she asked, with more bite in her voice than she'd intended.

He held up a folded note. "I almost forgot. I found this in the storage room."

Wendy's vision telescoped in on her name written in Alec's steady handwriting. Her breath stilled. Time seemed to go sideways at the sight of this artifact from the past. They'd probably left hundreds of these for each other over the course of their relationship. Never gushy, just silly things to make each other laugh, like *Shoot for the stars. Even if you miss, you might hit a bird.* Or *The early bird gets the breakfast burrito.* How long had that been here, hiding amongst the boxes of brochures and ghost shot glasses? How many more of these time bombs were out there? Grenades to the heart.

Julie appeared by Griffin's side and looked from the note to Wendy, eyes widening in recognition. "I'll take care of that." She snapped it up.

Wendy's stomach clenched. Why did a simple note from him affect her so much? Even when they hadn't seen each other in nine months. Especially after she was the one who couldn't get past her fears and had walked away.

She shifted in her seat. She should just let Julie take it and throw it away and try to focus on—what exactly? More work? More spreadsheets and group events. She was already set for the next two weeks. Stress knitting a new sweater? Her gaze landed on the novel jutting out of her purse. The graphic she was making for her friend Autumn's book! Yes, that was something happy to focus on. See, she was going to be just fine.

But as Julie tucked the note into her pocket, the hollowed-out part of Wendy's heart felt scraped raw. Maybe the schlocky sentiment of this time of year was getting to her, or maybe she was just a glutton for punishment.

"No." Wendy held out her hand. "I'll take it."

"Are you sure?" Julie held the note to her chest, and her features etched with concern.

Before she could change her mind, Wendy nodded.

"We're going to get out of here, but Paige is holding down the fort in the shop until your parents and Rayjay get here," Julie said after reluctantly relinquishing the note. "See you at your place in an hour?" Her eyes searched Wendy's for any sign she needed immediate backup. "Or I can wait, and we can grab a ride together."

Wendy gave Julie her best *I'm fine* smile and shooed her cousin and Griffin away. "Get out of here before you smell like patchouli, too."

Once they left, Wendy pulled her office door shut and returned to her desk. She picked up the note and rubbed her thumb over the year-old ink like she could somehow transport herself back to the time that was populated by private jokes and cheesy movies, and someone to dress up with at comic conventions. To a time when she'd somehow made it work. He'd calmed her suspicions, and she'd finally let him in. She missed him so much it hurt.

She lifted the corner of the paper, and at the sight of more of his handwriting and what looked like a drawing, resistance slammed into her.

It was only a few lines of text from days gone by. But it was also a Pandora's box of what-ifs.

What if she hadn't been so sure he'd eventually walk away? What if she hadn't been so chickenshit? Would she change things if she could go back and do it all over again?

Well, that was dumb to even consider because of course she couldn't.

She *could* call him, though. She could try to apologize again. Explain. He'd shot her down the first time after she realized the colossal mistake she'd made, but after all this time, he'd listen even if he was still hurt and angry. She knew him well enough to know that. There was a good chance he was even in town right now. The thought that he was here and not with her tugged at her. He might even find it in his heart to give her another chance.

But she knew herself too well, too. No matter how hard she fought against it, maybe it would always just be a matter of time before she panicked and shut him out again. And there was no way she'd do that to him a second time. Not if she wasn't absolutely sure she could stick it out despite the chance of being hurt. She cared about him too much.

But if she *could* do that.... She turned the note over in her hands. Her heart did a little skip, but then she looked at her new plant and frowned.

Right. That was about as likely as getting Prince to come back from the dead for a revival performance.

Wendy set the note back down on her desk unread.

Maybe it was time she started looking forward instead of back.

When Wendy finally felt like her legs wouldn't turn to Jell-O if she took another step, she poked her head out of her office. "Heading out?" Paige asked from behind the register.

"I'm going to see if we need anything else and restock the beads first," Wendy said. "Unless you need me."

"Nah, I got this." Paige repinned a loose blond strand that had fallen out of her ponytail. "So have you got any big New Year's plans now that you finally have a night off?" Paige said once the customers had left.

Wendy shrugged. "Just hanging out with Julie this afternoon. I'll probably fall asleep on my feet after that."

"I get that. Hey, have you seen that new holiday movie, *Wings of Love?* You should check that out if you get time this week."

Wendy stewed. This was the big schlocky second chance miracles blockbuster. There would be no second chances for her. It was pretty hard to come back from promising to move to Vancouver with someone and then not getting on the plane and breaking things off instead.

"Why does everyone think I need to see this sappy movie?" Wendy snapped. "You're like the eighth person today who's told me to watch it."

Paige gave her a confused look. "It's not sappy. It's about a back-up dancer turned climate scientist reunited with her lost love, the Prime Minister of Canada. They're stuck on a plane together circling the North Pole when elves attack. Sort of the *Snakes on a Plane* of holiday movies. But weirdly poignant at the end," she said. "Totally your kind of thing."

"Oh."

"And it has Will Morton."

"Well, maybe then." Wendy gave a half smile. Paige was just being nice. But planes, cheesy movies that were exactly her thing—her and Alec's thing—it was hard not to feel like the universe had planned every detail of this day to taunt her with reminders of Alec and how everyone else was making resolutions and traveling to new countries and trying new recipes and here she was, mired in the same place she'd always been.

"Your parents and Rayjay are coming in an hour, and Norman said to call him for backup if we needed another hand. And don't worry about the beads. I can do that later."

Wendy grunted her assent, sounding more like her father than she liked. She grabbed her purse and took a few steps toward the door, but when she spotted the anemic-looking bead rack, she doubled back to the storeroom. They'd probably be busy later. Best to get them stocked up, in case there was a rush before the night crew got there.

She was elbow-deep in a box of purple and green Mardi Gras throws when footsteps approached, and she anticipated Paige's protests. "I know. I know." She hung gold beads with attached shot glasses. "But really, I can't in good conscience leave you like this with a mob of drunken people who want their beads."

But instead of Paige's cheerful chirp, a low, soothing voice from Wendy's past stilled her hands on the rack. "Good to know you're still looking out for me."

Plastic beads clanged together. Heat and cold flashed inside her chest at the achingly familiar sound. Slowly, she straightened the last necklace and turned around, half convinced she was hallucinating from lack of sleep. But no.

"Alec," she breathed. He smiled his familiar smile, one side of his mouth tilted upward and a single dimple formed in his cheek. Dark brown curls fell just above his eyes and he fixed his steady gaze on her.

"Happy almost New Year," he said.

Words deserted her. Like she'd somehow conjured him, he was *here*. Her Alec who said "aboot" instead of about and *serviette* instead of napkin and gave her a run for her money at Trivial Pursuit. The same Alec who made her laugh and went out of his way to be kind to people others made fun of. Alec who ate hot sauce on everything and had to drink Red Bull to stay up past 11p.m.. She took in all six foot something of him standing there before her in dark jeans and a henley that looked so worn and soft that she had to fight the urge to touch him. The heather of his shirt made his sea glass eyes lean more blue than green. The fanciful parts of her—who knew those existed?—danced around like this was some sort of fucking sign, and she immediately put the smack down on that line of thinking. But... but part of her wanted to lay her head on his chest and breathe in the wintry aftershave scent of him and give up the fight that was always raging inside of her, warning her to keep her distance, keep vigilant.

"I've missed this place." His gaze flicked around the store, but settled firmly back on Wendy, roaming her face in a way that felt like he was memorizing every detail. The thrum in her chest edged out all other sounds. *Easy. Do not get so excited.* "I saw the new sign out front. You design that?"

She moved her eyes to the ground to steady herself and nodded.

"I like it. Still has the same charm as the old one, but looks like it will last."

"Thanks. That's what I was going for."

Alec toyed with one of the strands of beads on the shelf, and it felt for a moment like he'd never left, like he would always be a part of this place.

"You just missed Julie and Griffin."

"Ah, too bad. I would've liked to catch up with them, too."

What was she supposed to do here? She hadn't planned for a mini reunion. This was all uncharted territory.

"What are you doing here?" Wendy finally sputtered.

"I spent the holidays with my sister," he said. "I'm flying out tonight on a red-eye."

"I thought you might have." Wendy swallowed, her palms growing slick. She gathered her courage because she had to know. "But why are you *here*?"

He met her eyes, and a charge went through her like the electricity in the air before a coming storm.

No. No. No. This was a bad idea. She should send him on his way. Save them both the heartache.

"I wanted to see you, see how you were doing." Alec's gaze moved toward her office. "Could we talk?"

Bad idea. Abort. Abort.

"Sure."

He trailed behind her, and with every step she felt his presence.

"So, how've you been?"

We need to talk and then *how've you been*? Wendy blew out a breath. He always went for small talk when he was nervous.

Wendy, not so much. Small talk made her skin crawl. Maybe that's why she didn't have that many friends.

"Fine, I guess. Ghost tour biz. Rest. Repeat."

Alec regarded the canvases printed with her favorite quotations and the overflow from her bookshelves at home with a nostalgic smile and wandered over to the edge of her desk.

"I see you've got yourself a new plant to brighten up the place." Alec ran a finger over the tiny hair triggers inside the plant's mouth.

"Careful, that one has teeth."

"I'm a little tougher than its usual fare, I suspect." His gentle smile made her heart swell.

He looked at her with a question in his eyes before moving aside some of her papers and taking a seat on her desk.

The movement reminded her of a time they'd used this desk for more entertaining purposes, and heat dappled her cheeks. The part of her brain that dealt in tactile pleasures and instant gratification conjured the memory of the feel of his skin on hers and her fingers tangled in his hair, and bleated out a message: want.

But she schooled her features and sat down at least one coffee table book length away.

"So..." She chanced a glance at him, wishing he would just get to the point of whatever he'd come here to say. "How about you? How have you been?"

"It's nice to get away and be somewhere where I don't have to wear three layers of clothing at all times. It's eight degrees in Vancouver right now."

She shivered at the thought and tried not to think about the fact that he was wearing only one layer of clothing now.

"I, uh—" Wendy cleared her throat. "My *family's* missed you an awful lot." She wiped her slick palms on her pants.

Alec's smile grew. "I've missed them, too."

"My dad is very disgruntled about not having an ally at family dinners anymore," Wendy said, her own smile growing. "Claims you kept everyone from picking on him."

"Glad I could be of service. How is he? And everyone else?"

They chatted for a while, Alec catching her up on his exploits in the IT world, fishing trips, and life in British Columbia, and Wendy sharing the latest happenings with the business and her family, including her dad's recovery process. The whole time, she couldn't help thinking about how much she'd missed these talks.

"I cannot imagine your dad in a yoga class." Alec laughed. "I bet the instructors love him."

Wendy smirked. "Yeah, well, he's got petulant child pose down at least."

Alec looked over at her, a smile in those blue-green eyes, and it almost felt like nothing had changed. But as much as this stirred up memories of a simpler time, Alec was palpably different somehow, which was both dismaying because it came from a part of his life that she had not had a role in, and intensely sexy. She tried to put her finger on precisely what it was.

His thick chestnut hair was longer than she remembered, curling onto his forehead and around his ears. But that wasn't it. No. It had more to do with how he now carried himself, every movement more deliberate and purposeful. His presence had always been arresting, but now it was like he had his own atmosphere. Apparently, her absence had done him good. The thought caused a wretched pang of emotion she didn't dare name.

Alec's eyes searched hers, and he frowned at whatever he saw on her face.

"Was this a bad idea? I can go." He motioned to the door.

"No." Wendy shook her head. Something they used to say to each other to ease the tension popped into her mind, and the corners of her mouth twitched into a sad smile. "Just thinking about the price of Speedos in South Africa."

Alec laughed, and she saw the tension bleed out of his shoulders at the joke they'd once shared. It was something they'd overheard a stuffy British tourist say at Jazz fest, and they'd adopted it as their favorite saying.

Wendy's heart ached at the familiarity of it all.

"Are you seeing anyone?" Wendy knew she shouldn't ask. What business was it of hers now? But she couldn't stop herself.

"Sort of nursing a breakup," Alec said.

A pang of dismay arrested her at the thought of him with anyone else. "I'm sorry. What happened?"

He gave a rueful smile. "She wasn't you."

The breath flew out of her. A painful twist of longing wrenched in her gut.

"How about you? Are you seeing anyone?" Alec asked. Wendy watched the tops of his ears turn pink, his one tell besides excessive small talk that he was flustered.

"No." There had been guys she'd seen here and there, but they'd all been over before they really started. Same reason. Well, that and her big fat trust problem. But none could overcome the additional hurdle: none of them were Alec.

He seemed to relax at that. "I finally told that pesky coworker of mine where to stick it for stealing all my ideas."

"Yeah?" Wendy felt a sense of pride, followed by the dismal thought that he wasn't hers to be proud of anymore.

"Very politely, I'm sure," she said.

He gave her a sly grin. "You might be surprised."

"Look at you, all kicking ass and taking names."

"I don't know about that," he said, ever modest. "But I did get a promotion."

"Good for you."

"But I'm thinking about looking for work here."

He let the words hang in the air, and Wendy's mouth went dry. What was he saying? "You'd be in the same city as your sister. That's great."

"That's a big factor, yes."

Wendy felt the weight of his gaze, but it took a few panicked seconds before she could brave meeting his eyes. He couldn't want her back. He couldn't after all that she'd put him through. But what if that wasn't the case? Seeing him here had been a bright spot in an otherwise shitty, or at least numbly uneventful stretch of months. But could she trust herself to let go and give this another try if, against all logic, he asked her to?

Alec raked a hand through his hair and looked like he was steeling himself for a confrontation. A cold current of panic zipped through her. The Alec she knew didn't do confrontation, but it looked like this new Alec did.

"C-can I ask you something?" Alec said. Wendy's world narrowed in to those words, and her heart hammered. This must be something serious if it brought his stutter out. She'd only heard it occasionally, but she knew how self-conscious he was about it. Her eyes flicked to her desk, where she located a bottle of water and handed it to him. She knew it was one trick he'd learned from his speech therapist as a kid: drink, slow down, take a breath, try again.

He gave her a grateful smile and downed half the bottle before continuing.

"Why did you really end things between us?"

Wendy stilled, every breath she took, every pulse of blood rushing through her ears in suspended animation. She felt like she'd grown antlers and was staring down the high beams of an oncoming car.

"I... I couldn't go. The distance. And with my dad's heart scare again, I couldn't just leave."

Alec gave her a sad smile and continued gently. "Your parents were practically pushing you out the door. This was you."

"I..." Wendy's throat closed up. "Do we really have to stir up old painful topics?"

"Will you hear me out? I'll leave after if you want. But I didn't speak up before, and I've regretted it every day."

Wendy's heart beat erratically, but she couldn't see that look on his face—his eyes both soft and fierce—and deny him, no matter how much it would cost her. She motioned for him to continue.

"If it was about being away from your family"—he met her eyes—"you could've asked me to stay."

Warmth stirred in Wendy's chest for a brief respite from the guilt and discomfort.

"It might've been tricky, and we'd have had to do long distance for a while, and arrange visas and such, but I would've tried. But I think it was more than that."

It was hard to breathe.

"Look Wendy, when you didn't get on that plane, it crushed me." Alec looked away, and Wendy's chest tightened with the guilt of what she'd put him through.

"I was blindsided. After the time we'd spent together, I didn't get it. Sure, you can be prickly and stubborn, but underneath all that you're also one of the kindest people I've ever known. I don't know anyone who would sacrifice the way you do for the people you love. You were it for me. And I was so sure you felt the same. Did I get that so wrong?"

A lump rose in Wendy's throat. She blinked away the moisture in her eyes, but shook her head.

Alec ran a hand through his hair, and Wendy had an urge to lace her fingers into his to comfort him.

"When you said you wanted to move back with me when I finished my assignment here, I wanted it to be true so much that I didn't push enough to make sure it was what you really wanted. This is your home. You'd have been leaving your parents, Julie, your business. Even if you were going to work remotely, that's a lot to give up."

It was. But despite all that, she had wanted to. To take a chance and be with the person who reminded her she was allowed to find out what she wanted without the trappings of everything she'd ever known.

"And when you said it was over, I just accepted it. I told myself I was respecting your wishes. And I was. But I've realized that was also a way of shielding myself from more rejection. I should have fought harder for you. Tried to find another way." He looked up at her. "Then I wondered if you weren't doing exactly the same thing. I think you let your past get in your head and shut you down."

A cold sensation flashed in her chest. She hated that he could still do this. See right into her like he was some kind of x-ray tech of her heart.

"I was still so hurt and so angry when you called after and tried to explain and fix things. Even if you were trying to tell me that, I couldn't hear it. I couldn't hear it because I didn't want to get hurt like that again." He looked up at her. "I still don't."

For an agonizing moment, they held each other's gazes, both of their past regrets playing there like old home movies. But how could they go forward from here? Could he ever trust her again? Could she ever give him the guarantee he needed that she wouldn't run again?

"Wendy, I'm not those high school girls who hurt you. Even though we share some DNA, I'm not my sister. I wasn't going anywhere. I wish I'd done a better job of convincing you of that."

Alec covered Wendy's hand with his and squeezed, even with all the uncertainty. She should pull away, but God help her, it felt good, almost as good as his words. She wanted to believe him, to let herself trust him. But could she trust herself not to get spooked and run, even if she could trust him?

Alec rubbed slow circles into her hand, and she leaned into the sensation.

"I've missed this," she murmured before she could process what she was saying.

"Me, too." Alec shifted his hips and moved closer to her on the desk.

Her back stiffened abruptly. What was she doing? If she wasn't sure, she had to shut this down.

"So where does this leave us?" she asked.

"I don't know," Alec admitted, pulling away. "I miss you. You're like my phantom limb."

Wendy's lips twitched into a smile. "You're like mine, too. You can scratch all the hard-to-reach places, and you know how to do all the computer-y stuff."

His smile brightened before taking on a melancholy tilt again. "But I don't know if I can live with the constant wonder if you'll leave again."

She gave a slow nod. "I get that."

The impasse spread out like a chasm between them.

"What are your plans for the rest of the day?" Alec asked.

Wendy unlaced her fingers from Alec's and stretched, the few brief moments of bliss evaporating into reality.

"*Doctor Who* Christmas special marathon with Julie and then probably sleeping off the holiday overtime." She stood.

"My sister and I and some of the guys are heading to La Media Naranja around nine. Ringing in the new year from there."

Was he asking her to come too? Did she want to?

"Sure you can stay up until midnight?" she said, to change the subject. Alec reliably fell asleep before any of the late shows.

"I can make an exception." He shot her one of those achingly beautiful grins. "But I'll need to bail right after midnight to get my stuff and catch my flight."

She nodded, not sure what to say.

"No matter how much I try to talk myself out of it, I keep circling back to you and me. If you tell me you don't love me, and you don't think you can get over what made you leave in the first place, I'll respect that, and I'll walk away. But if it was just because you were scared..."

A muscle in Alec's jaw jumped as he met Wendy's eyes.

"If that's what it was, will you come meet me tonight? I don't know if there's a way forward from here, but if it's what you want too, let's at least talk about it."

"I—I'll think about it."

CHAPTER 2

"Why do we always have to watch the old ones?" Julie emerged from Wendy's kitchen balancing a bowl of Chex mix and two spiked eggnogs.

"Because the old ones are the best." Wendy accepted a mug and took a sip of the nutmegy goodness. She settled in on her couch, more than ready for their blessedly predictable tradition of watching *Doctor Who* specials—and for something to take her mind off of Alec's visit today.

"And come on, no Doctor will ever be as good as David Tennant," she said.

Julie scoffed. "Um, except for Matt Smith."

"Blasphemy." But Wendy smiled and pulled a blanket over her legs—her favorite, black with demonic pink unicorns.

"New one and then the one with Donna's grandpa you like?" Julie pointed the remote at the small TV in the midst of a wall that was mostly bookshelves.

Wendy pulled a face.

"Come on." Julie shook Wendy's leg before turning her attention back to the screen. "Ooh, *The Husbands of River Song*. That's a perfect compromise. Something old, something newer, something—"

"We're watching the Doctor, not getting married." Wendy laughed and then felt a strange tightness in her chest as she remembered how much other people's lives were changing all around her. "Well, *I'm* not getting married, anyway."

Julie's expression turned pensive, and she pulled her *Hamilton* pajama-covered knees to her chest. "My last Who-Year's marathon as a singleton." Then her thoughtful look took on a tinge of mischief. "Guess that means I get to pick the episode."

"Oh, alright," Wendy grumbled. She took another gulp of her drink and let the sweet mixture of cream and nutmeg and bourbon burn down her throat.

The show started and Julie tugged at the blanket and snuggled under it next to Wendy, hogging the covers as she'd done since they were kids. The familiar irritant made her smile. She'd needed this so badly. The comfort of tradition, the comfort of just eating Chex Mix in pajamas with the person who knew her better than anyone.

But as much as things were the same on the surface—Julie hogging the covers and trying to sneak in more eleventh Doctor episodes—she could already feel the shift. The light glinting off of Julie's engagement ring in its Victorian-throwback setting reminded her that soon Julie would have a husband. Maybe even kids. She could be an aunt. And they might move away to one of the cities where they'd been traveling for speaking engagements. Wendy knew they'd always be a part of each other's lives. But for so long, it had been the two of them, as close as sisters, against the world.

She wanted Julie to be happy, sure—no one deserved it more—but Wendy needed Julie so much. She just feared that as the new parts of Julie's life expanded, Wendy's part would get smaller and smaller until she was scarcely a part of her world at all.

"Hey Jules," she said after a while. "Will we still do this next year?"

Julie looked at her with a puzzled expression. "Of course. It's our tradition."

Wendy's voice caught. "Even after you're going on book tours and calling yourself Mrs. Durocher?"

"Deveaux-Durocher. I'm hyphenating." But when she studied her cousin's face, her playful expression turned earnest. "I know things are changing, but you'll always be one of the most important people in the world to me." Julie squeezed Wendy's knee and smiled. "You'll always be my sister-cousin."

"Not to be confused with sister-wife," Wendy said, relief loosening the lump in her throat.

"Right. I'm not good at sharing."

"Plus Griffin, just no." Wendy shook her head. "I grudgingly admit he's got his good points, but way too smooth for me."

"Hey, that's my fiancé you're talking about." Julie shoulder-bumped her. "Alec, on the other hand..." Julie waggled her eyebrows and let out a wicked laugh.

Wendy whacked her with a throw pillow. "I thought we agreed not to talk about him again. Still processing."

Julie rolled her eyes. "I think it might be time to change that, too. You're really not going to go meet him tonight?"

The tumble of nerves and misgivings Wendy had only just sent packing made an encore appearance.

"I've slept a grand total of ten hours in the last three days. I'm hardly in the mental state to be making life-altering decisions like this."

"So take a nap."

"Maybe we can revisit this if he moves back."

Julie rolled her eyes. "You can't expect him to just wait around indefinitely. If you still care about him, at least go talk to him tonight. It's not like you have to bring two goats and a fatted calf as dowry."

"Why are you pushing so much on this?"

"Because sometimes you need a push or you'll stay where you are forever."

Wendy scoffed. She could push herself just fine.

But maybe Julie had a point. *Could* wasn't quite the same as *would*.

"And I know how happy you were when he was in your life. You let the good parts of yourself closer to the surface when he was around."

Wendy swallowed. "But what if I freak out again and want to run? I can't hurt him like that again."

"So freak out. But don't run."

Wendy exhaled slowly. "Great. Easy. So glad you're here."

"Thank you." Julie gave her a cheeky smile. "Do you still care about him?"

Wendy thought about his note she'd found earlier. She'd brought it home and opened it. *Nothing is impossible. The word itself says, "I'm possible." It also says, "Imp! Ossible!" and "Some spilb."* Underneath, he'd drawn a picture of a pig next to a spider web with the last phrase woven in with the caption, *Arachnids aren't known for their spelling prowess.* She thought of all the days they'd spent in companionable book debates, how he'd encouraged her in her secret art and typography obsession. And of how it felt when he'd taken her hand in his this afternoon.

She nodded. But caring was never the issue. "What if I go all in, but this time... he's the one that leaves?"

It was the thought that had been haunting her ever since she'd first seen him today, and it felt even bigger and more ominous now that she'd voiced it aloud.

Julie shrugged. "No guarantees, I guess. There's no way to look into the future. Unless you want to ask Sophia..."

"No." She didn't need Griffin's psychic grandmother to confirm with grim certainty how miserable her future would be if she stayed this course.

"Fine. Just saying." Julie shrugged. "But what if he doesn't leave?"

Wendy hugged a pillow to her chest and turned back to the TV, watching River and the Doctor with his new face, recognizing each other again for the first time. It had been a while, but there was still that palpable spark, and they were no less willing to jump in front of an intergalactic weapon for one another.

Julie's question echoed in her mind, and she slipped her fingers into her pocket and ran them over the smooth edges of Alec's note. Maybe she could have everything she wanted. She just had to be willing to risk having it all snatched away.

CHAPTER 3

The sound of a window latch opening jolted Wendy out of a deep sleep. She only vaguely remembered Julie tucking the blanket around her and muting the TV before her eyelids drifted closed earlier.

She blinked awake again, eyes adjusting to the dark. How long had she been asleep? The darkness coming through the blinds said the sun had set, but she wasn't sure if she'd been asleep for hours or days.

A rustling at the front window snapped her out of her sleep fog.

"Julie?"

No one answered.

The window slid open from the outside, and Wendy's adrenaline spiked. She felt around for possible weapons, but only came up with a typography magazine.

"Who's there?" She crept closer, wielding the rolled-up magazine and its hopefully mighty sans serifs. "I know karate." Then she muttered under her breath, "At least, I saw *Karate Kid*."

A male figure tumbled through and onto her landing. Wendy jumped and her back slammed into the light switches on the wall. Heart hammering, she fumbled the lights on, only to find her cousin-in-law-to-be dusting off his chinos.

"Griffin?" She blinked and pressed a hand to her rapidly pounding heart. "What are you doing here?"

"Want to give me a hand? I think I pulled something." He rubbed his hip.

Wendy groaned and swatted him on the arm with her makeshift weapon. She pulled him to his feet, but he felt almost as light as air. Was she dreaming?

"P.S. There is a perfectly functional door about two feet to your right," Wendy said.

Griffin shrugged and gave her a roguish smile. "I thought this called for more of an entrance."

Wendy pressed a hand to her temple. "What are you doing climbing through my window on New Year's Eve?"

"I am the Ghost of Midnights Past," he announced before making his way to the living room and grabbing a pretzel from the bowl on the coffee table.

Wendy's brow furrowed, and she stomped after him. "Um, no. You are Griffin Durocher, enamored of my cousin and general pain in the ass."

"Tomato, to-MAH-to." Griffin flopped onto the couch and put his feet up on the coffee table. "But I'm going with the first one. See?"

Griffin waved a hand, and as he did, it went from solid to translucent and back again.

Wendy reached for his arm to see what trick he was pulling, and to her surprise her fingers passed right through where his forearm should have been.

He moved again, and her fingers brushed flesh. She jerked back, goosebumps and all the tiny hairs rising on her arms.

Wendy shook her head, trying to make sense of what was happening. Maybe Julie had been more heavy-handed on the bourbon than she'd thought.

"Believe me now?" Griffin asked.

"I..." She tried to finish the thought, but found her brain overloaded by the sheer ridiculousness of what was happening here.

"Close enough." He gave a jovial shrug. "So you're probably wondering why I'm here."

"You're not looking for Julie." Though it began as a question, it took a left and ended up as a statement before she could finish.

"She got home a while ago."

"Then care to enlighten me, Ghost of Interrupted Naps or whoever you are."

"Ghost of Midnights Past," Griffin corrected. "This is really good Chex Mix, by the way. I really need to get the recipe."

"It's on the box. Be my guest. Now do you want to tell me what you're doing disturbing my slumber?"

"Think of this as a sort of cosmic wake up call, Ebenezer Scrooge style." Griffin spread his arms wide, as if he were presenting some kind of good news on a game show. But it felt more like, Congratulations, you've won a colposcopy!

"Well, I'm awake. Reluctantly. So mission accomplished."

Griffin held a hand up. "This is a different sort of wake-up. You know, something to help shake you out of what's been holding you back. Before it's too late."

Wendy frowned. Even through her irritation, his words—cheesy as they were—echoed her thoughts from earlier closely enough that they skirted her defenses and found their mark. She hugged her arms to her chest.

"I'm not holding myself back," she bit out.

Griffin shot her a look that said, *Keep telling yourself that.*

Her throat went dry as she followed Griffin's gaze first toward the wall, to the artwork she'd done and then to Alec's note, somehow no longer in her pocket, but lying open on the table.

"So here's the deal. Tonight you're going to be visited by three spirits: The Ghost of Midnights Past—that's me—the Ghost of Midnights Present, you're going to love that one, very fuzzy, and the Ghost of Midnights Future. And hopefully by the end of the night you'll have what you need to decide if you want to stick to what you're doing or bet on something better."

A feeling that was part nausea, part thrill kicked up in her stomach. She shifted her eyes to the darkened windows, and a thought hit her, and with it alarm bells went off.

"Wait, what time is it?"

"Why? Have somewhere to be?" Griffin raised an eyebrow and gave a knowing smile.

"No," she answered automatically, but as much as she wanted to put off a decision of any kind, the thought that she'd slept right through her window of opportunity to see him again didn't sit well. "Maybe."

"Don't worry. We're sort of outside of the timeline right now. You'll have plenty of time to get there. You know, if it's *maybe*. Now, on to the fun stuff."

CHAPTER 4

I f there was one thing Wendy sucked at, it was waiting around, listening to details while her brain insisted on running through worst-case scenarios.

As Ghost Griffin went on about the dynamics of time travel on the ghostly plane, Wendy rolled and then re-rolled her typography magazine, willing him to get on with it, so she could think of anything other than the impending humiliation that would likely accompany this leap of faith.

"You skipped a step," she finally cut in. "The whole Jacob Marley cautionary tale part."

"I can go get the chinchilla lady down the street," Griffin said.

"Hey, leave Mrs. Hilliard alone. She's not doing so bad."

"She always smells like dry cleaning and broken dreams."

Wendy frowned, remembering the last few conversations while Mrs. Hilliard watered her petunias, the buxom older woman lamenting more and more frequently that she'd missed her chance at burlesque dancing. *I might've been terrible, but I might have been like a half-naked Audrey Hepburn. You never know,* her neighbor had said.

Was that where Wendy was headed? Without the half-naked aspirations, of course. To be an octogenarian upholder of responsibility destined never to leave the ghost tour circuit even in her afterlife?

Griffin studied her. "I think I know what you need." He abandoned the couch and rubbed his hands together.

Doesn't everybody? she thought, but before she could make a snide comment, the temperature in the room took a sharp drop. She rubbed her arms, her *Supernatural* pajama pants and tank top suddenly feeling insubstantial.

"How much longer before we have to get back to the gift shop?" Wendy's head whipped around at the sound of her own voice, though younger somehow, coming from somewhere else in the room.

Her heartbeats ratcheted up. Misty fog the luminous grey-purple of opals seeped up from the wooden floorboards. It curled and twisted, first around her calves and then around everything, filling the room until Griffin disappeared and only the tops of the walls were visible.

Then Julie's voice, but also younger-sounding, cut through the haze. "I told your dad we were coming back in an hour."

"Jules?" she called and choked on a mouthful of vapor in the process.

No answer. Wendy reached out for Julie or Griffin or anything to anchor her, but found no purchase. In that instant, the room spun away into a vortex of fog. Her hair whipped into her face in auburn streams, clouding her senses. The current upended any sense of stability, and it was hard to say what was down and what was up and what was real and what was only a dream. But whatever this was, it felt very, very real.

"Griffin?" She finally choked out. "You can cut the special effects now."

The spinning stream of cloud matter slowed, and she batted her hands in front of her face.

Griffin's smirking face materialized next to hers, along with the rest of his body. "But that's my favorite part."

Warmth came back into her limbs. The last tendrils cleared, and the moonlight through her window melted into afternoon sunlight. It filtered through the trees creeping over the edge of the park in Jackson Square. The smell of horses, chicory coffee, and sweet fried dough crept into Wendy's awareness, and she started. Though it was humid, typical New Orleans fare, a shiver danced up her spine at the abrupt change of scenery.

"Aww, look, it's the mini Deveaux cousins." Griffin nodded toward the two teenaged girls ambling along the sidewalk that ringed the park.

Wendy's breath left her. It made sense that she would see her younger self given the whole midnights past thing, but it didn't make it any less strange to see herself walking around while she watched from a few feet away. When she'd adjusted to the shock of seeing double, she tried to process what she was seeing: her younger self practically bouncing down the street in a breezy yellow dress. Wendy Deveaux did not bounce. Or wear colors associated with sunshine and rainbows.

But apparently this earlier incarnation of her did.

Mini-Julie's face split into a braces-filled smile and mini-Wendy brushed powdered sugar off her dress and handed the last bite of beignet to her cousin.

An amused smile played on Griffin's lips. "You used to be so... cheerful. It's weird."

Wendy rolled her eyes. "Yes, the cognitive dissonance abounds."

But as she watched her fourteen-year-old self giggle—*giggle*—at something her cousin said, taking in the open, unguarded look on her younger face, she had to agree. It was disconcerting. But also sort of nice. In a sappy alternate reality kind of way.

Without warning, an ache started and an expression that couldn't decide between a smile or a frown tugged at the corner of Wendy's mouth. How long had it been since she'd felt free to laugh this way? How long—? No. She shut the next thought down before it could take shape. That sort of thinking was for suckers. People who believed that there was no one out to hurt them in the world when there obviously was. People who saw all glasses as half full and hung inspirational posters unironically in their kitchens. People who didn't know any better.

She turned her attention back to the girls.

"Can they see us?" Wendy waved a hand in front of her younger self's face and fell into step with her cousin.

Griffin shook his head. "Nah, this is purely for your viewing and learning pleasure."

"And what exactly am I supposed to learn?"

"A good teacher never gives you the answers, only gets you to ask the right questions."

"This professor thing is really going to your head."

Griffin shrugged, his eyes still twinkling.

Wendy rolled her eyes and kept pace as the younger girls continued their conversation.

"Guess what I'm doing this Friday?" said fourteen-year-old Wendy.

"Reading *Neverwhere* again and going to the yarn store?"

Her younger self seemed to consider.

"No, but I might make a yarn stop on the way."

Julie smiled.

Wendy pulled herself up to her full height. "I happen to be going to a Rougarou concert at Molly's."

"Shut up. How did you get tickets? I thought they were sold out when you checked."

"I guess they're doing some kind of special small show. Kara Lynn and Aundrea asked me." Both pride and sheepishness made their way into her tone. "Aundrea's dad got tickets, and they had an extra one, so they asked me."

Julie frowned and made a noncommittal sound. If only she'd listened to her cousin then.

"What's 'hmm' supposed to mean?" Hurt tinged Wendy's words. She turned to her cousin and saw Julie wrestling with a wary expression. The protective look on her face was hard to miss, though.

Julie twisted her lips to the side, like she was trying to avoid saying something. "Aundrea, that's the tennis player with the smart mouth, right?"

Wendy snorted. "Smart mouth—who are you, Granddad? Besides, you're one to talk about smart mouths."

"Hey, I use mine for the forces of good."

"Whatever."

"Who's Kara Lynn again? The new girl with the perfect hair?"

Wendy nodded, the tension in her shoulders visibly relaxing. Kara Lynn's honey-blond hair was a thing of fascination. It was always immaculate and somehow singularly unaffected by the humidity that made Wendy's wave up despite any attempts to tame it. Kara Lynn also wore outfits that looked like something out of *Project Runway*. And not the weird kinds made of produce either. "She seems nice. She's sort of quiet, but she did a great job on her part of the project."

At first Wendy had thought Kara Lynn was aloof, but maybe she was just quiet, or like Wendy, not sure what to say around people that were not her family. And though Wendy was much more laid back, she'd thought the two of them might have been kindred spirits in their early teen awkwardness even if they came in much different wrappers. Present-day Wendy's stomach curdled at the thought of just how wrong she'd been.

"Since when do you hang out with them?" Julie asked.

"We had a group project in history last week." Wendy shrugged. "They've been so nice to me since then. It was kind of Twilight Zone at first, but maybe they just had to get to know me."

The girls passed the Saint Louis Cathedral and headed toward Saint Peter. Wendy's steps were still buoyant with thoughts of her potential new friends, despite her cousin's wariness.

Older Wendy squirmed, and a sick feeling came over her when she remembered how hopeful she'd felt that day, on the precipice of finally having some friends outside of her family, her stupid secret wish. Not that Julie wasn't enough, but Julie was two grades ahead of her and had a different lunch time. She wished for someone to make eye contact with in class and snicker at all the obvious innuendo in *A Midsummer Nights Dream* in English class or to have someone to eat with. She didn't mind reading at lunch and working on the sets for the school plays, but it would've been nice to have an actual friend instead of just acquaintances and people who pointed at her in the halls and snickered as they called her ghost girl.

Also, as much as she loved her family, sometimes she just wished for a relationship outside of them—somewhere where she wasn't Wendy, dependable daughter of Rob and Jacqui, tapped to take over the family business before she'd even gotten proper boobs. She wanted friends with whom she could just be Wendy who liked font pairings and loud angsty music and books where people got yanked out of their ordinary worlds and made a new way for themselves. A Wendy without all the expectations who didn't have her life all figured out yet, and that was okay.

Wendy looked over at her cousin, who had grown quiet again. "What?"

"Nothing."

Wendy arched an eyebrow.

"Okay, I don't like that Aundrea girl. She was the one who got in trouble for hazing the other tennis players last year, forcing them to drink alcohol and ketchup out of a dog bowl or something awful like that."

Wendy's smile faltered. "I don't think she would do something like that. Maybe you've got her confused with someone else."

When Julie's concerned expression remained unchanged, Wendy blew out an exasperated breath. "This is a chance for me to make some friends who haven't known me since I was in diapers and haven't decided all that they need to know about me. For once it would be nice to have someone to sit with at lunch and not be called ghost girl. Do you not want me to have other friends?"

"Of course I do." Julie's expression softened, and she looked chastened. "I just don't want to see you get hurt."

The defensiveness that had coiled in Wendy's chest backed down. "It's just a concert."

Julie sighed and smiled at her cousin. "Okay, tell me more about this concert."

CHAPTER 5

"God, this play is awful," Aundrea whispered to Wendy the next day after Mrs. Sloane, their English teacher, put on the *King Lear* movie. "I mean, Goneril, what kind of name is that?"

Wendy smirked at that, even though she didn't exactly agree with her new friend's assessment of the play. It was tragic maybe, but in a pretty genius way. And the villains were awesome.

"You're still coming tonight, right?" Aundrea said.

Wendy nodded and opened her jacket to show off a t-shirt with the band's last album cover on it.

Aundrea's face scrunched up at the sight of it.

"That's... enthusiastic of you. Anyway, 10 p.m. at Molly's. Oh, and the door-man's supposed to act like he doesn't know about it unless you've got the special tickets."

Aundrea grinned and exchanged a look with Kara Lynn, her eyes glittering with some shared secret before turning back to the movie.

Wendy flashed a smile at Kara Lynn, who was in the seat next to her, too, and felt a pleasant ache in her chest. Free tickets to see her favorite band. A real girls' night out with people who hadn't known her since birth. Maybe she'd get that friend group she'd always wanted after all.

Wendy had missed it the first time around—probably because she'd wanted this to work out so badly—but standing here watching it all play out from a distance, it was plain as day. When Kara Lynn gave younger Wendy a half smile back before letting a curtain of perfect hair cover her face, she wouldn't quite meet her eyes.

At 9:55 that night, Wendy stood in front of Molly's, decked out in a V-neck t-shirt, figure-hugging jeans, and ridiculously high heels with black and pink polka dots she'd borrowed from Julie's closet. Buzzing with excitement, she rocked back and forth in her toe-destroying heels, scanning the crowd mingling in the Quarter for any sign of Aundrea or Kara Lynn.

Under the glow of the streetlamp, she'd scanned the first floor of the bar and restaurant through a large open window, but hadn't seen them anywhere.

Wendy peeked inside her purse for one last look at the three matching photo mats she'd made for each of them to commemorate the night. She'd hand lettered each one in gold with a cool brush script she'd been practicing. She bit her lip. Was this too much? It was something she and Julie would do for each other, but she didn't know the protocol with outsiders. But she'd needed a project to channel her nervous energy into anyway, and why not channel it into a way to say thank you for inviting her?

A crush of bodies filled in the street bit by bit as the night got darker. Music—not Rougarou music though—and laughter from groups of friends poured into the street. Time ticked by.

By 10:30 they still hadn't arrived, and Wendy realized that in all of her excitement they'd never exchanged phone numbers. Maybe they were just running late, though. Thirty minutes was not a big deal in the grand scheme of things. And the band hadn't started yet. Maybe she'd even gotten the time wrong.

The bouncer raised his caterpillar-like eyebrows.

"Oh, right, you're not supposed to talk about that. Like the *Fight Club*."

He gave her another odd look, but it was not unkind. "You can go inside and get yourself a water or a cold drink while you wait."

"Thanks." She bit her lip. "They're probably just running late. I'll just hang out here for a little longer."

She fanned herself and thought about pulling the copy of *Anansi Boys* she'd been dying to finish out of her purse, but refrained.

People came and went, and the bouncer watched her with growing concern. By 11:00, her good-natured frustration turned to annoyance, and a sinking feeling began in her stomach. They wouldn't just stand her up like this, would they? This was not how this night was supposed to go. They were supposed to rock out to the concert and possibly whisper about cute boys and come back to school on Monday with inside jokes. And then Wendy wouldn't have to sit by herself anymore. They had wanted to be friends, hadn't they? What other reason could Aundrea possibly have had for inviting her?

Her borrowed heels pinched her toes, but Wendy squared her shoulders. They must have had some emergency come up, only they couldn't have called her because they didn't have her number. She folded her arms over her chest. The alternative was too awful to think about.

But as the clock ticked closer to midnight, her foolish hopes flickered into shame. She finally let herself see what she'd been too trusting to consider an hour and a half ago.

She replayed the morning's conversation again in her mind, and a sickening realization settled in her stomach like lead paint. The glee on Aundrea's face and the discomfort on Kara Lynn's started to make so much sense.

God, how could she have been so stupid?

She marched up to the bouncer.

"Still no friends yet?" he asked.

A lump formed in Wendy's throat. Yeah, that was the story of her life. "There's no secret concert here tonight, is there?" she asked, barely keeping the tremble out of her voice.

"Here? Nah, not tonight."

Wendy's stomach burned, and she blinked against the moisture in her eyes.

The bouncer called after her as she elbowed her way through the crowd of people with their violently green hand grenades and hurricanes, but she was too sick to face anyone just now.

Stupid. Stupid. Stupid.

And naïve. Why did she always believe that people's intentions were good? Aundrea had never said more than hello to her for three years of middle school and suddenly she invites her to a concert? Wendy should've shared some of Julie's skepticism. Of course Aundrea didn't want to be her friend. Wendy was just the weird ghost girl who actually liked the books they studied in English class. But Kara Lynn, too? That blow hurt worse.

Wendy felt around in her purse until her hands closed around the photo mats. The golden letters flashed in the streetlights. Wendy ripped the photo mats and all of her naïve hopes into pieces. She stuffed them into the garbage; then she stalked off as fast as her feet would carry her to Julie and Aunt Angeline's.

Griffin rocked back on his heels and let out a low whistle.

Wendy wrapped her arms around her chest as the scene faded away, wanting to disappear. She suddenly wished she'd had time to grab more than a tank top and her pajama pants to keep her from feeling so exposed. It was one thing to be so gullible as to fall for their BS in the first place, but it was a whole new level of humiliation to see it play out again with a witness.

With a shudder, she remembered Aundrea's cruel giggle in English class the next Monday and Kara Lynn's refusal to meet her eyes.

The scene took shape again, and everything in her body tensed up. The smell of fresh pencils and too-strong boy cologne filled the air.

"Have fun at the concert on Friday, ghost girl?" Aundrea had whispered.

Wendy's open, guileless expression hardened into the impassible mask that would become her armor, and she lasered in on the pages of *King Lear*.

They were supposed to be writing a diary entry for one of the characters. She picked the king with all of his backstabbing daughters.

Her tormenters giggled.

Why did she put herself out there for these awful girls to stomp on? Well, never again.

After class Wendy stayed behind to talk to Mrs. Sloane to beg off from set building for the spring play that afternoon. And also to avoid any further contact with Aundrea and Kara Lynn.

Wendy bristled when she looked up. Kara Lynn lingered near the door while the other students made their way to their next classes.

She smoothed her hair and straightened her ridiculous pink satin dress, looking like someone had kicked her puppy. Like she somehow thought *she* was the one who deserved pity.

"Wendy, hey..."

Wendy shouldered her backpack and kept walking.

Kara Lynn trotted after her, fuchsia heels clicking against the walkway.

"Wait, please," Kara Lynn's voice pleaded.

All the hurt and rage boiled up in Wendy's chest and she whirled on Kara Lynn and gave her the full force of her ire.

"What? Want to invite me to another nonexistent concert? Or maybe a nonexistent slumber party, this time. Hard pass."

Kara Lynn's eyes went wide, and she took a step back. "No, I..."

But she never finished. Retreating from Wendy's glare, she turned and fled the other way.

Maybe it was better this way. At least she'd learn early not to be so naïve and trusting.

CHAPTER 6

Aflurry of scenes followed and Wendy watched them flit past with the shame of that weakness still burning from the inside. In her high school classrooms and at home, she retreated more and more into her artwork and typography studies. The oranges and yellows of her technicolor wardrobe were slowly traded in for grays and blacks, and the open, guileless expression closed up shop and put up bars over the entrance. Especially when the teasing and pranks from Aundrea and Kara Lynn became more and more relentless. They graduated to splashing paint on her sweater and leaving various disgusting things to fall from the top of her locker when she opened it. And the ghost girl taunts meant to put her and her family in their place worked with cruel efficiency.

Only when she was around Julie or her parents or aunt or at the shop or working on sets for the school plays did she let some of the light slip back in.

She worked at the gift shop after school until she started giving ghost tours herself and saved until she could buy herself a copy of Photoshop. Whenever she had downtime, she watched design tutorial videos and taught herself to use brushes and effects.

When it came time to apply for colleges, everyone, herself included, assumed she would stay put and continue to help run the family business. It was the one place where she'd always belonged, the one place she always felt needed. In the four walls of that charmingly dingy little shop and through her well-worn tour paths, she was never the outsider or the one who got laughed at and stood up. And when you find that, it's not an easy thing to walk away from.

The barrage of scenes from her life slowed to a halt. The space around Wendy and Griffin reformed into the drama room at Wendy's old high school. Eighteen-year-old her, with ripped black jeans and kohl-rimmed eyes, sat cross-legged on a beat-up old couch, the glow from her laptop illuminating her face. She bit her lip and let a goofy grin break through her normally stormy expression.

Next to Griffin, Wendy's heart did a little flip. She was fairly certain what her younger self was looking at on that screen.

She let her fingers trail across posters advertising the one act festival and spring plays and navigated the props and set pieces she had spent much of her after school time working on during her high school years. She settled onto the cushion next to her younger self, and sure enough, she was right. A pang of loss for what could have been twisted alongside the memory. She looked at her younger self and closed her eyes, reliving the scene in her place. When she opened them again, The Chicago School of Art and Design admissions page stared back at her from the screen. It was a website she'd been visiting more and more frequently. She recalled the thrill that had zipped through her as she clicked and read more about their graphic arts program and the procession of thoughts that had followed. She had to submit a portfolio to qualify, and she hadn't been sure her projects were up to their standards. And also, her life had been here—how could she leave? But for that afternoon, she'd let herself daydream of a different path in a different place all her own.

"Thinking of applying?" The voice of Mrs. Sloane, her favorite teacher, startled her.

Both Wendys, in unison, brought a hand to their chests to still the rapid heartbeats. On young Wendy's other side, Griffin cracked up, and present-day Wendy shot him a glare.

"No. Um, just looking. Well, maybe." She turned toward her favorite teacher, who also oversaw the set design for the drama department.

"I'd have to do a portfolio," she continued. "Probably wouldn't get in, anyway."

"I don't know about that." Mrs. Sloane pushed her glasses up on her nose and took a seat on the arm of the couch. "The institution's job is to teach. I doubt if they expect you to have everything mastered before you even begin."

Wendy's heartbeat picked up again. "But Chicago, though. It's so..." But she didn't know what it was really as she'd never been. From the pictures she'd found on the internet, it looked like a big city with a beautiful lake and tall buildings that reflected the water, and museums and an elevated train. And hundreds of thousands of people who didn't know her as that weird girl who worked for the ghost tour business.

Her mouth went dry. "So... cold," she finished lamely.

"Humans are adaptable creatures," Mrs. Sloane said. "I'm sure you'd adjust. When's the deadline?"

Wendy bit her lip. "Still got two months."

"Why don't you work on a portfolio and think about it?"

Chicago. Art school. Was she really considering leaving this city she loved so much? A dizzying, giddy dread came over her.

"You know, my niece is a graphic artist," Mrs. Sloane continued. "Works in advertising now. She went there, too."

Too. As if getting in and going were a foregone conclusion.

"Why don't I arrange for you to meet? You can ask her all about it."

Without telling another soul, Wendy worked every spare moment on the required elements for her portfolio. A month and a half later, with anxiety buzzing in her chest, Wendy gathered the printouts of the pieces she'd been working on and trotted down the street to meet Mrs. Sloane's niece, Min. The busy café bustled with the afternoon crowd, and the smells of coffee and fruit pastries filled the air.

"These are some great first efforts," Min said, flipping through the pieces Wendy had prepared.

"Um, thanks." Wendy bit her lip and tried to keep her smile from faltering. That was probably a compliment. *I haven't had any formal training,* Wendy reminded herself.

But she'd worked for months on some of these, practicing new blending techniques and tweaking. She tried not to let it crush her.

"I especially like what you did here with the color fading out, but you could work on the proportions in this one."

Two weeks later, Wendy gave a surreptitious glance around the Deveauxs' Historical Haunts gift shop. Once assured that everyone else was otherwise occupied, she slipped into her dad's office to use the good printer. Swallowing her pride, she had taken in every piece of advice Min offered and made revisions to the best of her admittedly limited ability. The printer chugged to life glacially—had it ever gone so slowly?—and Wendy took another nervous glance around. Finally, they were all done, and she gathered the pages, warm against her fingertips. Here it was. Her chance at something new.

She eased her freshly filled out application into its waiting envelope.

"Whatcha doing?" At the sound of Julie's voice, Wendy fumbled the pages, nearly jumping out of her skin and becoming a permanent part of the family's haunted attraction.

"N-nothing." She shoved the designs in as quickly as she could without bending them.

"Wait. Those are nice. You've been holding out on me. Where are you sending them?" Julie tugged at the envelope, and Wendy snatched it back, but not before Julie could read the address.

"You're applying to school in Chicago?" Julie swatted her arm. "Why didn't you tell me?"

Wendy shrugged. She'd expected to hear hurt in Julie's voice, but if it was there, excitement upstaged it. "You're not... I don't know, disappointed?"

"Why would I be disappointed? That's a great school, right? You'd get to study what you love."

"My mom and dad expect me to stay here." Wendy bit her lip.

Julie waved the idea away. "They'll deal."

"Will they?"

Julie smirked. "They might take some persuading. But I can help with that." Her eyes twinkled with the promise of new trouble to stir up, and Wendy felt a surge of affection for her cousin and best friend.

"Let's not get too far ahead of ourselves. It's competitive. They might not want me."

"Of course they'll want you."

"I wish I had your confidence."

Wendy sealed the envelope and walked to the mailbox down the street. Nausea roiled in her stomach. Her palms grew sticky around the manila envelope for reasons that had nothing to do with the humidity. She stood in front of the blue postal box, unable to move. You can do this. Just lift the flap, insert the application. Other people do this every day. A little risk never hurt anyone. Swallowing, she lifted the envelope, and the contents of her stomach threatened to make an appearance. Maybe she could make a few more changes.

It was Julie who had snuck the envelope out of Wendy's backpack and sent it off after several more walks to the mailbox cut short by mental images of the admissions officers laughing at her work.

One day, Wendy came home to her dad frowning and tapping a large white envelope against the kitchen counter.

"This came for you," he said. "From Chicago."

Wendy blanched, and the rush of her pulse in her ears nearly blocked out all other sounds. She looked from her dad's furrowed brow to the envelope curled in his fist. It wasn't too thick, but not totally flat either. Acceptance or rejection? She wasn't sure which would be worse at the moment. The sick feeling that started in her stomach intensified when she chanced a glance at her dad's face.

"So you want to leave?"

She shook her head. "It was just a thought. I don't even know if I got in yet."

"I don't understand. I thought your plan was to stay here. Take over for your old man."

That was *your* plan, she thought.

"At least, you've always acted like you wanted to," her dad said.

That was true. Even if things had been decided for her, she'd never bucked the responsibility or acted like it wasn't her own idea to begin with.

Her dad set the envelope on the counter and scrubbed a hand through his hair. She watched the hurt seep through the rare crack in his bluster. There weren't too many secrets in the Deveaux family. They were sometimes overly involved in each other's business and voiced their opinions on it without holding back. But they also loved and protected each other with a ferocity that Wendy cherished. She saw Rob Deveaux standing before her, looking at his only daughter, who he'd practically raised in the back of their shop so they could spend more time together. He wanted her to learn what hard work looked like and to have a present father. Whenever she'd been in trouble at school, he or her mom came in, guns blazing, always at her side without question, even when she was at fault. And now how was she repaying all of that? By hiding her interest in art and possibly walking away from all that he and her mom had worked so hard to build for her?

"I thought this was your home." He met Wendy's eyes and then looked down at the envelope. "Did I—did I push too hard, make you want to go?"

Her heart crumpled at the break in his voice, and she shook her head. "It was just a thought."

Two nights later, after tossing and turning, her mind unable to quiet from her tempest of thoughts, she finally drifted off into a restless sleep. In her dream, Aundrea and Kara Lynn appeared in her bedroom and grabbed her still unopened envelope.

"Nice t-shirt," Aundrea said, and they both snickered.

Wendy wrapped her arms around her Rougarou t-shirt. "What are you doing? Give that back."

"You're obviously too chicken to open it," Aundrea said. "So I'm doing it for you."

The envelope ripped open, and Kara Lynn snatched the papers out. Her two tormenters exchanged a look.

"You got in!" Kara exclaimed.

"I did?" Wendy blinked the sleep away from her eyes, a lightness buoying in her chest.

She grabbed the letter, but Aundrea and Kara Lynn's cackling laughter turned the lightness into dead weight.

"No. Of course you didn't," Aundrea said.

Kara Lynn shook her head and gave Wendy a pitying look. "Didn't we teach you anything?"

Wendy shot up in her bed, chest heaving, in a tangle of sheets. Sweat beaded on her forehead, and it took her pulse several minutes to return to normal after the remnants of the dream. She flung off the covers and pulled out the art school envelope from the desk drawer where she'd stashed it. What was she even thinking? She had roots here, people who loved her and wanted her to stay. And on the other side of this envelope was what? A gamble. A city of two and a half million people who might meet her and find her wanting.

Guts thrashing, she knew what she was going to do. She'd stay here. Take on the mantle of the store responsibilities. She was a Deveaux and Deveauxs didn't walk away from each other when they were needed. That's who she was.

She might give up part of herself in the process, but maybe what she was keeping was much more valuable.

Resolute, but with an awful feeling, she ripped the envelope in half and then in half again and stuffed it in the kitchen trash can with the shells of last night's shrimp, so she wouldn't be tempted to fish it out again.

"Have you ever wished you'd opened that?" Griffin's voice brought Wendy back to the present.

He strolled over to the trash can and retrieved all four pieces, dusting off some stray cracker crumbs.

A buzz of resistance started in her chest, and she had to get away. She took the stairs back up to the loft, where moonlight shone through the open window.

After that day, Wendy had gone on steadfastly, committed to the choice she'd made, taking business classes at City College and some open source design courses when she could squeeze them in. But in her rawer moments, she had wondered dozens of times how her life would have played out.

Griffin approached from behind with the discarded pieces of letter fitted together. Again, she wasn't sure if she hoped it was an acceptance or a rejection or whether she wanted to know either way.

He looked up at her with a tinge of sadness in his smile, and she knew before he said it.

"You got in."

Wendy squeezed her eyes shut against the feeling of vertigo rising inside her. At that moment, her world seemed to cleave in two. One path was still safe and known, looping endlessly around the streets of the French Quarter, past the waters of the Mississippi, through City Park and the melodies of Jazz Fest, through the crawfish boils and heavy summer air in her parents' backyard. And always, always back to the little gift shop on St. Peter that was her family's livelihood. She'd made her choice that day and hadn't looked back. But now there was this whole other path unfurling in her mind, one where she'd let herself open the letter and gotten on a plane to unfamiliar territory. One where she shut down the voices telling her this was too good to be true. Where she let the part of her that wanted to be something all her own blossom and grow in unfamiliar soil.

She might have failed spectacularly or hated it and headed right back home. But she might have loved it.

What kind of person would she be today if she'd said yes? Would she still have ended up back here?

She opened her eyes and wandered over to the unlatched window as if the space inside were too small to imagine the possibility. Then a thought out of accord hit her, and she frowned.

"I wouldn't have met Alec," she said.

She let her gaze roam the streets she loved.

Griffin joined her and leaned over the window ledge. "Or you might've been a different person when you did."

A tangle of emotions that she didn't like knotted in her chest at the idea. Would that experience have made her into a person who didn't bolt when things looked too good to be true?

She blew out a breath. This was too much. She didn't know the answers to the what-ifs and could-have-beens. She was only the person she was now, the person she knew how to be, the one who knew how far you fell if you took too many chances or got your hopes too high.

After a moment, Griffin broke the silence. "Speaking of Alec, we've got some more ground to cover before midnight."

Griffin motioned toward the open air outside the window. The same ethereal fog that had brought them here drifted into the night sky.

Griffin hoisted himself up onto the sill and swung his legs to the other side. "Come on."

Wendy peered over at the twelve-foot drop to the ground below and frowned, but swung her legs over, anyway.

The fog came faster now in great purple-grey plumes, and Griffin held out his hand for Wendy to take.

She stared at it for a moment and thought of all the other chances she didn't take and where it had gotten her.

She slipped her hand into his, and with a twinkle in his eye, he pulled her forward.

Wendy's butt left the safety of the ledge, and her heart hit her throat as they fell into the fog below. Wind rushed by her cheeks and her ears, and the ground rose to meet her.

CHAPTER 7

Wendy braced herself for the second sighting of Alec in one day. Her feet didn't touch down where she'd expected, though. At the mention of him, she expected the fog to clear in one of the many places that had been their haunts during his year of working in New Orleans. Not... here.

Instead of their favorite café or the bookstore or her place or his, she found herself in the fluorescent haze of a dive bar off the beaten path she used to frequent. Low light reflected off bottles of alcohol and when she took a few steps, her feet came away sticky with spilled alcohol.

"Eww." She made a face.

"Nice place," Griffin quipped.

"I thought this part was about Alec," she said. "Did you need a pit stop first?"

"We're getting there." His eyes gleamed with mischief. "But first, we need a little Wendy's Dating Life montage. Just in case those memories have faded."

Wendy groaned, and it was at that moment that she caught a flash of auburn hair and spotted her younger self—presumably around legal drinking age since she'd never bothered with a fake I.D.—on the corner barstool. An imposing male figure set two shots in front of Wendy and slipped onto the stool next to hers. Some kind of tribal symbol snaked around his substantial bicep, and too much body spray that probably had a name like Ares or Battle Axe followed him like a cloud. He was good-looking in a too-obvious way and clearly had more confidence than sense. He looked familiar, but Wendy couldn't recall his name—Niko, maybe? Or was it Rico?

Young Wendy gave him a flirtatious half smile and threw back her shot and his besides. This seemed to please her companion.

Next to Griffin, Wendy pushed up the strap on her pajama tank top and shook her head, smirking at the exploits of her younger self. She also had more confidence than sense around that time.

At least that's how she'd tried to play it.

Several more similar scenes took shape before her, moving through the seasons, always brief, never letting her get close enough to any of the guys that they'd have the power to wound her the way the girls had years ago. She remembered telling Julie once that guys and relationships were like fruit. They could be indulgent and satisfying in their first few days of ripeness, but if you kept them around too long, they rotted. So she stuck to the ones with a built-in expiration date: those who were only in town for a short while, or were too cocky for her to stand in the long term. These were guys who would never get her *Firefly* references or pass muster at chaotic Deveaux family dinners.

A few more of her dalliances played out before her, and she felt her smirk dip into a frown. She'd lived through this, of course, and hadn't been unhappy with the arrangement in the least. However, somehow in a post-Alec world, the prospect of a future like this felt grim. Especially after being with someone who had gone to Comicon dressed as Wash to her Zoë and had become the designated peacemaker at family dinners.

"Aww, I miss that guy," Griffin said.

Wendy looked up. She'd been so lost in thought that she'd almost missed the change in scenery. The bare winter branches in the last scene gave way to new buds on the Quarter's magnolia and lime trees. The evening air hung heavy with their fragrance, and over the top of the buildings, the horizon took on the tangerine and rose flush of the last throes of sunlight.

Wendy's younger self stood leading a tour group on the street across from the white walls of the Hotel Provincial. Four flags fluttered in the breeze over the entrance to one of the most haunted hotels in New Orleans.

Gathered around her, a group of tourists fanned themselves and peered up at the mint green shutters on the second story as Wendy gave her spiel about the military hospital that used to stand in its place.

Among the tourists, a little apart from the rest, stood Alec, his chestnut hair curling in the humidity. A lump formed in Wendy's throat. She moved without really deciding to do so, and stopped next to her cynical former self, who was busy detailing reports of ghostly wounded soldier sightings. She had no idea what was about to hit her.

She watched her younger self's attention drawn to the tall stranger apart from the crowd. She couldn't quite put her finger on it, but there was something arresting about his presence, even with his air of politeness. He pushed up the sleeves of the navy henley that fit just south of snug across his well-defined chest and hooked his thumbs into the pockets of his jeans. His sea glass eyes crinkled at the corners at Wendy's attempts to add some macabre humor to the Provincial's ghostly history.

Alec's gaze moved in her direction and lingered a beat longer than polite tourist-interest dictated.

Wendy felt something shift in this moment. This day, this meeting was a pivot point in her life. The one time she took a chance and sent her life spinning in a new direction.

She looked into his eyes—gentle and earnest, but fierce when the occasion warranted—and swallowed.

Maybe because this wasn't real, and she didn't have to put on a brave, indifferent face. She let herself feel the full extent of how much she missed him.

How much she missed his laugh and his ability to know exactly what she was avoiding. And more than anything else, she missed having someone in her life who was just hers and who saw her as the girl who upheld her responsibilities and did what everyone expected of her, but also saw the possibilities that she scarcely let herself consider.

Griffin appeared at her side and studied her expression. Wendy schooled all of that naked emotion into a frown and looked back at her other self.

Alec had just smiled at her. It was not the sultry, almost-predatory smile of the guys who usually turned her head. Though no less sexy, his was open and earnest. Not exactly the qualities she was used to seeking out, lest the owner of said qualities expect the same in return. Younger Wendy brushed the hair out of her eyes with a vexed expression, clearly trying to make sense of the flurry that smile kicked up inside of her, like a thousand moth wings in her ribcage.

"Back in those days, there was no such thing as general anesthesia," Wendy Jr. said, talking about the practices in the hospital. "And soldiers came in here with some pretty grisly wounds. So, even if they had to get a leg or an arm amputated, they had two choices of pain relief: the whiskey or the mallet."

She met Alec's gaze again, and he raised an eyebrow.

Wendy mimed a mallet to the temple. "They might've woken up with a headache along with one less limb, but it did the trick."

"No wonder they never got over it." Alec's face lit in a way that said he was part horrified, part fascinated by this new information. It reminded her of the endearing way Julie and Griffin often looked when they were in one of their historical fervors.

Another familiar male voice with a robotic cadence piped up with questions about Civil War surgical procedures. Wendy looked up to see Steve Hanover, all long limbs like a puppy who had not yet grown into his body, and smiled. Her old teacher, Mrs. Sloane, had talked her into doing some volunteer work on the sets with some of her students who didn't work so well with the other kids. Steve was one of them. After learning about his fascination with true crime, Wendy had invited him to come on one of her tours.

Her younger self answered his rapid-fire questions, even when they wandered into excruciating detail.

"Hey, is that when it was popular to bleed patients in Europe?" Steve asked about eight questions in. "Did they do bloodletting here?"

A few impatient sighs came from the back of the group, and Wendy frowned. Since when was curiosity a crime? How quickly people dismissed others if their behaviors didn't fit into the norm.

"I think that was mostly out of favor by then, but there might have been a few doctors still doing it," she said.

"Did you know barbers used to do the bloodletting, not doctors?" Steve continued on one of his famous asides. "That's actually the origin of the barber pole. A red stripe for blood and a white one for bandages."

A few more heavy sighs came from others in the group who were clearly more interested in the landmarks and haunts than tangential history lessons.

Steve looked at the groaners with his brow furrowed in question and shrunk back. The others laughed when he turned around, and Wendy's blood pressure spiked. Her nails sank into the flesh of her clenched fists. Fuck people who made fun of others.

Wendy narrowed her eyes at the laughers, but she tried to rein in her temper before she went full on mama bear and did something that would sully her company's reputation. Instead, she steeled herself and beckoned the group on to the next stop. That way Steve could ask questions while they walked and the others could chill the fuck out.

He fell into step behind her as they headed farther down Chartres, going on about bloodletting practices in Europe. Thankfully, the impatient killjoys hung to the back of the group. Steve really was a sweet kid. Besides his fascination with true crime—and apparently bloodletting—he was one of the most talented woodworkers Wendy had ever met, especially for someone barely old enough for a driver's license. Last month he'd taught Wendy how to use a scroll saw, and he was always happy to share his encyclopedic knowledge of the woods of North America. Too bad most people missed out on that because of his struggle to read social cues.

"I never knew that about barber poles."

Wendy turned toward the sound of the voice. It was a pleasant voice, low and soothing, with a trace of an accent she couldn't place. And it had come from the handsome stranger who had caught up with Steve. Wendy eyed him warily. He sounded friendly enough, but she'd seen enough people chat Steve up only to mock him. It was hard not to be on guard about his intentions.

"My granddad was a barber and my great granddad, too. I've got his old-fashioned barber chair in my living room. And his barber pole, too, actually," Alec said. No hint of mockery. Wendy frowned, hoping none was forthcoming.

"I've got a different kind of pole in my living room," Steve said and then broke into a bout of laughter, which made both Wendy and Alec laugh, too. This barber's grandson had a great laugh, loud and unselfconscious. But was he laughing with Steve or laughing at him, Wendy wondered, eyeing the stranger. He smiled at Steve. With him, she decided. The thought made her stomach do a flip.

"You a pole vaulter?" Alec ventured.

"Nope."

"A fishing pole?" Wendy asked.

Steve shook his head again with a grin.

A stripper pole? Lord, she did *not* want to know if that was the case. Her eyes met Alec's, and his twinkled with shared amusement. For a second she wondered if he'd had the same inappropriate thought, and a buzzing warmth went through her at the thought.

"I have a firefighter pole!" Steve said, busting up again in such an exuberant way that Wendy and Alec couldn't help but join in.

"Seriously?" Wendy said once she'd caught her breath. "You never told me about that. You're holding out on me, friend."

Steve nodded vigorously. "When I was ten, I begged my dad for one so my brother and me could slide down instead of using the stairs."

"I'm going to your house after the tour," Alec said with a smile.

The street lamps illuminated as dusk turned the sky above a dusty azure.

"Uh, you can come over. But not tonight. I have homework."

"Maybe a rain check then," Alec said, still grinning.

Steve nodded. "Hey, you should ask your granddad if he knows about the origins of the barber pole stripes."

"I wish I could." Alec's smile dimmed.

"Is he dead?" Steve asked, to-the-point as ever.

Alec nodded. But unlike most other adult males she interacted with, save maybe her father, he didn't immediately try to change the subject and avoid emotion at all costs. He just walked on and let it be.

"I lost my grandpa about four years ago, too," Wendy said after a moment. Her heart jumped after the words were out. Where had that come from? She hadn't really planned to share that, particularly not with someone she'd just met twenty minutes ago, but there it was.

"It's been about five for me," he said, meeting her gaze. "I'm sorry."

"I'm sorry about yours, too."

"Well, guess you can't ask him then," Steve said.

Alec's lips curved upward again. "Guess not."

They turned a corner and came to a stop in front of the brick facade of Griffin's grandmother's former home and place of business.

"Ah, the famous Sophia Durocher house, right?" Alec eyed the intricate ironwork grates that lined the windows of the upper story.

"And psychic reading parlor," Wendy said. She raised an eyebrow at him again. It had been big news in the city last year when Julie and Griffin had discovered the truth about the murders that had gone down here sixteen years ago and cleared Sophia's—Griffin's grandmother's—name. But it always surprised her when outsiders were familiar with it.

"And the site of the brutal stabbings of Santero and Ackerman," Steve added. "They were dirty politicians who ran a"—he lowered his voice—"prostitution ring. I've read all your cousin's articles."

Alec's eyes took on the glint of curiosity at that comment, but Wendy only flashed him an enigmatic smile. His blue-green gaze heated in response to her smile. In Wendy's chest, a dizzying warmth unfurled, making her limbs go loose and languid. A warning signal blared from the depths of her brain, even as she reveled in the feeling and stole another glance at him with his sexy half smile.

She should probably stay away from this one. From all appearances, he was the kind who showed up on time and you could introduce to your parents. Not someone who was good for a week's entertainment, only to be sent on his way. And yet...

Still rattled, Wendy faced the rest of the crowd and slipped back into tour guide mode, detailing the scandal that involved two dead men, a faked ghostly possession, and an innocent woman sent to prison for fifteen years. Until the real culprit, Marie Renard, was discovered last Halloween.

Julie and Griffin had gone rogue and tracked her down only to wind up at knifepoint, nearly becoming victims themselves. The rest of the tale, which was so close to home, diverted her misgivings for a bit.

This was always a crowd favorite, and the entire group, even the sighers from the last stop, leaned closer, eyes intent on the sensational happenings. Alec was no exception, occasionally making side comments to Steve, which made the boy smile and on a couple of occasions guffaw.

As soon as she'd wrapped up with Sophia's recent release from prison, Steve dove in with questions again, this time from a list he'd retrieved from his pocket.

"How much sedative was necessary to subdue the victims? Do you think they were conscious when Marie stabbed them, or were they passed out already?" he asked. And then, "What did Marie's face look like after your cousin's boyfriend threw the teakettle of boiling water at her?"

Seven or eight questions in, the others got restless again. Several shifted, and others started with the exaggerated sighs.

"You know what Steve, I've got an idea," Wendy said in a low voice. "Why don't we come back here between tours after your school gets out one day. We can make it a private tour, and you can ask me as many questions as you want."

"Really?" Steve's eyes glowed at the possibility. "And I can actually go inside?"

Wendy shrugged. "I can ask Sophia. She hasn't sold the place yet."

Steve's body pulsed with excitement, and Wendy smiled.

"That. Would. Be. So. Awesome."

Wendy loosed a breath in relief. Everyone happy and taken care of. At least for the time being. She motioned for the rest of the group to follow her to the last tour stop.

"So your cousin really just went after this person she was fairly sure was a murderer," Alec said. They rounded the corner onto Bourbon Street, and the sounds of music and people out celebrating a fine Saturday night filled the air. "No police or anything?"

"Well, her boyfriend—fiancé," she corrected, "was in trouble. People do crazy shit when the people they love are involved."

Alec smiled at that, a complicated sort of wistful smile that made Wendy want to unravel the reasons behind it.

Next to him, Steve nodded sagely. "Like buy their sons a firefighter's pole."

They all laughed.

"So you're into crime stuff, too, aren't you?" Steve asked Alec. "Have you watched *Making a Murderer*? It's so good."

Wendy couldn't help but smile as the two chatted away about Steven Avery and Brendan Dassey.

"Have you ever watched?" Alec asked Wendy.

"Eh, I get my fill of true crime at work," she said. But their excitement was contagious and almost made her change her stance on that. Steve loved to talk, and it was so nice to see him have such an enthusiastic conversation partner. Big points for this good-looking stranger.

"You're missing out," Alec said. "That's good stuff."

The slightly different *ou* in the way he said *out* caught her attention again. "Where are you from? You're not local, are you?"

Alec shook his head. "Canada."

"What part?"

"I grew up in Newfoundland, but I'm in Vancouver now."

Wendy nodded, lips curling at this development. Maybe that explained his politeness-to-the-max vibe. And maybe if he was only here for a short time, they could spend some more time together without any kind of expectation developing.

"A lot of lumber comes out of British Columbia. They're a big western red cedar producer," Steve said.

"I suppose," Alec said shrugging. "We do have a lot of trees."

"Some people think cedar is a hardwood, but it's actually in the softwood category," Steve said.

"Steve is something of a lumber connoisseur," Wendy said.

Alec nodded with a smile.

"So, you here for business or pleasure?" she asked.

"A little of both. I'm here for work for a bit and figured I'd check the place out. I was told your tour company was a good place to start."

"You were told right," Wendy said, with a little flush of pride that always came with compliments about the family business.

"I was." Alec met her gaze again, and that sizzle of attraction between them reverberated in her chest.

Wendy corralled the group once more in front of the LaLaurie Mansion, hands down the stop with the most gruesome history. She let her eyes wander over the Alec's tall form as she turned to face them, lingering on his lips which were upturned more on the right side than the left in an easy smile. He caught her looking, and her whole body flushed as that smile widened at her attention, slow and sexy. In this exchange, she missed some of the errant chatter from the back of the group.

Then she heard a derisive tone and something about "the million ques-tion guy." She shifted her attention with a frown, unable to tell which of the tourists it had come from. With a shake of her head, she refocused and started into the story of the infamous socialite turned torturer and murderess, Delphine LaLaurie.

Steve interrupted with a query. She began to answer, and then she zeroed in on the source of the earlier chatter.

"God. Next time I'm going to make sure there're no freaks in the group before I do one of these," a girl with a bowl-cut muttered to her pinch-faced friend.

Wendy stopped mid-sentence, eyes flicking to Steve's wounded face and back to the girls. Fury boiled her insides. If looks could kill, these two would be a pile of mean girl ashes by now.

Bowl cut's face paled, and her companion's eyes widened. The rest of the group shifted uncomfortably.

When Wendy spoke, ice infused every word. "If you feel the need to be disrespectful to other people on the tour, you can leave. Now."

Silence hung heavy in the humid air.

"Are we all clear on that?" Wendy asked.

Fervent, wide-eyed nods came from both girls.

They were probably going to write a bad Yelp review, but Wendy didn't care. She would be damned if she'd let people treat Steve—or anyone else—like that. She took a deep breath to steady herself. "Okay then."

Steve stayed quiet for the rest of the stop, holding his questions in, shooting furtive glances at the two girls who had called him a freak. Wendy's heart sank at the sight, and she abbreviated her usual story, eager to finish up and check in on Steve.

Usually, she led everyone back to the shop at the close of the tour, but this time she announced everyone was free to come back with her or leave off here. Both bowl cut and pinch-face skittered off with most of the others.

"Don't worry about those jerks." Wendy stomped over to Steve as soon as most of the crowd had scattered.

Steve's half-hearted attempt at a smile gutted her all over again. Why were people such assholes?

He shrugged. "Maybe I do ask too many questions."

She hated the way words could cut like this and kill what should have been a fun night for him.

Alec lingered next to Steve. "Hey, in my book, you're much better company than they are," he said. "Besides, I bet they couldn't tell a softwood from a hardwood if it hit them in the face."

A tentative smile broke through the clouds in Steve's expression. "Yeah. Probably not."

"Back to where we started?" Alec asked, this time looking at Wendy.

She nodded, still fuming, but grateful to have another voice of reason nudging Steve away from feeling bad about himself because he didn't fit someone's narrow idea of "normal."

"Hey, have you ever listened to *Serial*?" Alec asked. He steered Steve after Wendy and farther away from judgmental eyes.

"I just finished the second season," Steve said, some of the light Wendy loved coming back into his eyes.

"Season one was way better," Alec said.

"Obviously."

Wendy's heart lifted. She let the sound of their animated chatter carry her back to the shop, Steve's robotic cadence and Alec's low soothing voice mingling together and rising above the other sounds of the Quarter. She stole another glance at Alec. He pushed back curls of hair that had fallen into his eyes and warmed her with his smile. Her skepticism was still strong, but for a moment, she let some of her iron guard down.

Maybe the balance of the world wasn't tipped so heavily in the favor of assholes after all.

CHAPTER 8

Back at Deveauxs' Historical Haunts, Wendy left Steve and Alec to the gift shop while she slipped back into her office to change and grab a blanket for the outdoor movie she planned to see. Once she'd changed into a fresh shirt and jeans, she spritzed on some vanilla body spray.

Still trying to shake off the last bits of residual fury, she peeked out the door. It dissipated a bit more when she saw Steve still hanging out with Alec, a smile on his face, still talking and making animated gestures.

Their laughter carried through the store, and Wendy let her gaze roam the planes of the friendly stranger and unexpected ally's face. She liked the way his lips drew into a smile, one corner turning up before the other. She also liked the way he was with Steve. He seemed like a good dude.

He caught her looking and gave her that same slow grin. Her face heated, but she gave a little wave and ducked back into her office to collect her purse.

Her pulse beat out at an erratic pace, and she flashed back to the look they'd shared during the conversation about the nature of Steve's pole. She wasn't sure why that one had snared her. It wasn't a look of heated longing, but when their eyes met, his somewhere between blue and green, alight with laughter, something had passed between them. It was a co-conspirators' look, and it had hit her somewhere she kept buried. It tugged at a longing that had eluded Wendy most of her life. Connection. Getting someone and having someone else get her.

She cradled the blanket to her chest, a disquiet seeping in to rain on that Mardi Gras parade. She didn't trust her instincts with that desire. It made her stupid and clouded her judgement, making her see what she wanted to be there rather than the stark reality.

It was probably nothing anyway. Sometimes a look is just a look. She'd just say goodnight, thank him for not being a dick, and head to the park as planned.

When Wendy approached, Steve and Alec were exchanging phone numbers.

"I've got to go. My parents are waiting outside. Thanks for the tour." Steve stuck out his hand and gave Wendy a firm handshake.

She smiled. "Anytime. Until Wednesday then."

"We can work on the ship's steering wheel." It was one of the props they were working on.

"If you don't finish it by then."

Alec quirked an eyebrow at this exchange.

"Nice to meet you, Alec," Steve said and shook his hand, too. "You have excellent taste in TV and radio programs. And people, obviously," he said with a laugh.

"You too, man." Alec smiled. "And tell your dad A plus on the fireman's pole."

Steve waved his goodbye, leaving only the two of them behind.

When Alec shifted his weight, there was little distance between them. He was close enough for her to pick up on the scent of sandalwood and masculine sweat that wafted off of him. She really shouldn't look up because those crinkles at the corners of his smiling eyes would ensnare her again. Non-dickhead, impossibly sexy smile, and that raw scent of him that made her want to lay her head on his chest. That potent combo addled her plans and won out over any chance of cool logic. At least for the moment.

"So, it's Alec, huh?" Wendy reached out to straighten a row of tarot cards on display next to them.

He nodded. "That's me. And you're Wendy, right?"

"Yep." Against her better judgement, she looked up at him and felt a flutter in her chest. Now that she'd traded in her boots for flip-flops, he was nearly a full head taller than she was. He had a cleft in his chin, and he looked back at her with those eyes so light that they were almost translucent. She felt suddenly shy without the buffer of Steve between them.

"Thanks for the tour," he said. "I wasn't sure what to expect from a ghost tour, but I figured I should take in some of the local fare while I'm here. It was really fun. You know your stuff, too."

"I try," she said with a self-deprecating smirk.

"So, what's the story with the captain's wheel?" He nodded in Steve's direction. "Side job as a pirate ship builder?" His eyes twinkled.

"Alas, no. I'm a one weird occupation at a time kind of girl. Just some volunteer stuff I do for my old favorite teacher."

"What sort of stuff?"

"Making sets for high school plays. Mostly with kids that don't always mix well with others." She gave a wry smile. "Because I know a thing or two about that."

Alec raised an eyebrow at this, like he didn't quite believe it. She felt another warm pang in her chest.

"Anyway, Steve's one of them. We're doing ship sets for *Peter and the Starcatcher*."

"So you *do* build pirate ships in your spare time."

"I suppose."

"A woman of many talents. I like that."

She met his gaze again, his smiling eyes intent on hers, and that delightful warmth spread out inside her like warm honey. What was she doing getting all susceptible to the touchy feely stuff tonight?

"So," he said after a moment. "I didn't eat before the tour, and I'm starving. Want to grab a late dinner with me?"

Wendy swallowed. Yes. Yes, she did want to get dinner with him. She wanted to keep talking with him, have him keep looking at her like this. Maybe go back to her place with him. Her eyes traced the strong cut of his jawline and the smile that still crinkled the corners of his eyes, desire vying with hesitation. Warning. That things weren't always what they seemed. But what if, in this one case, they were?

"I'm new around here, and I figured you probably know all the best places," he said.

Her fists clutched the blanket, and she bit her lip. "I already have plans."

"Oh." His smile dimmed for a moment. "That's too bad."

Her insides kicked up a storm of nerves. "But they do involve food."

The words were out before she'd consciously decided to forego her earlier plan. Just this once, she let what she wanted win out over what she'd trained herself to do.

His lips turned up at one side.

"Um, do you like movies?" Wendy asked, still abuzz with uncertainty.

"What kind of movies?"

"Bad ones?"

This earned a rich peal of laughter, and Wendy couldn't help joining in. "Bad like everybody dies of cancer, or bad like there's a new volcano about to erupt and the only ones who can save humanity are The Rock and his teacup chihuahua?"

"More like the second one," she said.

Alec gave a thumbs-up.

"So, good food, bad movie?" Wendy asked.

"My favorite combination."

"Me, too."

CHAPTER 9

Half an hour later, Alec spread out Wendy's blanket under an ancient live oak in City Park while Wendy unpacked their picnic basket. Shafts of moonlight peeked through the boughs overhead, creating a lacework of light through the shadows in their little alcove.

A sea of patchwork quilts filled with families, friends, and coolers spanned across the meadow, stopping in front of a jumbo movie screen playing previews before the main feature.

"Now this is what I've been missing." Alec reclined on his elbows and took in the expanse of green. His head swiveled from the screen to the art museum and sculpture garden to the water meandering through the space in the distance. This was one of her favorite places to walk and think and just soak in the city.

"And you said there's a forest in here, too?"

"Yup. On the other side of the park." Wendy handed him a mason jar of sweet tea. "And the world's largest collection of mature live oak trees. Some of them are 600 years old."

Her nerves settled as she watched his expression soften with wonder. It was one much like she got when she slid into her pajamas after a long day at the tour biz and started in on a beading or Photoshop project. She let out a contented sigh and pulled out the muffuletta sandwiches from her favorite deli. Not that she was trying to impress him or anything, but her heart gave an unfamiliar squeeze at seeing Alec react to this place the way she did.

"How long have you been away from your part of the world?" Wendy asked.

"Just a week so far, but I had no idea there were places like this in New Orleans. It reminds me of home a bit."

A week already. Maybe he was heading home earlier than she thought. An unpleasant sinking sensation accompanied the idea, but she forced herself to shake it off. Short and sweet was best, anyway.

"How so?"

"We've got a city park right near the water in downtown Vancouver, too. Great trails and outdoor stuff to do. Also, we have awful movies there from time to time."

She smirked and took a bite of her sandwich.

"Speaking of which—" Alec stopped and prodded dubiously at the bits of cauliflower and carrot in the relish under the assortment of meats in his sandwich. "Hey, is this some kind of vegetable sneak attack?"

Wendy snorted. "Yes. Tiny vegetable ninjas trying to sneak past your defenses." She reached for her drink. "It's just part of the olive relish. Why, you don't like vegetables?" She surveyed the defined ridges of his stomach outlined through his shirt. He certainly looked like he ate his vegetables. If he didn't, whatever he *was* eating was doing his body good.

"Vegetables are fine on their own. I just don't know about cauliflower on a sandwich."

"Relax, it tastes good all together. I promise."

"If you say so." He still looked dubious, but took a bite anyway. "Okay. Weirdly it works."

"Told you."

"So just how bad is what we're watching tonight?" Alec asked.

"See for yourself." She nodded at the screen, which was just flashing the opening titles for *Sharknado: The Fourth Awakens.*

Alec covered his face with his palm and shook his head. Wendy watched a dimple form as he laughed.

"I like to do my own *Mystery Science Theater 3000* running commentary in my head." Wendy's cheeks heated as soon as the words were out. That was not the kind of thing she usually shared. *By the way, my hobbies are reading, knitting, ghost tours, and talking to myself during movies.* But Alec only grinned.

"I used to do that when my mom would drag out her old Godzilla movie collection," he said.

"Now those are truly bad," Wendy said.

"Tell me about it. My mom was obsessed with them. And there was this bowling alley we'd go to when I was a kid that played all these awesomely bad 80's movies on the screens above the lanes. Everyone was in spandex or *Miami Vice* suits—the actors, not my parents and I—"

Wendy smirked at the mental picture of Alec in yellow spandex with a white suit jacket.

"We used to do these goofy voices and imagine what they were saying."

"Dork." Wendy laughed good-naturedly.

He winked at her. "At least I'm in good company."

She felt a swell of that feeling of kinship from earlier, chased swiftly by that awful dread in the pit of her stomach that she was imagining it all, like he imagined the lines of corny movies. She took another sip of her sweet tea to distract herself, and Alec shifted on the blanket until their thighs touched, and he gazed over at her with one of those open, earnest smiles of his. God, it was a nice smile. Reassuring. Sexy. And the hint of laughter in his eyes when he smiled at her like that made her feel included in some delicious secret, like with him she'd always be in on the joke. The warmth of the contact and the want for more of that feeling despite her reservations overloaded her circuitry. She leaned into him, but immediately stiffened.

"You okay? Is this okay?" He tapped his knee against hers. It was a playful movement, giving her an out, if that's what she wanted.

This is no big deal, she told herself. It was okay to enjoy his company as well as the sexy curve of his lips, right?

"Yeah." She forced herself to relax then and tapped her knee against his with a smile. "Just had a Godzilla flashback."

As Ian Ziering and company combated the latest outbreak of sharknados on the Las Vegas Strip, Wendy pushed away the plague of doubts and let herself be lulled into easy chatter with Alec.

"Seriously, you're going to 'surf' a car off the Stratosphere tower?" Wendy said.

"He's using the surf force." Alec wiggled his fingers.

"That's not how the surf force works!" she said. "Or the laws of physics."

"I'm pretty sure that there's no such thing as an actual surf force, so it can do what it wants."

Their eyes met in shared terrible movie delight.

"Oh my God, they're going to ride the pirate ship down the Strip, aren't they? No one can tell me this isn't pure entertainment gold," Wendy said.

"Look at the captain's wheel. You totally could've made the set piece for this."

A few scenes later, Wendy balked at the characters hopping from the top of one train car to another to fend off a freak shark attack. "Seriously, how can you do anything but hold on for dear life on top of a train going 60 miles per hour?"

"You know you want to have a shark fight on top of a dining car."

"Yep, that's me, Wendy Deveaux, train desperado."

Alec cocked his head. "Deveaux, like your tour company? Is that your family business?"

Wendy nodded.

"That explains your expertise about all of those places. So is this something you got roped into or something you've always wanted to do?"

Wendy paused. She opened her mouth to answer, and then frowned.

"Sorry, too personal? You don't have to answer if you don't want."

"No. It's just..." She looked up at him. It was nice to have someone care about what *she* wanted. "I don't think anyone's ever asked me that before. It's always been a given that I'd be a part of the family business."

"That sounds like a lot of pressure."

"Sort of comes with the territory in my family." But she shrugged. "It's nice to be a part of something, though. To have a place where I belong."

Alec nodded, and his gaze turned back to the movie screen. She could have sworn she caught a wistfulness in his eyes. She wondered where he belonged. And then chided herself for the thought that followed, imagining him as part of where she belonged, too.

After a few more scenes, Alec turned to her. "Do you always come here by yourself?"

She shrugged. "Sometimes. Usually my cousin Julie comes with me, but she has a strict no cheesy movie policy. Sometimes my mom and dad come, too."

"So you don't take all of your gentlemen callers here?"

Wendy snorted. "Gentlemen callers? Definitely no."

Alec relaxed a bit, and his fingers brushed hers, sending a tingle racing up her arms. There was a sort of vulnerability in his teasing that Wendy admired. How did other people do that? Just make it plain how they felt without worry that they'd be stomped all over?

"So, what did I do to make it into the secret bad movie club?" Alec said.

Wendy tipped her head back and watched the stars through the trees for a moment before looking over at Alec again. "Well, you're cute, and you're a non-asshole, so that was a good start."

Alec put a hand to his heart, and humor glinted in his eyes. "I think that is the nicest thing anyone has ever said about me."

Her chest shook with laughter. "Stick around. I've got plenty more where that came from."

"I'm on board with that plan." He held her gaze for a moment as he traced the back of her fingers with his fingertips. She tipped her head back and let her eyes fall closed. The sensation of his touch swirled inside of her, loosening her iron grip on the reins of her control. Maybe she didn't have to keep all of her emotions on lockdown after all. She snuck another glance at him and quickly looked away.

"Um, thanks for being decent tonight. With Steve. He needs more people around like that."

Alec shrugged. "He seems like a pretty awesome kid. I hate that those girls were making fun of him. Been there too many times myself."

I couldn't think of what people might find fault with in such a confident, funny, decent person like him.

"Oh yeah? What's your offense against the normals?"

Alec laughed. "I had a really bad stutter as a kid. It still comes out when I'm really nervous. Thank God for speech therapy. Middle school kids are merciless."

"Tell me about it."

"So, what about you? You have any offense against the normals?"

"A family who makes their living from paranormal activity. Actually liking the stuff we studied in lit class. Except for Hemingway, of course."

"Who likes Hemingway?" Alec mimed, putting a finger down his throat.

"Not me."

They grinned at each other.

"You said you're here for work, right?" Wendy said. "What sort of work do you do?"

"Computer stuff. Nothing nearly as exciting as yours."

"What, you don't get to talk about paranormal activity all day and occasionally fend off assholes?"

"I guess there is the occasional asshole. Maybe not *so* boring. I mostly took this assignment because my sister lives here," Alec said.

"Really? Older or younger? You seem like you could be an older brother."

"Well, I guess I am technically five minutes older."

Wendy's eyebrows spiked. "No way. You have a twin? Did you guys have a secret twin language growing up?"

Alec's expression clouded, and she wondered if she'd said the wrong thing.

"I'm sorry. Do you not get along or something?"

"No, no, we do. It's just sort of complicated." He sat up and laced his hands together. "I had no idea I even had a twin until last year."

"Seriously?" This was intriguing. But it also seemed personal. Not the sort of thing she might share on a first date if their roles were reversed.

"We were both adopted."

"And your parents never told you?" Wendy breathed. She imagined having a sibling she never knew existed. Or growing up with a Julie-shaped hole in her life, never having had that closest confidante who was more like a sister than a cousin to her. What would her life have been like without that bond?

"They didn't know. Well, until—my dad passed away a few years ago. And then my mom got sick, too." Alec frowned, and a muscle in his jaw ticked. "Anyway, she did some digging before it got really bad and found out about my sister."

The breath seemed to still in Wendy's chest.

"She didn't want me to be alone."

Wendy's heart constricted. Instead of trying to deflect or brush away the emotion like so many guys in her experience, he just let it be.

"I'm so sorry," she said in a small voice.

Alec gave her a smile that chased some of the clouds away. "Thanks."

"I'm glad you found your sister, though." She slipped her hand into his and squeezed, uncharacteristically giving what she would need. "And that you're not alone."

"Me, too."

They sat for a moment, letting the sounds of the movie wash over them.

"Well, this conversation got intense fast," Alec said with a grin.

"I think this calls for more David Hasselhoff and a cyborg woman," Wendy said, nodding to the screen.

Alec's thumb traveled over her wrist. She'd never realized how sensitive the skin there was. Their gazes met. Hers shy. His steady. "I haven't really talked about that with anyone."

She squeezed his hand and leaned into him, a rush of emotion inundating her at being taken into his confidence.

On screen a chainsaw-mobile took care of an oil/firenado.

They both laughed.

As if she were a compass needle, and he the true north, their eyes locked on one another. She let the emotion well, and while his gaze roamed her face, she felt it like touch. As his eyes moved to her mouth and back to meet her eyes, desire mingled with the other tangle of feelings. Her lips parted. She shifted closer and leaned into him. He met her halfway, gaze alight, never wavering until their lips met.

He gripped the back of her neck and pulled her to him. In the crush of mouths and breath and skin, her consciousness seemed to spin away, leaving only this one clear desire for *more*. More touch, more time with this polite Canadian and his sexy laugh and broad hands exploring the skin at her waist who also liked cheesy movies and was kind to strangers, and maybe just maybe was the same kind of weird as she was.

His lips moved slowly, teasingly, over hers, drawing out a contented sigh. Every part of her seemed to melt into honey. This was not the lust-drenched frenzy she was accustomed to—though there was certainly lust involved—the kind that burned hot and bright in a rush to consume everything before the fizzle. This was slow and languorous, with a promise of more to come.

Alec pulled back and looked at her, his translucent eyes heavy-lidded and chestnut curls mussed from where Wendy's fingers had threaded through them.

"I already want to kiss you again," he said. His voice was pitched low, so low that she had to sway closer to hear.

Wendy flushed and gave him a coy grin. "I fully support that idea."

She leaned in for another taste that was not nearly enough.

Giggles erupted from the group of pre-teens a few blankets away.

Wendy and Alec separated, still grinning at one another.

"If we keep this up, we might scare away the children, though," Alec said.

He reclined on the blanket and drew Wendy to his side. She joined him, breathing in the woodsy scent of him as she pillowed her head on his chest. Alec stroked her hair, and the cicadas sang over the sounds of the movie. A contented sigh escaped her lips.

"A blanket under the stars, a Texas chainsaw massacre of sharks. It doesn't get more romantic than this," Alec said.

Wendy laughed.

They settled into a comfortable silence as the movie played on. She traced the lines of his chest with her fingers. Each time a rumble of laughter reverberated through her cheek, a warm happy feeling danced through her chest under their blanket of stars.

After a long while, the rise and fall of his chest grew slow and steady.

"That's like some terrible Transformers cosplay," Wendy said.

No answer.

"Alec?" She pushed up to her elbow to see his eyes closed in peaceful slumber and lips slightly parted. He'd fallen asleep. It struck Wendy as an oddly charming thing to do. And a trusting one. With a grin, she snuggled back into his side.

When the credits rolled, she shook his chest gently. Alec let out a gasp. His eyes blinked open, getting his bearings. His expression softened when he looked up at Wendy. He nestled into her and covered her hand on his chest with his own.

"Did I really fall asleep? How did it end?"

"The sharks ate all the original cast members of *90210*, and Tara Reid saved the world with laser lipstick."

"Totally called it." Alec gave her a sleepy smile.

Wendy laughed.

"Sorry I zonked out. Am I the worst date ever?"

"I assumed I was when the snoring started."

"Pssh. You gave me a vegetable sandwich and took me to see sharks on a train. That's hardly a bad time."

Alec propped himself up, aligning his body with Wendy's. Every place their bodies touched ignited, and she suppressed a heady groan.

"I was up early today." He stroked a hand across the swell of her hips, and she loosed a breath. "Actually, I'm up early every day. I'm sort of an early to bed early to rise kind of guy."

"How early is early?" Wendy asked.

Alec's fingers twined in her hair. "Six most days, but today I was up at five thirty."

Wendy made a face. "I don't trust anyone who voluntarily gets up before seven a.m.."

He shrugged. "I can't help it. My body just wakes up. What time do you get up?"

"Nine or ten if I have a late work night. "

"Seriously? You're missing out."

"On what?"

"The world is quiet and still in the morning. I love it. Also, sunrises. Early morning donuts." His lips brushed hers with a sleepy kiss.

"It's perfectly quiet and still in my house at nine a.m. And we can have donuts at any time of the day."

"Not fresh from the oven."

"Meh. Still not enough to tempt me."

Alec's eyelids fell heavy, like sleep was ready to reclaim him at any moment.

Wendy planted a feather-light kiss on his nose and slipped away to repack their picnic basket.

"Come on, sleepyhead. Let's get you home before you get a citation for sleeping in the park."

"Mmm," he murmured, but eventually pushed to his feet. He hefted the picnic basket with one hand and laced his fingers through Wendy's with the other.

"You could come back home with me," he said, turning his sexy, sleepy-eyed gaze on her. Something hammered in her chest at the thought. He looked way too tired for any recreational activities, so was he just being hopeful or inviting her to just sleep next to him? She imagined settling under unfamiliar covers with him, resting her head on his chest, trusting, just feeling the warmth of him next to her with that same sleep-mussed look on his face, waking up tangled up in him. She'd never done that before—just sleep with someone. Her chest tightened. The intimacy of the prospect overwhelmed her. That would open her up to all kinds of *feelings* that would only have to be retracted after he went back home.

"So you can pass out on me and then wake me up at 5:30 a.m.?"

He grinned and nodded.

"Tempting. But..."

"How about another night, then? You, me, vegetables in their proper place. I'd love to see you again."

Wendy swallowed and unlocked her car. "Yeah, okay. I'd like that, too."

Alec sat the basket in the backseat and cupped Wendy's cheek. The warm metal of the car pressed into her back. The pads of Alec's fingers trailed the lines of her jaw, setting loose shivers down her spine, and sending her mind reeling. Her hands moved of their own accord, grasping his hips and pulling him to her. She might be moving into dangerous territory, but for the moment, she didn't care. Her lips parted and Alec sighed against her and pressed into her for another slow, mind-melting kiss. His groan reverberated through her. And she wanted so much more. When they parted, chests heaving, he kissed her forehead and leaned in to whisper in her ear.

"I promise not to fall asleep on you next time." His breath on her neck sent arousal unfurling in every part of her.

"I'll hold you to that."

CHAPTER 10

"Lapped you!" Wendy leapt triumphantly on her treadmill, sending her ponytail flapping against her back. When in doubt, Wendy always found it best to sweat out her feelings.

Next to her, Julie's face took on a disbelieving look, and she squinted against the late morning sun at her cousin's virtual track screen to confirm. Wendy's tennis shoes slapped a steady rhythm over the sound of music videos playing on the big screens of the gym. "Someone's got some serious sexual frustration to work out today."

Wendy adjusted her speed from beast mode down to a comfortable jog and sipped from her water bottle. "Who says it's not work frustration?" she shot back.

"Nuh uh." Julie shook her head and mopped her forehead with a towel. "You're in too good a mood for that. You didn't even make a smart-ass comment when the guy at the counter told us his boss made a 'mute point'"

Wendy gave a mock innocent look and shrugged. "Maybe the point was made in writing."

"Or maybe—" Julie watched her with a sly grin, no doubt picking up on Wendy's cheeks heating even under the flush of exertion. Wendy could get away with deflection with everyone else, but Julie saw through it every time.

"Maybe what?" Wendy said.

"Nothing." Julie shook her head, eyes still glinting. "So he really invited you back to his place after this magical date, and you said no?"

Wendy'd filled Julie in on the details of last night when they'd met up for a run this morning. "He was tired. I was being considerate. And who said magical? That was *not* my word."

"It was implied." Julie's eyes twinkled.

Wendy scoffed.

"Maybe you want more than a Mountie with your new guy from up north."

"Har har."

Wendy trotted on, relishing the burn in her calves and runner's high and the way the physical exertion quieted her nagging worries. Including the worry that Julie's suggestion had a grain of truth to it.

A few minutes later, her phone screen lit up with a text message notification.

Hey, it's Alec from last night. Tall, pale, owner of an antique barber pole.

Even though she'd kicked her speed down several notches, her heart rate sped up. Last night he *said* he wanted to see her again, but you never knew.

Can't stop thinking of kissing you goodnight.

Wendy's mind traveled back to the sensation of his lips grazing hers, of her pulling his hips against hers until her back was pressed to the car. She could still see the sleep-kissed look on his face before his lips brushed her forehead. Fire seeping back into her limbs, she snuck a glance at Julie and picked up the phone to answer.

Good thing you added the last part. I was a little hazy on the rest. =)

At least something made an impression.

You could say that.

Hey, do you have any plans for tonight?

She glanced at Julie, who had gone back to reading her book as she walked at a steep incline. *I'm hanging out with my cousin this afternoon, but we'll finish up about 4.*

I know you said you got enough true crime at work, but how do you feel about fictional crime? And dressing up.

Wendy's mind raced, gleefully puzzling over what activity might involve both crime and cosplay.

"That's him, isn't it?" Julie peeked over Wendy's shoulder, angling for a look at her phone.

Wendy started and looked over to see her cousin's sly grin spreading.

"So what if it is?" Her cheeks flushed.

"You really like him," Julie declared with a note of shock and delight.

"Yes, we already covered that. He's very attractive."

"Yeah, but you don't get all flustered like this over just any Jared Padalecki look-alike." Julie waggled her eyebrows. "You like his brain. His big sexy brain."

Wendy huffed a laugh. "Whatever. He's only here for a little while. Sadly, I cannot get overly invested in his brain."

Still, she slowed to a cool down pace and turned back to her phone.

I'm intrigued.

My sister got us tickets to this Murder Mystery Dinner Experience tonight, but she had a last-minute work event come up and had to cancel, so I was wondering if you wanted to go with me. It's an interactive thing. Everyone gets a role and a costume and we try to figure out whodunit. K said it has a 1920s theme.

Oh. Yes. Wendy thought back to watching the movie *Clue* as a kid and thinking of how much fun it would be to dress up as Ms. Scarlet for Halloween. Except she was a generation or two too late for anyone to get who she was in an emerald dress, even with the cigarette holder and a candlestick.

Who do we get to be? she typed.

Let's see... I'm Henry Astor, oil tycoon with secret dealings with the FBI and a pet tiger. And you'd be Astrid Hollingsworth, survivor of the Titanic's maiden voyage, suspected diamond thief, and regular at the local speakeasy.

Ooh, can I wear a garter and tuck my flask into it? There is a prohibition, you know.

I will personally procure both of those things if you will.

Wendy laughed. *I'm in.*

CHAPTER II

At 6:25, Wendy rolled on the silky black stockings she'd picked up earlier. She didn't have many occasions to wear things like this, but she couldn't resist the opportunity to add a little of her own 1920s flair to the evening. And okay, the memory of Alec's body pressed against hers while he promised not to fall asleep on her next time had definitely played in her mind when she'd picked them out.

She smoothed her dress over the lacy bits that stopped mid-thigh and peeked out the window. No sign of new cars on the street yet. She spritzed on perfume that smelled like vanilla and honey, and then clenched and unclenched her fists. It was still five minutes before Alec said he'd pick her up. Nothing to worry about.

But a tremor of uncertainty passed over her. And then those awful thoughts droned around her head like flies. What if he doesn't show up? He'd given her no reason to suspect that, she reasoned, but she'd missed the signs before. Though it was entirely possible she'd projected more than was really there onto whatever was happening between them. Probably a guy who was sweet to Steve and laughed at ridiculous movies with her and kissed her like he was just getting warmed up for more was just too good to be real. She'd never admit to anyone how these misgivings dogged her and wreaked havoc on the cool mask of composure and snark she presented to the world. But she couldn't help it. It had never quite left her, that feeling that she was always one step away from being the butt of someone else's joke. Not that she'd given many people the opportunity to let her down.

The sound of tires crunching over the gravel in front of her house brought her attention back to the window. A car engine stopped, and Alec stepped out of the SUV in front of her house in dark jeans and an olive green shirt. Wendy's breath whooshed out of her, and she watched him walk to the stairs to her porch. See? Nothing to worry about.

But she couldn't quite shake the traces of that uncertainty as she trotted down the stairs.

Moments later, Wendy opened the door, and at the sight of him clean shaven with that note of humor in his eyes, she felt the pull again.

"Hey," he said, his dazzling smile spreading as he took in Wendy's stockinged legs and black dress that flared at the waist. His gaze lingered on her face, the weight of it searing through her nerve endings, and the breath caught in her throat.

"You look beautiful," he said.

Her cheeks warmed. She reached for one of her usual snarky deflections but couldn't quite come up with one. Beautiful: it seemed like a normal thing that people said to each other, but she wasn't used to it. Unlike its cousins, hot or sexy, beautiful seemed to imply something beyond just a physical pull.

"Thanks. So do you." Her eyes wandered over his upper body, appreciating the way his shirt showed off his chest. She flipped a hand. "I mean good. Nice. Handsome. Pick your positive adjective."

"Too bad there are costumes involved tonight," Alec said. "Or maybe you could skip that."

"Oh, hell no," Wendy said. "When life hands you a chance to dress up as a 1920s diamond smuggler, you take it."

Alec smiled. "Speaking of which, I brought something for you."

He produced two items from his back pockets.

No, he did not. Wendy practically bounced with glee.

"As promised. I had a harder time with the garter than the flask, but I found this beauty in a tourist shop."

Wendy laughed as he twirled the garter in a sparkly whoosh of green, gold, and purple around his index finger.

"Metallic and elastic. Sexy." Wendy accepted it. She read the word printed on its ribbon and laughed. "*Lagniappe.*"

"I'm not sure what it means," Alec admitted. "But I figured I'd roll with it."

"It's Cajun French. Sort of like the cherry on top. A little something extra to sweeten the deal."

Alec's smile widened, and he handed over the flask. "*Lagniappe*, I like it."

"What have we got here?" Wendy said, feeling the weight of the liquid sloshing inside.

"Sweet tea," Alec said, "with a little kick."

"Cheers." She held it up, took a sip, and offered him one.

He shot her a grin. "Don't let the coppers see you with that."

Indulging in her shenanigans: major points for Alec.

"You want to come in for a sec? I just need to run upstairs and grab my purse."

"Sure."

A few minutes later, she trotted down the stairs, putting on her second earring to find Alec examining one of her paintings.

"Just checking out your artwork." He motioned to the canvas behind him where a girl stood in the foreground, apart from everyone else under a wide black umbrella. Around her, rain splashed in a riot of colors, dripping like a torrent of melted crayons.

Wendy stopped in her descent, her pulse stuttering. Seeing his possibly critical eye turned on the things she'd created stripped her earlier brazenness away. Her work was an extension of her, like her inner workings out for display. The urge to run back up the stairs or rush him out the door without comment pulsed through her. It felt like being naked and inspected for imperfections. She hadn't prepared herself for this kind of exposure tonight. Maybe at all.

She swallowed and forced herself to keep going.

"I think this one's my favorite." He nodded to the umbrella girl.

Her held breath rushed out. Some of the ball of rejection anxiety building in her chest eased.

"It's sort of sad and whimsical at the same time," he said. "Like if you saw a centaur riding a motorcycle in the park, but no one else will ever get it or believe you because you're the only one who saw it. And that's sad." He met her eyes, and they both laughed at his ridiculousness.

"Shall we?" she said, still wanting to get some distance from this vulnerable feeling. She stepped into the living room.

"Where'd you get that one? Local artist?" Alec asked.

"Um, yeah." She worried her lower lip, ready to leave it at that, but with an ever increasing drumming of her pulse in her ear, she admitted, "Me."

"No kidding?" He looked at her with wonder, like this was a new artifact in the archeological dig of Wendy's life. A flush of pleasure crept up her neck and cheeks.

"It's a digital painting. I was working with some new textures."

"A woman of many talents. I can barely fingerpaint."

A feeling of relief flooded in again, but not enough to keep her from her long ingrained habit of deflecting once again.

"I don't think centaurs could ride motorcycles." She shot him a wry smile.

"Says who?"

"They couldn't reach the handlebars. And they'd have two extra legs and a giant ass hanging off the back. That would be an ergonomic nightmare."

"Don't kill their motorcycle dreams."

Their gazes met again, laughter in both of their eyes. Then they set out to solve a murder.

CHAPTER 12

A short time later, Wendy stepped out of her dressing room dripping in 1920s glory. She brushed the cascade of crystals from her fascinator out of her eyes and scanned the room, eager to see if Alec had gotten as much of a kick out of playing dress-up as she had. She adjusted the beaded strap of her dress, unable to stop the totally unironic smile from overtaking her face. It felt good to have a night away from work doing something out of the norm with someone who didn't have to be coerced into playing along.

Light glinted from the dripping crystals of the parlor chandelier, and another eight or nine people milled about. She caught sight of Alec standing behind a potted plant. He wore a suit and bow tie, and he lifted his straw boater hat in greeting as he spotted her. Wendy grinned at the exaggerated, genteel grin on his face. His hat wildly mismatched with the elegance of his suit, but it somehow worked, as if Alec had a way of charming all disparate things into working together. She'd never really gotten the fuss other women made about guys in suits, but as her eyes swept over the way the crisp, dark fabric lined his long legs and biceps, she could see the appeal.

She approached and made a little curtsy. Polite though he may be, the way Alec's gaze heated as it traveled over the gossamer and beadwork, trailing over the low neckline of her dress, and finally up to her eyes turned Wendy's insides to honey butter.

"I take back what I said before about the no costumes thing," he said, his blue-green eyes holding hers.

"Told you." She unleashed a coy smile.

Alec hooked his thumbs under his suspenders and popped them forward. Who knew suspenders could be sexy, but they were definitely working for him.

"Speaking of getting into character, I almost forgot." He faced away from her and turned back with a stick-on mustache. Its bushy ends curled over the edges of his grin, and Wendy's chest shook with laughter. "What do you think? Too much?"

She reached up to tweak one side of it, grateful for the levity. "I don't know. Should I be worried that you're going to tie me to some train tracks later?"

"Never can tell." He grinned at her.

"Ah, Mr. Astor, Miss Hollingsworth, I see you two are already acquainted." A man in a brown suit and derby hat—one of the actors, Wendy presumed—approached them with a bemused look on his face.

"Indeed, we are," Wendy said, already getting into character.

Alec nodded.

"Horace Brown." He stuck out a hand for Alec to shake. "Though *you* already know that." With this he flung a disgruntled look at Wendy, and she grinned, eager to find out what this was all about.

Alec's palm grazed the small of her back, and the possessiveness of the gesture sent new tingles of awareness zinging pleasantly through her.

Mr. Brown moved his attention to Alec's hand on her back with a pronounced frown. "This will be interesting." He shoved a slip of paper at Alec. "Cocktails around the corner at The Jake. This password will get you in."

"Do you have a jealous fiancé I should know about?" Alec said.

"Not that I know of. But you never can tell."

A few moments later, another an actor in a champagne dress who introduced herself as Tina whisked the two of them behind a curtain into a small alcove. Dim lights flickered overhead, casting the walls and door surrounding them in a crimson hue. A small door about eye level slid open and a pair of green eyes regarded them from the other side.

"Yeah?" The green-eyed man said. Jazz and laughter floated through from beyond.

Wendy and Alec traded an amused glance.

"Maybe he needs the password," Wendy whispered.

Alec unfolded the paper Mr. Brown had given him, his lips curling into a smile and read, "The great bambino wants some giggle water."

Chains clinked out of place and the door swung open into a dimly lit speakeasy with a mix of actors and guests gathered around a makeshift bar and tall tables.

"Make yourself at home. Grab a drink," Tina said, once they were inside. Then she turned to Alec. "You might need it. You're a brave soul stepping out with Mr. Brown's lady. He's likely to make an example of you."

With a bootleg lemon drop and whiskey in hand, Alec and Wendy gathered around one of the unoccupied tables. "Apparently I do have a jilted fella." She shrugged. "Hard to keep up, what with surviving the Titanic and the diamond smuggling and all."

"How exactly did you manage to survive the Titanic?" The ice in Alec's glass clinked as he took a sip of his drink.

"A friendly dolphin carried me to shore. And then she came to live with me on my country estate."

His eyes glinted. "Lucky dolphin."

Wendy snorted. "And how did you get into your dealings with the FBI?"

"That is a really funny story, too, which also coincidentally involves a sea mammal and a vending machine that did not contain Coca Cola."

Wendy nodded sagely and ran a finger over the sugared rim of her drink.

"It's too bad your sister couldn't come tonight. I mean, selfishly I'm glad to take her place, but I'm sure you probably want to spend time with her."

Alec gave a half smile that seemed to dull the gleam that had been in his eyes only a moment ago. Had she touched on a nerve? But before she could ask or consider what had caused it, his smile had returned full force. "I'm glad you could come when she couldn't."

"So what's she like?" Wendy couldn't contain her curiosity. She'd been thinking about the way it might feel for him to have an unknown twin and have a chance to make up for all the lost time. "Did it feel familiar meeting her for the first time, or bizarre?"

He shrugged. "She's like a female version of me."

"So... likes corny jokes and can really pull off a fake mustache?"

"Yup." He gave her a wry smile.

Wendy took a drink.

"Well, I don't know if she'd be into the mustache. She's sort of fancy."

Wendy cocked her head. "What do you mean?"

"You know how all the women dress for the cocktail parties on *The Bachelor*? She dresses like that all the time."

Wendy couldn't help giggling. "Wait, you seriously watch *The Bachelor*?"

"Says the girl who admitted to seeing *Scary Movie 1, 2,* and *3.*"

"Fair point."

"Occasionally." Alec shrugged.

"Let me guess, your mom liked it and you played along?"

"Nope. That one's all me."

Wendy continued to crack up, and Alec's cheeks colored. But other than that he didn't look the least bit embarrassed about his TV choices.

"What? It's a fascinating look at human nature."

"Watching thirty women fight over one dude?"

"Hey, I don't discriminate. I'll watch *The Bachelorette,* too."

Wendy rolled her eyes, her smile curving all the while.

"You've got to admit the editors are pretty genius. I always try to guess what's real and what's a show for the cameras. Plus, I've got to take a break from true crime once in a while."

"Well, in that case, I'll have you know, I'm here for the right reasons." Wendy placed a hand on his arm and gave a mock earnest look. "To get discovered so I can be on a shampoo commercial and eventually get my own daytime talk show. And possibly go bungee jumping in the process."

"I knew it."

They grinned at each other, and Wendy just wanted to keep talking to him here, keep up the easy banter that didn't seem so easy or natural with anyone else.

"So, back to your sister. You hold the key to the nature vs. nurture debate in your hands here. What's she like besides all *Bachelorette* all the time?" Wendy said.

"She's really dedicated to her job." This sounded like a diplomatic answer, masking something else.

"But?" she asked.

"I get the feeling she doesn't like it very much. Or at least parts of it."

"Sounds like we'd get along great."

Alec smiled at that. "Her family runs some restaurants here, and she has a food blog that she's really into."

"Oh yeah? What sort of food does she blog about?" Wendy asked.

"Southern comfort food and sweet afters. That's the tagline on her blog." The pride in Alec's expression when he talked about something important to his sister endeared him to her even more.

"Have you gotten to spend much time with her since you've been here?"

A crinkle formed between his brows. "I came for a couple of weeks last fall after we'd emailed and talked on the phone a lot. She took the whole time off then."

There was definitely more going on than he was saying. "She must be thrilled that you're here for a while now."

His lips formed a thin smile. "Yeah."

"What is it?" Wendy frowned. "Are you not getting along?" She imagined herself in his situation: no family left except for this new person who should be the person who knows him best, but was still in so many ways a stranger. Could she be rejecting him? The thought boggled her mind. She couldn't imagine anyone being around Alec with his quick wit and easygoing curiosity and not wanting to spend more time with him. Her chest constricted at the thought.

"No. No, we get along fine. She's just cancelled for work stuff the last few times we made plans to get together." His lips turned up again, but she could still sense the sore spot.

"That sucks."

He shrugged a shoulder. "I get it. She always calls and tries to make it up to me. And I'm glad she's doing something important." He ran a hand through his hair and looked down. "I'm just used to a family that's all up in my business. Sometimes it feels like I'm more of an afterthought to her."

"I can't imagine you being an afterthought to anyone."

His smile softened as he met her fierce expression. "Just growing pains, I'm sure. She grew up differently than I did. Her parents love her, but they're also sort of distant."

Actors came by their table in turns, dropping pieces of gossip about the other players in the room. The newspaper reporter who got mixed up in a gambling ring. The overlord he owed money to. The love triangle between them and Mr. Brown. Alec seemed relieved to have a murder investigation to take his thoughts away from his sister, and they speculated on who might be the one to drop dead during dinner and who might be the one to do the deed.

They were trading theories about Mr. Brown and the owner of the speakeasy when Wendy's phone buzzed with a text notification. She glanced in her purse. It was from her dad. Probably some work problem he wanted her to take care of tomorrow. She reached for it out of habit, and then changed her mind and tucked it away again.

"Do you need to get that?" Alec asked.

She shook her head and continued their conversation, but the phone buzzed again. Wendy sighed, trying to ignore it, but a few minutes later, the buzz of a call came through.

"Sorry, it's my dad. Probably a work thing. Do you mind if I see what he needs?"

Alec motioned for her to go ahead, and she stepped into a quieter corner.

"Hey, why aren't you answering my texts?" her dad's voice boomed through the phone, with no greeting or preamble.

"Um, maybe because I'm in the middle of something." Irritation edged her voice. "Is everything okay?"

"It's Sunday night. Yeah, everything's okay."

"And I'm in the middle of Sunday night plans."

"Doing what?"

"Murder mystery dinner theater."

"With Julie?"

Her chest fluttered a bit. "No, with a... date."

He grunted. "Anyway, I need your help. The producer from the *Alt History* show that's coming tomorrow called and wants to have a briefing tonight and have you send her the detailed itinerary notes ASAP."

"Claudia?" Wendy rubbed her temple. "I did all of that last week."

"Well, apparently Claudia left and took her computer with her, and no one is prepped. So I need you to call Kim, the new person in charge, and get her all the stuff she needs. I'll give you the number. Can you run into the office and get this taken care of? It shouldn't take long."

Alec shot her a concerned look from across the room, and that pleasant hot-air balloon feeling in her chest felt weighted down with sandbags. It's not like this was an abnormal occurrence, fielding a work request late at night, zipping off to take care of things. Normally it made her feel needed, important. Like staying had been the right choice and that the creative touches she'd added to the business were worthwhile. But at the moment it just felt like someone pissing in her Cheerios. Not to mention the fact that her running off to do work stuff would only rub salt in the wound left by Alec's sister doing the same thing.

"Can you call her? Or can this wait a couple of hours? I'm right in the middle of something."

Her dad's heavy silence added several more sandbags.

"You're the expert on this. You've got all the details and materials. And, you were the one who was pushing to branch out into new appearances and events like this."

She gritted her teeth. It was true. Getting the company to branch out in new directions—making connections with people who could get them some media buzz and partnering with reader and writer group events in New Orleans—had given her an outlet for her drive to create. Her old-school dad had been less enthusiastic. Not to mention hands-off when it came to her pet ventures. If she wanted to keep doing the parts of her job that made her happy, maybe this was the price.

"Fine. Text me the contact info, and I'll take care of it."

"Thanks, Wen."

She looked over at Alec again, whose shoulders were swaying to the music, and hated the thought of leaving him on his own like she'd been left so many times. Her disappointment veered into irritation, and suddenly she was in the mood to push back against these expectations.

"Speaking of new stuff, did you get a chance to look at the mock-ups for the brochures and rack cards I sent you?" *Two weeks ago. That you've been continually putting off.*

His sigh was audible even over the jazz notes in the background. "Yes."

"And? They look a lot more professional, right?"

"Honey..."

"What?" she bit out.

"I know you want to make your mark on the business, but we trade in history. Our marketing stuff doesn't have to be all sleek and new. The corny kitschy look is part of our charm."

Wendy's blood heated. "Have you seen the stuff the other tour companies are putting out? When people see theirs and then see ours, they'll keep on walking to the other places."

"But they don't have our reputation. This business runs on word of mouth."

Wendy rolled her eyes. Yeah, maybe for the locals. However, most of their revenue came from tourists who had nothing to go on but a quick look at advertisements. Though it was no use arguing further tonight. It would only stoke her already flaring temper.

"Let's just talk about this another time."

There was no hiding the irritation or the misery on her face as she walked back to Alec.

"Everything okay?" he asked.

"Just a work crisis." She had half a mind to ignore everything until they finished, but she wouldn't let her petulant attitude affect her relationship with one of the biggest paranormal history shows on television. She explained the *Alt History* debacle.

"Do you need to go take care of it?" Concern drew Alec's brows together. It was clear he was thinking about what she needed, which made her curse herself even more, but she didn't miss the way his smile tightened, becoming ever so slightly more guarded.

She looked longingly around the room at everyone draped in their 1920s furs and suits and dresses, laughing and gossiping, getting into the ruse. Then she looked up at Alec again and twisted her lips to the side. She really didn't want to. But she also couldn't let down her family and prove her dad right that they didn't really need to expand like this.

"I probably should. I've been pushing my dad to do more publicity stuff like this." She met his eyes again. "I'm sorry. Will you hate me if I leave?"

He went quiet for a beat.

"Only if we can't check back to see whodunit." He gave her a dim smile, but a muscle ticked in his jaw, like disappointment was all too familiar. She hated the thought of anyone disappointing him, especially herself. "Come on. Let's go change." He nodded in the exit's direction.

Oh God, this was terrible.

"No. No, you don't have to leave, too. I'll call a ride share. Maybe I'll even be back before the body's cold." She attempted a smile.

Alec's brows drew together in an unreadable expression. What did that mean? He seemed almost offended that she didn't want to inconvenience him.

She chewed on her bottom lip, unsure what to do. She settled for lifting to her tiptoes to brush a kiss on his cheek. "See you in a bit?"

He gave a half smile. "Sure."

Wendy made it as far as the dressing room before the full force of the indignation hit. She slipped off her beautiful fascinator and flung it onto the dressing table with enough force to send the feathers and crystals scattering. She always left. Her whole life, she always dropped everything and showed up at all hours to help her family with whatever needed fixing. Tonight she'd finally been doing something she wanted to do with someone who made her feel like the entire world wasn't divided into Wendy plus her family and everyone else.

When was the last time she'd shown up for her own desires? Certainly not during her whole art school phase. She chose what was expected of her. She chose what would best serve the people who were most important to her. And they sacrificed for her in return; there was no mistaking that. But just once in a while, couldn't they see she needed a night off and a push toward something that made her happy for a change?

She considered walking back out again and going radio silent until she was done having her fun, but the prospect felt akin to walking out of her own skin, like her world shifting off its axis.

Then a thought hit her, and even though the guilt still preyed on her, maybe there was a way to take care of her responsibilities and still not ruin her night, too. Maybe it was time to set some boundaries and come up with a more healthy balance.

She took a deep breath, shot off a few messages to Julie, and then picked up her phone and dialed the number for the newest *Alt History* producer.

CHAPTER 13

When Wendy strutted back into the speakeasy, it was with her shoulders rolled back and a defiant tilt to her chin, lightened from the burden of having to be at everyone's beck and call at all hours of the day.

Across the room, a pretty blond in a coral dress had struck up a conversation with Alec.

He looked up with a tentative smile. "That was fast. Problem solved?"

"I got Julie to give her some background information on the sites we're visiting, and asked the *Alt History* person if I could brief her and send the detailed itinerary in a few hours."

"And that won't cause any problems?"

"Nothing that won't keep for a few hours."

Alec's tentative smile relaxed into the real deal, and his eyes crinkled at the corners. "Did you tell her you were in the middle of solving a murder?"

"I told her I was in the middle of something important." The words were out before Wendy had consciously decided to speak them, and her stomach did a flip.

She pulled it off with a cheeky grin, but some of the honesty leaked through her wry demeanor, leaving her feeling exposed. At this, Alec's expression softened, and he covered her hand on the table with his and squeezed. His gaze traveled her face like he wasn't used to other people finding him important enough to choose. That thought struck her as terribly sad. But just now, he didn't look sad. Her insides warmed at his touch and affirmed her decision to come back.

"Speaking of important, Sandy here is an equestrian stunt rider and has been sharing some very interesting speculations about our dinner companions." Alec nodded to the woman in the coral dress. She looked a little less happy about Wendy's return than Alec. But who could blame her?

"Is that so?" Wendy shifted her attention to the woman.

To Sandy's credit, she only missed a beat before painting on a smile and leaning in conspiratorially. "I have it on good authority that Mr. Brown has some compromising photos of Mr. Jepson, the newspaper reporter, that would probably lose him his job if they got out."

Before long they were all whisked into a dining room for soup and filets, the actors carrying on and exposing each other's misdeeds and the various feuds between everyone gathered there tonight. Wendy and Alec played along, whispering hunches to one another and catching each other's stolen glances.

After the chocolate crème brûlées were cleared away and tension was reaching a breaking point between Mr. Brown, Mr. Jepson, and Sandy, the lights went out.

A loud bang sounded, and screams echoed from around the room. Lightning fast, as if on reflex, Alec wrapped his arms around Wendy and pulled her close. She giggled with delight and fitted her arms around his waist, enjoying the spicy smell of his cologne and the faint hint of chocolate at this close range.

"I'm not dead. Are you dead?" Alec said with humor in his voice.

Wendy shook her head with a laugh.

"Good."

"But I'm pretty sure someone's dead," she whispered. "Ten to one it's my no good fiancé."

People shifted around in the dark with a mix of nervous laughter and shrieks. Without her sight, Wendy's other senses intensified. She could almost feel him smile against her temple, his breath tingling the exposed flesh there. His hand gripped her waist, sending a wave of wanting curling low in her core.

With blinding clarity, the lights came back up, leaving Wendy and Alec blinking. She reluctantly unraveled her limbs from his and craned her neck to see the spot where everyone had gathered. She turned back to Alec, a mischievous grin forming, and felt a flutter at the way his eyes held on her before taking in the scene himself. Sure enough, there was Mr. Brown lying on the linoleum with a bullet-sized hole in his jacket, a pool of faux blood surrounding him. The game was afoot.

Everyone remaining leapt from the table in a frenzy, and Wendy's chest lightened with anticipation as she joined the fray. She tugged Alec along with her to check for clues and figure out the mystery du jour. When they stood over the body, his hand slid to rest on her waist, the warm weight of his presence causing a dizzy lightness.

As the night went on, she found herself reaching for him over and over again, for the connection when their eyes met in shared delight or when she pulled him along to look at the victim's ledger book to see if they could confirm one of the suspect's stories. He found ways to keep touching her, too: resting his hand on the small of her back, grazing her arm, holding her hand. The casual intimacy of it all had her feeling like a part of something, a story meant for two, and greedy for more of the sensation his touch flared up in her. The fact that he was so game and all-in for the silly stuff and that he could match her determination to find investigative words that could double as innuendo only made her want to be near him even more.

"I would very much like to *examine your evidence*," Alec said in a low, teasing voice. He'd rejoined Wendy after investigating another clue, and stood with his chest nearly touching her back, peering over her shoulder. She gave him a coy smile laced with mischief and pulled the correspondence she was reading out of view.

"I might have to penalize you for that," she said.

They traded another few quips back and forth before they devolved into pure silliness and Alec slipped an arm around her waist.

"Reprobate. Dossier," he whispered into her ear, starting a shiver of pleasure along with a wave of laughter.

"Now you're just saying all the crime words you know."

"Restitution. Subpoena. Restraining order." His lips brushed the shell of her ear. "I can go on."

She giggled and leaned into the warmth of his chest. He nuzzled her neck, wrapping his arms fully around her, and inhaled her scent. Her breath caught, and she had to restrain herself from pushing her backside into him.

As soon as the murderer was revealed, they fled the scene so fast one would've thought they were making a getaway.

"Meet you out here in five?" Alec said in front of Wendy's dressing room door. The hungry look that prowled in his eyes while he looked at her did delicious things to her body.

She cut her eyes left and then right. People were milling around talking to the actors, but suddenly Wendy didn't care.

Heart pounding and with a mischievous glimmer in her eyes, she grabbed Alec by the shirt and pulled him into her dressing room.

As soon as the door slammed behind them, Alec had her pressed up against the nearest wall. The soft scrape at her back and the sweet pressure of his body from the front sent her senses tumbling upside down. Her lips sought his, a groan escaping as they finally had full access to one another. She threaded her fingers through his hair and rocked against him. Lips and breath and mint and costumes and pliant bodies all jumbled together in one pulsing beat of want.

"I would very much like to have you as my accomplice tonight," he said in a husky, teasing voice as his lips claimed her neck. She let out a helpless whimper.

"And I'd like to put my fingerprints all over you." His fingers glided over the sides of her breasts and over her ribcage, then grasped her hips before pulling her closer.

She breathed out, "I'd like to request a thorough cross-examination." She hitched a leg up and hooked it around his waist, needing the solid weight of his body pressed more firmly against hers.

"Oh, I can be very thorough." He sucked and bit at the tender flesh just below her ear, making her lose all sense of time and place. Her head lolled to the side, but her hands kept up a thorough investigation of their own.

A knock pounded at the door. "Hey, no funny business in there," a male voice called from the other side.

Wendy's head fell forward, and she laughed into Alec's neck as his chest shook against hers.

"Busted," he said. He leaned his head against hers.

"Were we that obvious?" Wendy said.

"We did make a run for it as soon as they announced the murderer."

He shrugged, then skimmed his hands over her shoulders and took her hands before taking a step away.

"Guess you'll have to keep it in your holster for the time being."

She pulled him in for one more knee-weakening kiss before letting him go on his way.

CHAPTER 14

Back in Alec's car, it was all Wendy could do to keep her wits about her for the phone call with the *Alt History* person. Especially as Alec stroked her thigh and ran his fingers under the lace at the top of her stocking. And mouthed words she'd said on the phone like they were lascivious innuendos, even when they were things like "nunnery" and "cockatrice."

She wasn't sure whether to lean into his shoulder and shake with laughter or tell him to recline his seat and pounce on him as soon as she ended the call. Or maybe during...

The two desires had always been mutually exclusive before, but with him she felt the line shift and blur, laughter and desire all tangled up in one very sexy package. Maybe for once she could have her cake and eat it, too.

The call was still going as they pulled up to Wendy's house. Alec followed her up the steps to her porch. As she fumbled with the keys and tried to wrap up the call, he swept her hair to the side, and his mouth met the side of her throat, leaving a trail of exquisite kisses that started a powerful ache in her center. Her breasts tightened. She was nearly panting with want by the time she finally managed to undo the lock.

Once inside, she held the phone with one hand and used the other to lift the back of his shirt, exploring the flesh of his waist and back, needing the sensation of his skin under her hands.

"Where's your computer?" he whispered.

She reluctantly broke contact to point, and he jogged over to bring her laptop to the coffee table in front of the couch. He settled in behind her as she pulled up the right files. He brushed tender kisses over her bare shoulders and lightly traced her arms and then her thighs with his fingertips. The teasing feather-light touch only made her crave more, and she rocked back against him. The exhalation from his resulting groan sent more shivers of pleasure all over her skin.

"Okay. I just sent over the files," Wendy said to Kim on the phone. She pushed the computer away and straddled Alec, holding his smoldering gaze the whole time. Her garter and stockings rubbed over his thighs, and Alec's head fell back against the couch, and his eyes went heavy-lidded. He gripped her backside and guided her more firmly against him. Wendy had to stifle a moan.

"Are you okay?" Kim asked on the other end of the line. "You sound a little out of breath."

Alec's chest shook with laughter, and he rocked up against her again. Her lips parted, and another ragged breath escaped.

"Yeah, fine. Just... asthma. Gets me sometimes."

"Okay, well, I should let you get to your inhaler, then. I think that's all I needed. Thank you so much again for being so accommodating. I know it's late."

"No problem. Glad we could work it out. I'll see you tomorrow."

Wendy flung the phone aside, locking her gaze on Alec's. She shifted her thighs and reveled in the feel of his body pinned to the couch under hers and the way his eyes seemed to brew a tempest of desire every time he raked his gaze over her. "God, I thought that would never end."

"Me, too."

She leaned toward him, cupping the back of his head. That was all the encouragement he needed. He crushed her to him, and their lips tangled together, greedily taking as much of each other as they could get. Even in their urgency, she still got a sense that Alec was pacing himself, like he was in for the marathon and not the sprint.

The thought caused a trill of alarm alongside the warm flood of satisfaction, but as he scraped his teeth along her bottom lip and sucked, it was all she could do to hold on to conscious thought. She caught the painting at the foot of her stairs out of the corner of her eye, and thought of the girl she was when she'd made it. Fiery passions burning bright, but also isolated. Adrift. Desperately wanting not to be alone anymore.

"Do you want to move this to my bedroom?" she said suddenly. A nervous sensation twisted in her gut. She didn't invite guys into her room very often. She usually liked to keep them out of her personal space with a clear exit route, but....

"I want to move this wherever you are." He kissed her earlobe and then dropped a kiss on her forehead.

She slid off him and stood. The switch from touching to talking sent a flutter of shyness back through her, and her voice dropped lower. "It's this way."

She took his hand and pulled him to his feet. He brushed her cheek with the backs of his fingers, and her eyelids fluttered closed. Then he enveloped her in his arms, and sensation cocooned around her, light and warm and wistful. And right. She'd always wanted to be touched, but afterward to spring forward and run free. But for the moment, she wanted to be touched, *and* she wanted to be held. To stay in the moment with no thoughts of the nearest exit. She wanted more of this.

This would not end well. With him only here temporarily, how could it? But for the moment, she didn't care. She only led him upstairs and gave in to what they both wanted. And needed.

CHAPTER 15

"Was that a thorough enough examination for you?" Alec teased when they both collapsed onto the pillows of Wendy's bed, utterly spent. Wendy's body felt languid and limber as she curved her body toward him. Moonlight streamed through her blinds, illuminating the light curls of hair on his chest and torso. She traced a trail from his collarbone to his navel, unable to stop touching him. He pulled her close until she was flush against him and stroked her hair.

"At least for the time being." She bit her lip to contain her smile and glanced at the clock on her nightstand. "Look at you, staying up so late."

"I took a nap just in case I needed some extra energy." His eyes fell closed, and that lazy, sleepy smile she'd seen on him at the park overtook his face.

"Well, you did expend an awful lot of energy."

"Totally worth it."

She breathed in the spicy, masculine scent of him, and they both fell silent. The music of the crickets and Alec's steady heartbeat had nearly lulled her to sleep when he spoke.

"It feels good to be playful again."

"Mmm," she mumbled, coming back from the brink of sleep. "It's hard to imagine you not being playful."

"Tough couple of years."

She stroked his chest and stole a glance up at his beautiful face. Though his eyes were still at rest, his mouth tilted into a melancholy smile.

That pierced Wendy right to the heart: the thought of him without that playfulness that seemed so much at the core of who he was. Stolen away by the loss of both of his parents in quick succession—all the family he had in the world. Being left unmoored with none of his people left to anchor him. And then getting excited about getting to know his twin sister, only to have her constantly cancelling plans on him. She couldn't even conceive of how lonely that would be to lose her mom and dad and Julie and Aunt Angeline.

"I imagine," she said.

"Thanks for coming with me tonight." He looked down at her. "And thanks for staying."

She held him tight against her, wishing she knew what to do to comfort him. "Of course. And thanks for staying up late for me."

He leaned forward far enough to kiss her forehead before drifting back to his pillow and off to sleep.

Wendy awoke late in the night, half-surprised to find Alec still next to her. He curled up behind her, his chest tickling her back, and tucked her body into his. The warmth of him underneath the pillowy comforter might be her favorite newly discovered pleasure.

It was strange to have someone share her bed with her, just sleep next to her. This was not usually a bed for two. A light rain pattered the rooftop and greenery in the yard. Before drifting back to sleep, she thought of her painting downstairs, the lone girl always shielding herself from the downpour. She threaded her fingers through Alec's, and he kissed her neck sleepily. A warm, dizzying feeling seemed to melt over her at the contact.

At least for tonight, there was one more person in her bubble.

Back in the present, Wendy's throat constricted as she noticed Griffin materialize beside her. Coming back with all of this so far in the rearview mirror was a bitter pill to swallow. She could still smell the scent of Alec's cologne that lingered on her pillow after he spent the night. And she could still remember the feeling that she was no longer flying solo.

To have all that and then let it go—Wendy shivered and tucked her arms around herself.

She turned her attention back to Alec sleeping soundly on the pillow next to her younger self, and that unguarded, contented smile on her face. How could they ever get back to *that place* after everything that came next?

"I think there's a way," Griffin said with a roguish smirk.

Wendy narrowed her eyes at him. "I didn't say that out loud."

"I know. I'm in your mind reading your thoughts."

Wendy glowered, but her lips twitched upward at his attempt at cheering her up with cat meme humor to pick up her spirits.

He nodded back to past Wendy and Alec tucked close together in slumber. "I'm going to let you watch the rest of this with no more commercial interruptions."

The scene faded back to the Deveaux family gift shop the next morning.

CHAPTER 16

At her office the next morning, past Wendy sipped her green smoothie and leaned against the counter of the gift shop, a goofy smile spreading as she relived the previous hours. She could picture Alec with vivid clarity, freshly showered with a towel around his waist, before teasing her awake to enjoy the treasures of the wee hours of the morning. He'd even tried to make omelets while she got ready, though he freely admitted that his sister was the one who'd gotten the cooking gene.

She imagined more mornings like this, lounging in pajamas while reading, tucked into each other's sides. Her grumbling about being up so early and his plying her with donuts and giving her reasons to change her mind...

"What is that smile for?" Julie sauntered up to the counter and leaned over next to Wendy.

Wendy jumped and tried to school her features. "Nothing."

"Oh? Just delighted to be at work today?"

"Yep."

"Bullshit," Julie said.

"What are you doing here so early this morning?"

"Nice deflection," Julie said. "Working on an outline and sample chapters for my book proposal. It's hard to think about ghosts and murder when Griffin's got a *Voltron* marathon going all morning. So, I take it your date last night with Mr. Sexy Brains went well."

"You could say that." And she knew her flushed cheeks and undeniable grin belied her nonchalance.

Julie exacted the details and proceeded to walk around with a self-satisfied look on her face.

"Whatever. So we had a good time."

"Mmm hmm," Julie sing-songed.

Wendy harrumphed and was grateful for the chime of an incoming phone call.

"Morning pumpkin," her mom's voice greeted her.

"Hi Mom."

"Hey, do you think you could take the meeting with the new tech company this morning? Your dad's been having some chest pains since last night."

"Is he okay?"

The answer took a beat too long. "Probably fine, but I finagled an appointment with Dr. Constantine this morning just in case, and I want to go with him so he doesn't just grunt when I ask him the prognosis." Her overly flippant tone sent a tremor of worry through Wendy's own heart-region.

"Yeah. Um. That's fine. I'm in the office already. Let me know how it goes, okay?"

She promised she would. Wendy frowned when she hung up. It was probably fine, she told herself. Indigestion from those mozzarella sticks he insisted on eating on the regular. But she couldn't quite convince herself to believe it. Her dad was too stubborn and proud to admit when he was hurting, so it must have been pretty bad for him to complain and accept a doctor's appointment.

She went to the stockroom and called out for Paige, who was working on restocking some inventory. She knew she'd be checking her phone obsessively for news, but there was no use sitting around and worrying about something that might be a false alarm if there was something to distract herself with.

"Can you get me the contact info and notes on the new tech company we're using?"

Paige clicked away at the keyboard of the computer in the stockroom corner. "Just sent it your way."

"Thanks."

"I thought your dad was going to be here to — what did he call it? — lord his primitive influence over all unnecessary technological advancements."

Wendy smirked. "That sounds about right. Luckily I'm here, so we're not all using dial-up and dot matrix printers."

Maybe it was the combination of opportunity and her own inherited stubborn streak that made her make the call to Andi, their rep from the small business tech solutions company, but she did it before she could talk herself out of it. "Do you have anyone who does app development? I have an idea for a self-guided ghost tour app I might like to put together, and I'd like to see what kind of work and budget that might entail."

She wasn't committing to anything or "selling her soul to the technology devil," as her dad was fond of saying, but when she pitched the idea to him again, she'd have a better idea of the costs and logistics.

"Yeah, we actually have someone who's done a fair bit of app development. Hang on."

In a muted voice she called out to someone in the office with her, "Hey, can you see if McKinley is available for an eleven o'clock with a client today for an app development consult?"

The line went silent for a moment before she returned. "He's out right now, but if he's available, I'll send him over instead of myself. He can do all the other tasks we've talked about as well."

By ten to eleven she'd made sure everything was in order for the *Alt History* crew who'd be there by three, and she'd drawn up some notes on the app ideas for the meeting. She trotted to the mini fridge in her dad's office to grab an apple. Despite running on little sleep, today's work tasks had her floating around in a sort of buzzy exhilaration. If she could do stuff like this every day, she'd never want to leave.

She'd just taken a bite of her apple when she spotted Alec coming through the front door. His hair had that freshly tousled look, and the faint line of stubble along his jawline was the only hint that he was still wearing yesterday's clothes after leaving her place this morning. The clothes she had very much enjoyed taking off of him.

He'd been here in the shop just a few nights ago, but the dreamlike quality of the nights in the Quarter was no longer present. She was braver during those witching hours, inhibitions looser, less a slave to her strict defenses and her insecurities when there was only the haze of the lamplight to contend with. The veil of night blotted out everything else. Now here, in the stark light of day, she could see the whole picture, a shelf that had evaded Paige's last dusting endeavor, the chipping paint of the doorframe and her too-good-to-be-true companion of the last two nights with all the warning signs she'd suppressed.

She wiped the errant apple juice from her lips and went to meet him.

"What are you doing here? Did you forget something at my house? I thought you were working."

His eyes brightened at the sight of her, and her insides fluttered.

"I am. I hear someone here is interested in putting together an app."

Breakfast soured in Wendy's stomach as that reality further invaded her happy little bubble.

"Andi said she was sending someone named McKinley."

"That's me. Alec McKinley, at your service."

Her eyes widened as she processed all of this. Her fling had just gotten a whole lot more complicated.

Alec's lips curved into that slow smile of his, and a tingle low in her belly intruded on her apprehension. She tried to keep her voice even, though this whole thing seemed like something out of the *Twilight Zone*.

"Well, my dad had a last-minute doctor thing, so I guess you'll be meeting with me."

"Great. I can look at the system we'll be updating, and then we can talk about your app ideas." He gave her another amiable smile, and a crease formed between her brows. Unlike Wendy, Alec seemed completely unfazed by the fact that they'd gone from tangled in each other's limbs a few hours ago to embroiled in an unexpected employer/consultant relationship.

"And who do we have here?" Julie appeared at Wendy's side, a Puckish look in her eyes. Great.

"This is Alec. He's from the small business tech solutions company that's going to be helping with our website upgrade and some other tech stuff."

Julie offered her hand, her eyes still sparking with interest at the name.

"Alec, this is my cousin, Julie, who literally cannot resist insinuating herself into everyone else's business."

Alec's eyes lit in recognition. "So you're Julie. I've heard a lot about you."

Julie preened. "Like what?"

Wendy swatted her cousin's shoulder.

"Like that you two are like the female versions of Sam and Dean Winchester. Minus the messy demon-hunting thing."

"I'm the Sam, obviously," Julie said.

Wendy's heart warmed momentarily, crowding out the buzz of anxiety, both at the *Supernatural* reference and the way he'd picked up on their sisterly dynamic from their conversations.

"Well, I have also heard good things about you and your brain," Julie said.

Alec looked from Julie to Wendy, eyes lit with curiosity about the meaning of that comment. Wendy's cheeks flared again, and she gave Julie another swat.

"Like what?" Alec asked.

"And let's get started, shall we?" Wendy hooked a thumb toward her office.

"You're the boss."

"I'll tell you later," Julie whispered to Alec. Wendy rolled her eyes.

Julie, still oblivious of when to quit, stuck her head in after Wendy and Alec had entered the office. "You guys both must be tired. I'm going on a coffee run. Want some?"

"Yes, if it makes you mind your own business," Wendy said.

"The usual?"

"Sure."

"What about you, Alec?"

"Uh, sure, thanks. How about a double double?"

Both cousins cocked their heads to the side.

"Coffee, two creams, two sugars," Alec amended.

"Got it." Julie skipped out, making a show of shutting the door behind her like they were about to have some illicit tryst on her desk instead of revamping their outdated network situation.

"Is that a Canadian thing? The double double."

"Apparently so."

Wendy pulled up a second rolling chair in view of her computer monitors, this new dynamic making her feel suddenly uncertain where to stand or where to put her limbs in his presence.

"Here's what we're working with now," she said, sliding her mouse over to where he could control it.

Alec took the offered chair and rolled it until they were knee to knee. There wasn't a ton of space behind the desk, so it was almost unavoidable, but her shoulder stiffened at the closeness.

She stole a look at Alec, who was now clicking and scrolling through parts of her computer she'd never accessed before. A little wrinkle of intense concentration formed between his brows as his clever fingers worked the keyboard. He was cute when he was so wholly immersed like that. She'd never been one to mix business and pleasure before. Sure, she'd indulged in the occasional tourist flirtation, but then they went away, not scheduled to repeatedly be in her office in the daytime. She did the only thing she knew for sure how to do—revert to business mode.

Eyes on the computer. That's it. He went through their systems and website functionality with minimal eye contact. God, this was awkward, sitting here watching him work.

"I've been on my dad for years to bring us at least up to the 20th century."

The mention of her dad revived her earlier worries, but she reminded herself again not to panic until she had more information.

"Yeah, some of this is pretty bare bones," Alec said, looking up from the screen.

"That's a very diplomatic way of putting it."

"Most of it will be pretty easy to get used to after the upgrades, though. I can walk your dad through everything, if that will help."

They made it through almost an hour and got through Julie's coffee delivery and all the dad-approved items before she cracked the all-business-all-the-time front.

Alec had taken over her workstation and gone deeper into some of his tasks while she attacked a stack of paperwork on the other side of her desk. But it was still close quarters, and her every sense was aware of his presence at every turn.

After a while, he looked up. "So, tell me about this app you're interested in making."

Wendy clutched the invoices in her lap. She was going rogue here, and her dad—who was now at the doctor's with chest pain—would definitely not like this. A sheen of guilt covered her earlier excitement. She swiveled in her chair and scooted closer.

"This part is kind of on the down low for now."

Alec raised an eyebrow, and she couldn't help appreciating the clear blue green of his eyes.

"As in, you cannot mention this side venture to my dad yet. I need more information before I can give him the hard sell. He's perfectly fine running this place like it's 1792, so he's not on board yet."

Alec rubbed his chin thoughtfully. "So you need to convince him this 'newfangled' thing is valuable."

"Exactly. I think we could tap into a whole group of people we're missing who want a different tour experience."

Alec shifted to give her his full attention, leaning forward conspiratorially. "Okay, tell me more."

"Promise this stays between us until I give the okay?"

"Circle of trust." He gestured to the ever-shrinking space between them.

"Can you expand this circle of trust to include Andi and anyone else y'all might send over? I'll still pay you consulting fees, of course."

"I'll talk to Andi."

Wendy pulled out her notes. "Okay, so one would be like an interactive, self-guided tour. I'm thinking each stop would have both a written and an audio component with some photos. And if people wanted more in-depth info, we could expand it to include exclusive interviews and video footage. This would be great for people who wanted to go at off-peak times or do a few stops each day of their trip here, or people who wanted to take one of our guided ghost tours and then do a self-guided Voodoo tour."

"Or for people like Steve who want to really soak up all the details before moving on," Alec said.

"Exactly."

"Sounds great. We could definitely set up something like that. We'd have to have you create all the content to include, and we can talk about contracting audio/visual services if you're interested in that."

Wendy's heart jumped at the idea of this project she'd been working on in the back of her head for months coming to fruition.

"You could even do a junior version for school field trips." Alec leaned forward and jotted down some notes.

"Yes." Wendy's eyes lit at the prospect. "And speaking of kids, the other idea I had is something like *Pokemon Go*, but with ghosts."

"I already want that one," Alec said, grinning at her. "You could have them fill up an ectoplasm meter, add in little jump scares."

Some of the apprehension about exploring these ideas dissipated at Alec's shared enthusiasm.

He went into detail about what each might entail and promised to put a proposal together by the end of the week. They'd still have a lot of details to iron out, but the idea of having a creative project at work energized her in a way she hadn't felt since putting together her art school portfolio.

Alec's knee brushed hers, and she reached out to squeeze it before thinking. When she realized what she'd done, she stiffened and withdrew it. "Sorry."

Alec frowned, like he didn't catch her meaning.

"This is weird, right? Tell me you see that this is weird. Last night we were..." *Licking every inch of each other's bodies, spooning*—neither of those seemed right to say in her place of employment. His eyes smoldered like he was filling in the blanks of her naughty Mad Lib just fine on his own. "And today we're working together."

"It is an unusual turn of events, yes."

"So this"—She gestured between them—"is probably now very inappropriate."

"This?" A note of confusion echoed in his voice. Her eyes shot to the floor, and for a moment her stomach did a sick slide, like she'd read much more into whatever had passed between them than was really there. Maybe this time it was he who just wanted a no-strings fling, and she was no longer in on the joke.

But when she finally dared to look up, she saw the gentle teasing in his eyes, followed up by a look of concern when he registered her expression.

"You're only here for a few weeks anyway, right?" She shook her head, chiding herself for feeling so much already when she knew this at the onset.

"Who said weeks? I've got nine more months here. Possibly more if they need me to stay on."

"Oh. *Oh.*" She wasn't sure if this was good news or bad news anymore, just that he was now out of bounds.

"It does make things more complicated," Alec admitted, running a hand through his hair. "But I can ask Andi to take over your account again."

She blew out a breath. "But you're the only one who does app development."

"Here, yes."

Wendy chewed her bottom lip. Of course she could find any number of app developers to work with. But doing so now after this conversation would be like declaring her intentions of something more serious than she cared to contemplate. "I don't know."

"Then come to lunch with me, and you can think about it. And I can dazzle you with my knowledge of French Canadian swears."

She twisted her lips to the side.

"As friends, if that makes you more comfortable."

She had to let things take shape before she could decide anything. Thoughts swirling, she bent to grab her water bottle at the same time Alec leaned forward for his messenger bag, and they nearly collided.

As she straightened, her cheek grazed his chest. If she was gathering up her resistance, she would've done better not to breathe in the scent of him, a clean citrus and clove smell that made moisture pool in her mouth. Her eyes dropped to half-mast, and as she looked up at him through her lashes, that craving for his touch came slamming back into her.

Alec studied her expression with renewed interest. "I'd give all the Coffee Crisps my friend just sent me to know what that look means."

"You smell like my soap," she said, her voice low and breathy.

His eyes went heavy lidded, and the heat flared between them again. The idea took hold of her and called forth memories of him on top of her, playing her body like a steel guitar. It was one of the sexiest things she'd ever smelled. Like he was branded. Hers.

But things were a lot more complicated now.

His throat bobbed, and Wendy stood abruptly, needing some air before she did something that was not kosher. She exhaled deeply. Why, why did this man have her forgetting all logic?

Alec stood too and took a step backward, as though to honor his words. *As friends, if that makes you more comfortable.*

She knew he'd go along if it was what she wanted. The distance helped her cool off, but her brain was still not functioning fully with this overload of sensation. It was not good judgement to go forward with this. But. *But.*

"I have to be back to meet the *Alt History* crew at three," she said.

He shook his head and gave her a quick smile. "All the more reason to head out now."

"How do you feel about oysters?"

CHAPTER 17

Lunch went... fine. Ish. If fine is awkwardly trying to curtail flirtations after an offhand comment that oysters were considered an aphrodisiac. Wendy continued to think about it, and for the next week or so they drifted into a weird quasi-platonic business relationship between the times she spent fussing over her dad and his worrisome test results. Though the elder Deveaux insisted everything was fine and that they had nothing to worry about, he wasn't off the hamburgers or sodas the doctor cautioned him against, and Wendy spent her time off rounding up vegetables from the farmers market and feeding them to him every chance she got. Alec had called or stopped by several times and asked her to the movies or to see places in town. Despite her fledgling feelings for him, she dodged some invites and redirected the others into getting together to talk about plans for the apps they'd be working on together. She needed the buffer to give her time to think, both about crossing the business/pleasure line and putting herself in a position where she might get hurt.

But despite her pulling back in some areas, Alec was quickly becoming one of her favorite people to talk to. He got her jokes and provided a much-needed outside perspective on work-related tensions with her dad. He was singularly fun to tease, and his mellow nature balanced her tendency to let her temper flare up.

So your favorite show is on, Wendy texted him one night.

Making a Murderer?

Nope, the other one. Almost time for a group date. He's bringing both of the girls who had a fight and poured Tequila on each other. They're going cheese making.

No way. Searching for my remote now.

I have to admit, this is pretty entertaining.

Told you, he wrote.

We could make a drinking game out of this. Drink every time they say, "Can I steal you for a second?" or "I'm not here to make friends."

I hope you have a lot of wine.

A glass of wine actually sounded pretty nice after the long day she'd had. She walked to her pantry and poured herself a glass.

This guy is kind of a tool, pitting those twins against each other like that, she observed after at least one glass and more commentary traded back and forth.

What, not your type?

Not even close.

What is your type then? he asked.

She swallowed. This could come dangerously close to flirting again. *Hmm. I don't know if I have one. Let me think.*

He didn't respond right away, so she mulled over her real answer. She'd spent so much of her adult life guarding herself against what she didn't want that she hadn't stopped to consider what she did. *Smart, obviously. And someone who gets the low-key comedic brilliance that is The Rock, and all things Riff Tracks.*

And maybe because she was curled up in the safety of her house with a full glass of wine in her and the buffer of a work relationship between them, but she typed the rest out, anyway. *Someone that feels like a part of my family that I've been missing. But with kissing and stuff.*

He sent a happy face emoji back. Then a picture of himself with his own glass of beer tipped to his lips. *Missed one.*

Wendy's pulse jumped at her throat. She cradled the phone in her hands, letting herself admire the crinkles next to Alec's sea glass eyes and the dimple that came out when he was amused. His shirt was unbuttoned at the top. Why couldn't she just admit that she wanted him and figure out the work stuff?

Pageant queen from Iowa is not here to make friends, he added.

Duh, Wendy answered. She snapped a goofy picture of herself taking a sip of wine and fired it back, along with another inadvisable question brought to you by liquid courage. *So, what's yours?*

Beer?

No. Type.

Cheese-making tequila thrower. Natch.

An irresistible combination. She laughed, and then a flutter of nerves hit as she wondered if he was looking at her picture the way she was shamelessly ogling his. *Really, though?*

Stubborn. Pretty. Likes the outdoors. Makes me laugh and doesn't mind my mediocre cooking skills. Gets along with my sister. Someone who always looks out for the people she cares about.

She couldn't help comparing her own attributes to his list. *Sounds like you've thought about this a lot.*

I guess I have, he answered.

You really like stubborn?

Sometimes to my detriment.

Can I ask you something? she typed. She curled up under her blanket and surrendered to her quiet, contemplative mood.

Yes, I will go to the fantasy suite with you.

She laughed. Different question. What's the biggest risk you've ever taken?

She poured another glass of wine and waited for his answer. She'd need more than liquid courage for what was on her mind, both to pitch this new app idea to her dad—she'd called him up and chickened out twice already—and to stop hiding from what she was feeling for Alec.

Probably contacting my sister for the first time and coming to see her.

Did you ever worry that it might go terribly before you called her? Or that it might hurt less not to try?

Wendy swallowed. She always made a good show of being unfazed and bulletproof, but these were the questions that plagued her underneath all of that. The ones she kept as far from view as possible. But if she was ever going to quiet them, she needed some kind of guidebook on how to do it.

I had her contact information for months before I actually picked up the phone. It was a weird feeling. Like if she rejected me when I'd already lost my mom, I'd have no family left.

God, that must have been awful, Wendy typed. How did you convince yourself to do it?

I guess I decided it was too important not to.

Too important not to. Her throat tightened at the thought. Nothing thus far had been important enough that she'd let go of that safety net to do it. Since she'd torn up that art school response letter, she'd just been going along, working and being reasonably happy. But the things that really lit her up from the inside when it came to her job were making creative changes, taking what the family had built and growing it, shaping it for the present and the future. When she worked with the TV crews or the groups of thriller writers or paranormal romance conference attendees, or brainstormed about these app ideas with Alec, she'd had the best of both worlds: the power to have those creative challenges without ever having to leave the home she loved so much. Unfortunately, those were the aspects of her job that her dad gave her so much pushback on. He wanted to groom her to take over some day, but whenever she took the initiative, he grumbled and put the brakes on her efforts. She'd have to decide if this was enough or if she should keep pushing because it was too important not to branch out.

And then there was the matter of the person on the other end of the telephone.

What's the biggest risk you've ever taken? he asked.

She blew out a breath and tried to calm the battering of butterflies in her chest. Had she ever done anything at a big risk to herself? Or had she always just gone with what was easy or comfortable?

I'm not sure I've ever done anything really brave.

You stood up to those girls who were making fun of Steve on your tour, he replied. He says hi, by the way. We had milkshakes and talked about Truman Capote the other day.

Wendy smiled at the thought of her two friends bonding over chocolate milkshakes. *I'm not sure that counts as bravery. Just doing the right thing.*

It's not something everyone would have done, though.

Anyone worth knowing would've.

Agreed. But I think you're a lot braver than you give yourself credit for.

She looked from the stack of audio tour notes on her coffee table to Alec's picture. Maybe it was time to rethink holding back on everything.

I hope you're right.

CHAPTER 18

"So I brought up the idea of the audio tour app with my dad this morning," Wendy said. Her footsteps echoed on the wooden planks of the trail through Jean Lafitte National Park's Barataria Preserve, with Alec close behind. Birds called, and crickets added their song to the bustling stillness of the bayou. Moss-laden branches dipped close overhead as their path wound through the dense greenery of the wild wetlands.

"Oh yeah? How did that go?" Alec wiped his brow and turned to look at her. He'd tempted her into taking today's quasi-business meet-up into the outdoors after the clouds finally let up from five solid days of rain.

"I told him I wanted to investigate the costs and possibilities."

"And?"

"And he grunted and said, 'That again?' and went back to his project." Wendy sighed and took a drink from her CamelBak straw.

Alec gave her a commiserating look.

"I suppose in his defense, he's extra grumpy about the new low-cholesterol diet his doctor put him on. But it wasn't a no, and he didn't go into full argument mode, so baby steps, I guess."

It was a day for baby steps, it seemed, as she'd also accepted Alec's invitation to go "hike through the bayou preserve and hopefully not wrestle alligators" even though it was only tangentially business-related. She'd been mulling over their conversation about things that were too important not to do, but she still couldn't make herself take that next step with him.

Maybe she could just let things drift and develop naturally. How that would happen if she kept holding herself back, she wasn't sure, but, hey.

"At least you tried, right?" Alec said.

"You saw our computer systems. He does not like change, so I'll have to expose him to it a bit at a time until he gets more comfortable with the idea. Kind of like easing into a freezing swimming pool."

"What about your mom? Does she run the business, too? Could you win her over to the cause?"

"Maybe. But she usually goes all Switzerland on us when my dad and I butt heads. She's still involved, but she's pulled back a lot the past few years. Her real love is fixing up classic cars and selling them. She'll talk your ear off about the '67 Mustang convertible."

"What's she like? Are you guys close, too?"

Wendy nodded. "She's where I get my smart mouth. I once got sent to the principal's office because my P.E. teacher told me he wished I'd make more of an effort at climbing the bleachers. I told him if wishes were horses, I'd have one to climb up the stairs on. I heard my mom say something to that effect to our realtor the night before."

Alec chuckled.

They turned a corner into a dense section of the marshlands. Trees grew out of the water, canopies tangling together up above. They both stopped to stare at the scaly brown head moving through the greenery on the surface of the water.

"Is that what I think it is?" Alec asked, his eyes going wide. He wandered to the edge of the walkway to get a better look. The reptile changed course right for them, and Alec took a comically large step back as the tail became visible.

"If you think it's an alligator, then yes," Wendy said, suppressing a grin.

"It won't come up here, is it?"

She shrugged. "I've seen pictures of them on the pathways here."

"We should've brought something to feed it so it doesn't get tempted to use us for a snack."

"I think we'll be okay. I'll protect you from any rogue alligators in our path."

"With what?"

"My disdainful stare and ability to run the hell away from them."

"Okay then," Alec said with a grin.

"Speaking of tenuous situations, how are things going with your sister?" Wendy asked.

"We had dinner the other day," he said. Wendy was about to make an encouraging comment, but judging by the troubled expression on his face, maybe not so much.

"Is that look about your sister or the alligator?"

He shook his head, like he was trying to shake off whatever it was, and gave her a wry smile. "Maybe both. We're both still figuring things out, I guess. It seems like she's interested in having a relationship with me, but it's like she doesn't know how. I think she has trouble relaxing."

Wendy frowned, considering.

Alec continued, "I keep thinking, she's my twin, she's going to get me and see family things the way I see them, but we've had very different upbringings. There was a leaky faucet at her house, and I told her I could come help fix it. But she called a repair person, said she didn't want to put me out." He frowned. "I don't think she's had a lot of friends—real friends she relies on, anyway. It's like she doesn't feel like she's worthy of that kind of relationship."

"Not even with her parents? Or cousins or anything?"

"I don't think so. Like I said before, they love her, but they're distant."

"That's so sad," Wendy said. "To never have had anyone. I always wished I had someone outside of my family to be my special person, but even though I never really found that, I always had my family. Julie, my mom and dad, my Aunt Angeline."

"I want to help her, let her know she can rely on me if she wants to, but I'm not really sure how."

Wendy thought about this as they walked on through the mossy green and several herons swooped into view, coming to rest in the water. Overhead, dark clouds gathered. Maybe a full day of sunshine wouldn't happen after all.

"What if you asked her for help?" she said.

"With what?"

"I don't know. Anything you needed advice or help with. Picking out a shirt, teaching you how to cook something. She'd probably feel valued if she had the chance to do something for you. Then the next time she needs help, she might be less hesitant to ask you."

Alec turned his pensive gaze on her. "Yeah, maybe I'll try that."

Thunder rumbled overhead, and the surrounding air hung heavy, charged with the coming storm. Light rain spattered their cheeks.

"You didn't happen to bring an umbrella, did you?" Wendy asked. Lightning tore through the air, and the sky opened up. Torrents of rain sheeted down, soaking them in an instant.

"No. Did you?"

Wendy shook her head and walked faster. "How far to the end of this trail?"

Alec pulled the map out of his pocket. "Probably at least half a mile."

Wendy surveyed the swampland around them and nodded to a place up ahead. "There's a big tree over there. We could probably wait it out under there."

They both jogged until they were under its canopy, but though it provided partial cover, the rain still ran in rivulets down Wendy's cheeks, and soon her shorts, bra, and shirt were soaked to the skin. Alec rummaged through his pack and came out with a thin silvery blanket. He unfolded it and swept it over their heads, providing some cover at last.

Wendy exhaled in relief at the respite from the relentless pelting of the downpour. "What is that?" They had to huddle close for it to cover both of them, and her rain-soaked arm pressed into his.

"Thermal blanket for emergencies." He smiled. Rain plastered chunks of his hair to his forehead, and Wendy suppressed the urge to run her fingers through them. Being this close under the thin blanket, it felt like they were in their own adult blanket fort.

"Glad at least one of us came prepared."

"If I was really prepared, I would've packed an umbrella," he said.

They were silent for a few moments in their hideaway, with nothing but the sound of rain pelting the leaves and the earth and plinking off of the water for a soundtrack. The scent of wet earth wafted up. Wendy cut her eyes to Alec. Raindrops clung to his lashes and his t-shirt had plastered to him, leaving the contours of his chest and stomach on display. She should look away, but she couldn't drag her eyes from him, and wanting stirred inside of her. Her own thin t-shirt was probably clinging as well, leaving little to the imagination. Not like they hadn't explored each other the other night, but things had changed. And become more complicated. Alec was here for way longer than she'd anticipated, taking the easy way out off the table, and then there was the working relationship to contend with.

"Let's think dry thoughts," she said, to distract herself from that line of thinking. "If you could be anywhere in the world right now, where would you be?"

Alec huffed a laugh. Lightning streaked through the sky, and Wendy caught a flash of heat simmering in his eyes. His gaze dropped to Wendy's mouth, and her stomach fluttered.

"I don't know that I should say that out loud." By necessity, they were so close that his breath caressed her face.

Wendy flushed. "Why not?"

"Because I want to respect your wishes."

Wendy swallowed, and her heart thrummed. "That's very gentlemanly." Was this the time to break past the fear and just go for it again? She wasn't sure.

"But other than that," Alec said. "There was this cabin we used to go to for the Christmas holidays when I was a kid. I would get up and go snowshoeing until I couldn't stand up anymore and then sit by the fire and watch the snow fall. That's a pretty nice place to wait out a storm."

"That sounds nice." She wasn't sure whether to be relieved that he was being polite and not pushing to take things back in a romantic direction or supremely frustrated.

"What about you? You have a dream destination to hole up in for a storm?" Alec asked.

She couldn't help her awareness of the nearness of him. She could think of several options that involved him and a lack of clothing. "I don't know. Some place cold sounds nice right now. A place with no alligators. Maybe someplace I've never been before."

"Where haven't you been?"

Wendy snorted a laugh. "Pretty much everywhere outside a 300-mile radius. Not much time for long trips when your parents are hustling small business owners." She looked up at him. "I wouldn't mind checking out Vancouver after hearing you talk about it."

"Well, if you ever plan a trip, I'd be glad to show you around."

"I'll keep that in mind."

"So, what's your least favorite place to be?" Alec asked. He looked at her and then away, perhaps struggling with the same thing she was but having more luck in the self-control department.

Wendy pursed her lips, thinking, and then smiled. "Stranded out here without you and your Eagle Scout blanket for starters."

He mirrored her smile.

"But also stuck in traffic. I get some serious road rage when I know where I want to be and I'm trying to get there and keep getting held up. You?"

Alec frowned and said in a quiet voice, "The hospital." The humor went out of his eyes, and Wendy felt a pang of sadness.

"Did you spend a lot of time there when your parents were sick?"

He sniffed and nodded. "Not much worse than being in limbo *and* potentially catching MRSA." A smile cracked through his muted expression. "I still break out in hives and stutter again when I think about it."

"I imagine." Wendy met his gaze with a commiserating look. Once again she marveled at how freely he talked about such personal things that clearly still hurt. Was that just his way? Or was that his way with *her*? Because they shared something, some kind of connection between them. Her heart did a somersault at the thought. She wanted to reach out and comfort him, but hesitated, not wanting to blur the lines until she'd had more time to think. She looked over at him, his back hunched so she could be more comfortable and protected from the rain, his sea glass eyes so open and vulnerable.

"But I guess being out here at the mercy of the gators and creepy birds without you would be pretty miserable, too."

"Don't worry, I'll protect you from the birds, too," she said, and bumped his shoulder.

His smile widened, and his gaze traveled her face like in the silliness and in the seriousness, he'd found something that spoke to him and he was trying to memorize it all. Her heart skipped a beat at how look on his face pierced her.

Rain continued to pelt down on them. Thunder rumbled overhead. A steady stream of water sheeted off the front edge of the flash blanket, creating the illusion that they were in a private alcove behind a waterfall.

She spoke without thinking. "What would you have said before if you weren't being so gentlemanly? About where you'd like to be." Her heart knocked against her ribcage.

He gave her a questioning look, tinged with heat. *Do you really want me to go there?* it said. *Because I would love to go there.* She felt it all the way down to her toes, which curled in remembrance of his hands on her body.

She bit her lip.

"In your bed with both of our clothes in the dryer." Alec held her gaze, and Wendy let out a ragged breath.

He pushed a wet strand of hair out of her eyes, and the whole rest of her body reacted with a heady anticipation.

She breathed out and hovered there in the moment. Wanting. Waiting. And then the doubts whispered in her ear.

It wasn't settled. *She* wasn't settled. Why had she let herself take this out of an office environment before she knew how to proceed? It felt like she was walking on a tightrope. It was easier to balance moments ago, when she wasn't looking at the ground so very far below.

Alec hung back. There was still no mistaking the desire in his gaze, but he also wouldn't push if she wasn't ready. That she could also read in his eyes.

What if she gave in? The way she'd felt this week, having him to fill the empty hours, to talk to and laugh with and provide an outside perspective on things with her family: it was a good feeling to have that kind of kinship with someone. But then there was the undeniable fact that she didn't have the best romantic relationship track record. What if she screwed things up? This feeling of not being solo, this companionship would be gone. And then there was also the other thought, one that crept back to her, with the contamination of the past sting of disappointment: What if it was more to her than it was to him?

She dipped her chin. Then thunder crashed, reverberating through the ground beneath her feet. Wendy and Alec both jumped, and the silver blanket flopped to the ground. The moment was broken, and they both dissolved into sheepish laughter. The thunder's rolling boom rumbled on through the preserve, shaking the ground and rippling the water.

CHAPTER 19

T HREE DAYS LATER

Things could change in an instant. And not always for the better. Wendy sat numb in the hospital waiting room, the uncertainty and her complete lack of ability to make things better sitting heavy on her jittery limbs. She cast a glance at her mom, who had finally fallen asleep in the chair next to her. Covering her sleeping form with the hoodie she'd brought, she blew out a long breath. Other waiting families milled around the seating area, munching on stale hospital food. She guessed it was dinnertime, but couldn't quite bring herself to care.

Now that her mom had nodded off and Wendy was alone with her thoughts, the events of the last twelve hours played on an endless loop in her mind. The early morning phone call that her dad was having a heart attack and was being prepped for surgery. Not being able to see him, even though this might be her last chance to see him. Sitting with her mom, trying to soothe and comfort her when Wendy could barely speak for the blinding panic in her own chest. And now more waiting. More not knowing.

The hyperalertness from the adrenaline surge was lagging and her hands trembled against the pages of the book she'd splayed open in her lap. She'd been staring at it for the last hour, waiting for news and reading the same paragraph over and over. None of the words made their way into her mind, though, with so much else there to crowd them out.

She swallowed against the thought of her big strong dad, who always seemed larger than life and able to bend the entire world to his will, lying helpless on an operating table with his chest open.

The sliding doors at the entrance drew back, letting in a gust of muggy air, and Alec walked in with several bags over his shoulder. Wendy did a double take. What was he doing here? She hadn't answered any of his texts from earlier. Hadn't even been able to bring herself to read them with all the tumult going on inside her. But somehow, here he was.

Alec looked around the room with its institutional walls, cheap watercolors, and exhausted, waiting families, and a muscle ticked in his jaw. He seemed to gather his resolve, and then his gaze found hers.

"I've brought provisions." He smiled at her once he'd made his way over.

"How—?" But she couldn't finish her question around the lump in her throat. She was so brittle, so raw, with her emotions hovering close to the surface. The sight of that smile, and his presence here, was a comfort she just wanted to sink into after the events of the day.

"I went by your shop after work, and Julie told me what happened."

Wendy managed a shaky smile, grateful for her cousin's meddling this time.

"How are you holding up?" He set down his bags and rubbed her arm.

Instead of contemplating the inappropriateness of fraternizing, she let his warm hand on her air-conditioning chilled arm soothe the parts of her that felt so broken they might be beyond mending. Especially if her dad didn't make it out of this. "I've been trying to hold it together for my mom."

Wendy nodded at her sleeping mother and gestured to the row of chairs across the way, indicating they should move so they didn't wake her up.

Alec followed with his bags. She'd held onto her brave everything's-going-to-work-out-fine face for the last twelve hours, for her mom's sake. If she needed a rock, Wendy could make herself into granite, but little by little, even that was cracking.

Before she could think, she'd wrapped her arms around Alec's waist and buried her head in his chest. He wrapped his powerful arms around her and gathered her close, the wintry smell of his aftershave a balm. She breathed out a shuddering breath, but managed to hold a fresh sob at bay.

With his arms around her, holding her close, stroking her hair, she could finally let the granite crack, could finally shift from being the comforter to being the comforted. "She finally fell asleep." Wendy gestured to her mom slumped back in her chair. "She's been here since 6 a.m."

"Any news?" Alec asked.

"He's still in post-op. They haven't let us see him yet."

He squeezed her close again.

"So what's this I hear about provisions?" Wendy asked when her breathing had steadied.

"Oh, I've got all sorts of things." Alec stepped away and unzipped his duffle bag. Wendy sat next to him as he pulled out items.

"Neck pillow, *Uno*, *Mad Libs*, change of clothes."

Fresh tears brimmed in Wendy's eyes at the sight of this whole thoughtful spread. "Where did all of this come from?"

"My sister was in on it, too." He looked up to meet her eyes and wrapped the U-shaped pillow around her neck. "I took your advice and asked her for help."

Wendy's watery smile widened. Not only Alec, but also his sister—a complete stranger—had jumped in and done all of this for her.

"These are hers." He held up black lounge pants and a soft pink shirt. "I think you're about the same size. She also sent something called facial cleanser and baby wipes. She said it was a girl thing. Like the closest thing to a shower on the go. For the record, I think you smell just fine, but she was looking out."

Wendy smirked. "Give me another couple of hours, and you might change your mind."

She looked around and then met Alec's eyes, humbled once more at his thoughtfulness. "This is a grade A hospital bag. Thank you. And please thank your sister for me, too."

He nodded, a spark of pleasure in his eyes at her warm reception.

"And what's in this mystery bag?" She nodded to the one with the delicious smell that had her stomach growling.

"I thought you might be hungry." He reached inside and pulled out several takeout containers.

"You are the literal best," she said. "I think I grabbed some Fritos around lunchtime, but other than that it's just been a steady stream of hospital coffee."

"I wasn't sure what you'd like, so I went with a variety of comfort foods. Also courtesy of one of Kara's restaurants."

"You two were busy."

"She had it sent over to the house while we were packing. Let's see, we've got calamari—that's my favorite—fancy schmancy PB & J on brioche, and crawfish mac and cheese."

"Crawfish mac and cheese?" Wendy pressed a hand to her heart. "How on earth did I not know that was a thing?"

Alec handed her the container and dug into the open box of calamari. "Apparently that's Kara's specialty."

"I already like your sister." She closed her eyes and let the comforting cheesy goodness melt onto her tongue. Alec stole a bite from her container with a sly smile. She reached into his for some calamari rings. They smiled at one another, and for the first time on this awful day, when everything else seemed to be falling apart, Wendy found a moment of peace.

"So will it help more to talk about it or get your mind off of it?" Alec asked after they'd finished their feast.

Wendy let out a long exhale. "I don't know. Both. Neither." But she fished out the *Uno* deck and shuffled.

"I know the feeling."

Another tangle of emotions caught in her chest. She remembered how much he hated hospitals. And why. Yet here he was. And he'd been through all of this not just once, but with both of his parents.

"I think the uncertainty is the worst part," she said. "The not knowing and not being able to go in there and do anything to help."

Alec nodded, and she dealt the cards.

"Sometimes certainty is worse, though." He met her gaze, and a mixture of empathy and fear hit Wendy in the gut. Certainty that your parent is dying—of course that would be worse.

Her dad could die. The ending of everything she knew. Icy dread leaked through her, and it hit her with ominous clarity. She hadn't let herself consider the possibility, not really. But Alec's own experience was an awful reminder that sometimes people didn't get better. Sometimes things didn't work out.

"I'm sorry, I wasn't thinking," she said. "Of course that's worse."

"No, it's okay. I get what you're saying. Knowing someone that you love is hurting and not being able to do anything to make it better is pretty fucking awful, too."

She blew out a breath and focused on the brightly colored cards.

"I meant that with uncertainty, at least there's hope," he said, laying down a yellow four.

Wendy nodded. That was true, and she'd cling to that shred of truth and hope with everything she had.

"I know I complain about my dad and his Luddite ways a lot, but he's a lot more than that. He's mostly a big grumpy teddy bear." She smiled to herself. "He taught me to read. And he always made a point of getting me all the banned books so I'd never be censored. He named me after Wendy Darling in Peter Pan. I pretty much grew up on his knee in the office of the ghost tour shop. And when he and my mom were first starting out, he had to take a second job stuffing envelopes to make ends meet. So every night after dinner, he and my mom and I would sit around stuffing envelopes together and they'd tell me stories. Some they made up and some from their lives. I was eleven before I knew that *Goldilocks and the Three Bananas* was not a real thing."

She searched her hand like it somehow had the answers to all this. "He's always been such a presence in my life, sometimes a pain-in-the-ass presence, but mostly a loving, reassuring one. It's hard to imagine anything else."

It felt good to process what she'd been feeling all day without worrying about upsetting her mom even more. The tightness in her chest unraveled by degrees. She laid down a card and drew another.

They continued to talk and play card games, weaving laughter in with the pain and trading childhood stories, his about his mellow outdoors-loving dad and stubborn indoors-loving mom, who somehow fit together just right, and hers about growing up in the French Quarter chasing ghosts on every corner. He even shared about the dark years after losing his entire family in one fell swoop before he was even twenty-five.

"I thought they'd always be around, to see me get married, to see their grand-kids. But they missed all of that. Sometimes it feels like I got cheated."

"Uno." She laid down her card sheepishly. "Sorry, that was ill-timed."

"It's okay." He drew and slapped down three Skips in a row. "Because that's Uno for me, too." He gave her a challenging smile. "And then all the well-mean-ing people start with the platitudes." He rolled his eyes. "'Time heals all wounds,' and 'Everything happens for a reason.' Really? Because I would like to know what the reason is for two of the best people on the planet to not get to grow old together and leave their son an orphan."

She nodded. "I feel like we should rewrite all of those. Everything happens for a reason. Sometimes the reason is the universe is an asshole."

He grinned. "Shoot for the stars. Even if you miss, you might hit a bird."

"Yep. These are much better. We should start a greeting card company."

Wendy's phone buzzed, and she picked it up to look at her messages. "It's probably Julie checking in."

Alec made a show of trying to peek at her remaining card, and she swatted at him before giving Julie an update.

Glad your mom finally got some sleep. Are you remembering to eat? Griffin said he could run over with some food.

Thanks, but Alec brought a whole gourmet spread. He's keeping me company.

A winky face emoji popped onto her screen, followed by five heart emojis. *Tell him I said hi,* Julie added.

Wendy smirked and shook her head.

"What?" Alec asked.

"Nothing. Julie says hi. Aunt Angeline, her mom, took a few days off of work to help cover in the shop if my mom and I are still going to be here."

Alec drew another card, and his face took on a wistful expression. "It's nice. How you all look out for each other. I miss that."

"It is." Wendy twisted her lips to the side, imagining once more having all of her family wiped away one after the other and being left all alone. She'd been asking so many questions about his family tonight. It seemed so normal for her to do so, but maybe she should have been more sensitive. "Does it hurt to talk about your family?" she asked finally.

"It did for a long time. But now it's sort of like keeping them with me." Alec laid down his final card, and Wendy groaned as he did a silly victory dance in his chair.

"I want a rematch later," Wendy said.

"Done. Anyway, I think the change of scenery has done me good." Alec stood and stretched his long legs, and Wendy followed suit. "I feel better than I have in a long time. Too bad my assignment is only temporary."

This reminder deflated something inside of her. She hated to think of him even leaving later tonight, let alone permanently. "Could you stay? I mean, are there permanent positions if you wanted to? With your sister here and all."

He laced his fingers together and stretched his arms up into the air, exposing the trail of hair on his stomach. Wendy rolled her neck and shoulders and tried not to linger too much there. "Not as of now. They're trying to hire locals and avoid sponsoring too many work visas if possible. We're mostly here to set up the satellite office, make contacts with clients and prep for the transition."

"Then what?" she asked.

"Then back to Vancouver. We're opening up satellites in some other US cities, too: Denver, Seattle, Portland. They might send me to set up one of those next."

The thought of going some place for a few months and then hopping around to the next place and then the next made her hands clammy.

"Doesn't the impermanence bother you?" she asked.

He shrugged. "I guess it might if I still had roots somewhere." He took a drink of the soda he'd gotten from the vending machine. "But it's weird. No place really feels like home anymore. Same streets, same places, but missing two very important inhabitants."

He gave her a sad smile that tugged at her heartstrings. Any place without her family would feel cold and empty.

"And even if I wanted to settle down in a place they sent me, the whole Canadian citizen thing puts a damper on that possibility." He looked over at her, a touch of mischief returning to his eyes. "Unless I can get a job that will give me a sponsorship for my specialized skills."

Her lips turned up, and she couldn't help taking the bait and giving him a chance for more playfulness to soothe the wounds the last few years had marked him with. "And just what are these specialized skills?"

Wendy winced at a twinge in her neck from the stiffness, and she rubbed at the sore spot. Alec reached over and kneaded away the hurts in her neck and shoulders. His capable hands on her body didn't take away the pain of her situation, but every press into the places she couldn't get to on her own made her feel less alone. She leaned into the movement, and her body relaxed almost to the point of going boneless at the firm pressure of his fingers on her skin.

"Maybe I can show you again sometime," he said, still with a teasing lilt to his voice.

Wendy laughed. "Not if you're going to use those skills to get a visa right after."

"I'm talking about computers. What are you talking about?" he said with mock innocence.

"Me too. Software. Hard drives."

Soon after, they drifted into conversation, and before she knew it, Wendy looked at her phone: midnight. And Alec was still awake, though just barely.

"It's getting late," she murmured, stifling a yawn and pulling the blanket from the bag of provisions they'd been sharing up to her chin.

"Mmm." He leaned his head onto hers.

"Don't you have to work in the morning?"

"I asked Andi if she could cover my morning appointments."

"You did?"

He nodded and snuggled closer to her. An unfamiliar emotion swelled in her heart region, and she swallowed and sat up to face him. "Why are you doing this?"

Alec frowned and looked at her for a moment with sleepy eyes. "What do you mean?"

She shrugged. "You've only known me for a few weeks. And you hate hospitals."

"I figured as long as you were here, we could hate hospitals together."

Wendy gave him a fatigued smile, and Alec's teasing features turned earnest.

"And I know how it feels to sit in a waiting room with a parent in there, not knowing. I didn't have a lot of company, and I got into a very bad headspace. I didn't want you to have to do this alone."

Could it be that there was truly no ulterior motive here, no other shoe hanging over her head waiting to drop? Just that he knew what she was going through and didn't want her to have to face it alone?

Emotion blossomed in her chest until she wasn't sure she could contain it all.

He gave her a sleepy grin. "Now can I have my pillow back?"

He patted his shoulder, and she laid her head there, not sure what to do with all this deluge of feeling building inside her. He smoothed her hair and laid his head to rest on hers. The comforting sound of his breathing lulled her even as everything else swirled around in her head: fear for her dad, bone-deep weariness, the need to stay strong, and overwhelming everything else this deep, deep gratitude that at least for tonight, she had a shoulder to lean on, too.

CHAPTER 20

"Family of Rob Deveaux?" The doctor's voice intruded on her sleep and seemed more like something out of a dream until Alec shook her leg gently.

Wendy started awake with a gasp, and her surroundings came back to her. She lifted her head from Alec's shoulder, where she'd finally drifted off to sleep, and stretched her neck back and forth.

"I think you've got some news," Alec whispered. She extracted her arm from her hold around Alec's waist.

Wendy's stomach gave a nervous lurch at the sight of the cardiologist. She studied the woman's face for any sign of that grave, pitying look that was surely the harbinger of bad news, but her features remained annoyingly neutral, if tired.

Alec gave her knee a squeeze, and she joined her just-waking mom and braced for the news.

"Rob's sore and still a bit out of it, but recovery is looking good. We're going to move him to a room in the CICU. You can probably see him in an hour or two."

All the breath whooshed out of Wendy's lungs, so great was her relief. Next to her, her mom's chest shook with oncoming sobs, and Wendy wrapped her arms around her, gripping her thin frame.

"He's going to be okay?" her mom said.

The doctor nodded. "He's going to have to make some lifestyle changes, but it looks like yes, he'll be okay."

"Dad?"

An hour later, as soon as they were allowed back, Wendy and her mom said their goodbyes to Alec and followed the nurse back to her dad's room. After letting her parents have their tearful reunion, Wendy approached.

"Hey, pumpkin." Rob's eyes crinkled, and he rubbed the overgrown black hairs of his beard. He held a hand out to her and looked like he was attempting to get up. Strings of tubing ran from the IV in his hand to a metal tower next to his bed.

Wendy patted his leg. "Don't go stretching out your stitches. I'm coming."

She reached down gingerly to wrap him in a hug, and nearly cried at the feel of his heartbeat against her chest.

"Did you get me any clothes? They cut off my shirt, and this gown thingy they gave me has no backside."

Wendy smirked. "Don't worry. I can go by the house and get you some clothes." She pulled up the chair and sat beside him, holding his hand. He squeezed her hand and looked her over, like he was seeing her for the first time.

"I'm so glad you're okay," she said, her voice nearly breaking.

"You and me both. I love you, kiddo."

"I know. I love you too, Dad."

"For a while there, I didn't know if I was ever going to see you two again." He wiped at the tears streaking down his cheek. The sight of her dad crying unleashed tears of her own.

On Wendy's next visit, she brought him back some clothes, but not the chocolate pudding he'd angled for later. Now that he was more coherent and more rested, he'd obviously been reflecting on his priorities. He took Jacqui's hand and announced, "I've been thinking. Jacqui, as soon as the doctors give me the okay to travel, I'm going to take you on that honeymoon you always wanted."

Wendy's mom smiled and shook her head. "Let's focus on getting you well first, okay?"

He grunted. "I'm serious, though. We'll go. Two weeks in Havana, with those colorful buildings and all the classic cars you can handle."

"Two weeks?" Wendy raised an eyebrow at him. He'd never left anyone else in charge of the shop and the tours for more than three days. She turned to her mom. "This brush with death has gotten him all loosened up."

"I'm not complaining about that," Jacqui said.

Rob turned to Wendy. "We've got you and Julie, and even Paige, now taking on extra responsibility. There's no reason we can't take an extended holiday once in a while."

Wendy and her mom exchanged an incredulous look. Rob had just ceded more control in five minutes than they'd been able to wrangle out of him in Wendy's lifetime.

He poked at his chest and pulled at the tubes leading into his IV. "All this made me realize how foolish I've been. Never taking time off and keeping such a tight leash. Especially when there were things that both of you wanted that we could never do while I had us working around the clock. I wanted to build a legacy for you, but I probably still could've done that if I'd let up a little."

Wow. Wendy could hardly believe what she was hearing.

"I'm serious now. Don't you two go looking at me like I just ate the biggest batch of crow there ever was. Even a proud man can admit when he can do better."

Wendy nodded in agreement.

"And I'm sorry I threw a fit about you going to art school. I hate that I held you back."

"Are you sure this isn't still the anesthesia talking?"

He grumbled something under his breath that contained more than a few expletives.

"Okay, there's the Dad I know." Wendy grinned. The edges of the old wound threatened to open again against her will at the mention of art school. But she didn't want to get into it now. Not when her dad was here, and he was alive. She'd skip every opportunity if it meant having him alive and healthy. "I probably would've come back after, anyway. "

"But I put you off from even trying. In my defense, I wanted my only daughter to be in the same town as me, but that was selfish. And I don't want to get in your way anymore. So, make your brochures and your rack cards your way."

"That's so far down on the totem pole of what's important to me right now," Wendy said, but she appreciated the gesture just the same.

"I'm trying to do better. Are you going to keep sassing and stopping me?"

Wendy's grin stretched in response to the affronted look on her dad's face. "No, Dad."

"Good." He nodded like that was settled.

Wendy got up to bring him some ice chips and see about some food that he wouldn't deem inedible. "That sweet potato whatever they brought me before you got here was nasty," he groused.

Wendy and her mom exchanged a relieved grin. If he was complaining, he was back on the road to getting better.

After a while, the doctor insisted that Rob needed some time to rest and told them they were free to come back later. Jacqui kissed Rob goodbye, but Wendy hung back when her dad beckoned her.

"Will you promise me something, pumpkin?" he asked.

The earnest look in his eyes took her aback.

She hesitated, her stomach doing a little flip of uncertainty. "Sure. Anything."

"I want you to think on this, and I want you to think hard."

Wendy nodded.

"I don't want it to take a heart attack for you to realize this," he said.

"Okay."

"If there is anything you're hesitating or holding back on, do it now," he said. "Even if it takes you away from here. Don't wait until it's too late and you spend your whole life looking back and regretting not doing it."

Wendy sucked in a breath and nodded, her heart hammering.

"You still promise?" he asked.

She was too worn out for more soul-searching at the moment, but thoughts of one newly important person floated to the top of her mind.

She leaned over to give her dad one more hug before leaving. "I promise."

CHAPTER 21

Later that night, after the visit with her dad, Wendy's hands shook as she pushed the doorbell to Alec's corporate apartment. *Deep breaths. Deep breaths,* she told herself, but her heart ran wild in her chest.

With her dad stable and her mom on hospital vigil, Wendy had run home to take a shower and to do something she didn't want to spend her future regretting not doing.

The door opened, and Alec appeared in lounge pants and a t-shirt that said *Sorry ladies, I'm already like a brother to someone else.* His expression warmed at the sight of Wendy on his doorstep, and she let her eyes wander over the lines of his jaw, the crinkles at the corners of his eyes. His sleepy but luminous eyes turned on her.

"Hey, I was just about to call and check on you." He stepped to the side and ushered her into his place. "Any news?"

"He's still stable. Sore but bitching to the nurses about the food and the clothes, so he's on the right track."

"And how are you feeling?"

"Good. Still tired, but good." She was jittery with nerves and fatigue, but also flushed with a new clarity.

"You want a drink or anything?" Alec moved through the kitchen holding up options, and the sight of him relaxed in his pajamas and in his element flooded her with affection. She wanted to see more of that, more of him.

"I wouldn't mind some of that," she said when he held up a bottle of whiskey and another of Coke.

He poured two and slid one to her.

"How was your day?" she asked.

"Good. Spent the afternoon getting caught up and thinking about you." He clinked his glass against hers and took a seat next to her at his dining room table. "To your dad getting better."

She raised her glass and let the warm sting of the whiskey burn down her throat, willing the languid, floaty feeling to infuse her with courage. She twisted her still-wet hair in her fingers.

"I wanted to say thank you for last night at the hospital. For staying with me." She looked up at him, and he held her gaze, eyes soft with emotion. It was all still so close to the surface from the scare. "I've never had anyone show up for me like that. Outside of my family, I mean."

"I'm glad I could be there," he said.

"Me, too." She rummaged in her purse and handed over an envelope. "I made you a card."

He took it, and his smile spread as he read her corrected platitude. "Friends don't let friends sit in the hospital without mac and cheese. Thanks for being there with me. Love, Wendy." Her heart skipped at the last lines uttered aloud.

"I actually made one for you, too. Well, not a card, but a note." Alec stepped away from the table to and retrieved a piece of notebook paper from what must have been his bedroom and handed it over.

Wendy looked at the doodles and the words on the page: *It's always darkest before ~~the dawn~~ you find the light switch.*

The feeling struck again that he got her, that he was the same kind of weird as she was and that they—two people from different parts of the world who might never have met except for some weird twist of fate—fit somehow. Her heartbeat fluttered as she rallied her courage. She spoke, even though her voice shook. "I think I was wrong before. When I freaked out about us working together, and you know, dating." She swallowed. "But we can find a way to work things out, right? Like you said before, put Andi back on our account except for the app stuff. Or maybe even table that for the time being until we figure out what to do."

"Are you saying what I think you're saying?" Alec asked. He leaned closer and covered her hand with his. "Because you don't have to go making decisions like this when there is so much going on in your life right now."

"Are you trying to dissuade me? I'm declaring my feelings here." Her cheeks flushed.

"No. No, please declare away." The dimple appeared in his cheek. "I just don't want to be one more thing you're worried about with all that's going on."

"Alec," she said, heart aching at the sight of the tenderness and protectiveness in his eyes. "I want to be more than friends with you." She swallowed again. "You know, if you want to."

His smile turned radiant, and he wrapped her in his arms. "Wendy, I want to be more than friends with you, too."

CHAPTER 22

The next weeks passed with visits to the hospital, helping her dad with the transition back home, and a string of blissful, glorious nights wrapped up with Alec in her bed or in his. They put the whole app business on hold—still a problem, but one that could wait for another time.

When Rob was finally feeling up to more company, Wendy's mom decided it was time for one of their famous crawfish boils.

"You going to invite your young man?" Rob asked. Wendy served him a bowl of baby carrots, and he frowned down at them like they were nuclear waste.

"I don't know." Despite the dreamlike quality of their relationship over the last few weeks, it still felt too soon, like there was an invisible line she shouldn't cross. She'd been living in her happy bubble with Alec, and if this went badly, that would pop and it would be back to reality. But if introducing Alec to the boisterous family all at once went well... she might be even more scared of where that possibility would lead.

"Your mom and Julie tell me he's the one keeping you fed and making sure you sleep on your ridiculous dad vigil."

"It's not ridiculous, Dad. What if something happened, and you needed me?"

He took a bite of carrot, and his face screwed up in distaste. "That's my girl. Always looking out for everyone else. But I'm made of stronger stuff. I'll be back to normal again before you know it."

"Only if you keep your blood pressure down and start eating some green vegetables."

He screwed up his face at the mention of greens.

"And pickled jalapeños on movie nachos don't count."

He muttered something under his breath that sounded like "killjoy."

Wendy rolled her eyes. "This is why you need me to look out for you."

"Fine. Bring your new boyfriend for me to harass—I mean make polite conversation with,"—Wendy rolled her eyes, "and I'll eat a whole plate full of broccoli."

"Every day?" Wendy said.

Rob frowned. "That day."

"For a week."

"Three days."

Wendy gave an exasperated sigh. "Fine. I'll ask Alec to come." Her heart jumped into her throat at that. "But I can't make any guarantees. This is like throwing him into the lion's den the way you and mom and Aunt Angeline, not to mention Julie, love to interrogate people." She thought of the way they'd all pounced on Griffin his first few times at family dinners. *When do you think you'll want to have babies? You're not into that* Fifty Shades of Something *stuff, are you?*

"You could tell him I can fire him if he doesn't come," Rob added, with merriment dancing in his eyes.

"You will do no such thing. You're incapacitated, and that means I'm making all the business decisions."

"Okay, okay. Don't tell him that."

Wendy met her dad's eyes, and for a moment it hit her how glad she was that he was back to his normal obnoxiously joking self.

"So, I'll see you tomorrow then?"

Wendy bit her lip, unable to speak, and nodded instead. She leaned down to kiss her dad on the cheek and turned to go.

"Wendy?"

"Yeah?"

A rare moment of seriousness passed between them. "Thanks. For holding your vigil and looking out for your old dad."

"Always." After a moment, she smiled. "Don't think that's getting you out of the broccoli."

CHAPTER 23

Wendy had never felt nerves the way she did when she made her way up the familiar road to her parents' house the next day. Alec's hand slipped into hers, and her stomach tied up into pretzels. She'd brought a guy home with her on exactly zero occasions, and although she wanted her two worlds to collide here, that inner resistance still kicked up a potent force.

She dis-entwined her fingers from Alec's and wiped her sweaty palms on her jeans. She ducked under the sweep of the magnolia tree in front of the white-paneled house in uptown and spotted her mom under the hood of her newest project: a *flaming* orange '67 Mustang convertible.

"Mom, what are you doing out here? I thought you were seeing to the boil."

"Your father said I was hovering. So I sent Julie to hover and came out here." Jacqui wiped a swath of red hair that matched her daughter's out of her eyes. She winked at them both and fixed them with an everything-is-fine-just-fine smile.

Still, Wendy caught the crease of fatigue in her brow. Playing full-time caretaker and trying to balance everything out was taking its toll. Wendy hugged her mom, and her stomach clenched in memory of that first unending day in the hospital when it had all been touch and go. It was hard to imagine either of her parents without the other. They bickered and razzed each other mercilessly, but together they were unshakable. And seeing them both shaken, these two people who had been her rocks, tore at her.

"Nice to see you again, Alec," Jacqui said. She pulled him into a hug before he could protest, but he seemed to roll with it, like he did with most things.

He pulled out a bottle of motor oil from the package under his arm and presented it to Jacqui. "I was going to bring flowers, but Wendy said you might like this more."

Wendy's heart swelled. She'd been teasing when she made that comment, but he'd listened.

Jacqui squeed. "This one's a keeper," she said with a teasing look at Wendy.

Alec's smile widened.

"Go on in. Everyone's already out back."

In the backyard, amidst the sprawling greenery, Julie and Griffin spread layers of newspaper over the picnic table and traded verbal volleys with Wendy's dad, who was holding court in his favorite camping chair at the head of the table. The smell of Cajun seasoning bubbling over crawfish and sausage and corn and potatoes wafted over from where Aunt Angeline and her boyfriend Dean looked in on the progress of the boil.

Wendy opened the screen door and lingered on the threshold.

"What's got you all jittery?" Alec raised their interlaced hands to his lips and kissed her knuckles.

"Nothing. I'm not jittery," she protested, a little too quickly.

Alec's gaze moved to the fingernail she was gnawing to the quick, and she pulled her hand away with a flush.

She mumbled something, and Alec raised an eyebrow. She sucked in a breath. "I've never brought anyone home before. To a family thing."

"Never?"

"I said never." Even though she'd snapped at him, he pulled her close and rubbed slow circles into her back. She let herself relax into him a bit, but it didn't kill all the nerves. Not even close.

"Don't worry, I won't ask them to tell me all of your embarrassing childhood stories," Alec whispered.

"Oh, I'm sure they'll offer those up with little or no encouragement."

"What are you nervous about?" he asked. "That they won't like me or I won't like them?"

She shrugged. Both things felt like a *big deal,* though she wasn't ready to admit that. "I do want you all to like each other."

"They're your family. Your people." He met her eyes, and his mouth turned up into a smile. "I'm pretty sure I'll like them."

"They're going to ask you embarrassing questions."

"I come from a family of embarrassing questioners."

"Come on then. Into the lion's den."

Half an hour later, everyone gathered around the table, which was now slathered in a delectable layer of crawfish, corn cobs, sausage, and potatoes.

"What am I meant to do with these now?" Alec held one of the crimson shellfish up to examine it.

"Pinch the tail and suck the head," Wendy said. "Like this." She demonstrated and licked her fingers after.

A "that's what she said" followed from somewhere down the table, and Wendy smirked. Alec tried the food, unfazed.

As promised, the Deveaux family commenced their lunch conversation and mild interrogation of Alec. Griffin and Dean, the two other newcomers to the group, jumped in to run interference from time to time and commiserate. But if Wendy expected Alec would hang back and feel intimidated during the raucous conversation and teasing that was a Deveaux family get-together, she would've been wrong. He jumped right in, like he'd always been a part of this, self-possessed, engaging, and even daring to disagree with her dad a few times—in his trademark respectful way, of course.

When Julie teased them about their "tawdry work affair," though, Wendy stiffened. Her parents were sticklers about above-board conduct with the business they'd built from the ground up. Over the last few weeks, they'd been so consumed with her dad's health scare that it hadn't really come up, but she wasn't sure they'd be all that thrilled with the idea.

"We're going to have Andi take over our account again. As soon as we finish with a few things," Wendy said. We. That was new. A new flock of nerves stirred up to join the work worries.

"What are you working on?" her mom asked.

Wendy and Alec exchanged a glance, and Wendy shook her head. To buy herself some more time, she stuffed another crawfish in her mouth. Her dad might be all carpe diem about some things since the accident, but she had a feeling bringing up the app proposal again and pushing for more changes too soon might sour his newly good mood.

"You probably don't want to talk shop when you've all got the day off," Alec said, saving her from coming up with a diversion. "Now that you've got my life story, how did you two meet, Mr. and Mrs. Deveaux?"

"So polite," Wendy's mom said with a teasing smile. "You can call us Jacqui and Rob."

"Okay, Jacqui and Rob, then."

"We met at work, actually," Jacqui said. "In a way." She stood and draped her arms over Rob's shoulders.

"I was twenty and working for Tony's tour company down the way," Rob said. "And every day on my tours, I would walk past this ice cream shop and see this gorgeous redhead with a look on her face like she didn't take lip from anyone."

Jacqui snorted at this.

"We'd smile and wave at each other from a distance, and I kept circling back after my tours, but she'd disappear. So one day I went in early and asked her if she'd meet me after my tour. And we ended up talking all night. But we had opposite work schedules to it was almost impossible for us to see each other."

"So then this guy," Jacqui jumped in, "even though he was working fifty hours a week at Tony's, applied for a part-time job at the ice cream parlor, just so we could spend time together. The big dork."

"Hey, can you blame me? I finally got to see you as much as I wanted."

Jacqui's smart-assed smile softened.

"And when there were no customers, there was a private back room," Rob said, pumping his eyebrows.

This brought a chorus of, "Dad!" and "No" and, "Lalala, I can't hear you" from the younger generation.

"What? It was the perfect place to steal a kiss or two." Rob pulled Jacqui onto his lap and wrapped his arms around her. She gave him a swat on the arm, but also nuzzled into his beard and fluffed his hair with a goofy grin. Then she speared a broccoli floret from his specially prepared plate and fed it to her gloriously recovering husband, earning an exaggerated frown.

Wendy looked on, her heart growing full at the sight of the patriarch and matriarch of her family. Seeing them together warmed her heart, doubly so after one of them was so nearly taken from her.

A bird sang in the distance, and she looked over and caught the wistfulness and affection in Alec's expression as he watched the same scene.

"How long have the two of you been married?" he asked.

"Twenty-eight years of blissfully driving each other crazy," Jacqui answered.

"My parents just celebrated their twentieth when my dad passed. It would've been twenty-two when I lost my mom."

Rob assessed Alec with a fatherly concern and newfound softness in his features that seemed to be new since the heart attack. "Sorry to hear that."

"Thanks."

"I bet they were good people with a son like you," Rob said.

"The best."

Alec tackled a potato, and Wendy goggled at her dad's open praise of someone he'd only just met. But maybe it shouldn't have surprised her. Alec had a way about him, with his good nature and willingness to be vulnerable, that had sneaked past her own defenses in rapid succession, too.

"Twenty-eight years. So, what's the secret?" Alec asked.

"When you can pee in front of someone, it's pretty much all good from there," Jacqui said.

"Ah, yes. Nothing says love like open-door peeing," Wendy deadpanned.

"It's a metaphor, honey." Her mom reclaimed her own seat and grabbed a corn cob.

"A colorful one," Julie said with a smirk.

Jacqui only shrugged, not looking the least bit embarrassed. "I bet even our sweet mysterious Julie pees with the door open now."

"She does," Griffin confirmed with a wink.

Julie scoffed. "Maybe metaphorically."

Griffin opened his mouth to further comment and wisely shut it at Julie's red-faced glare.

"Okay, can we stop talking about bodily functions as a stand in for lifelong commitment?" Wendy said. "Alec is probably second guessing his decision to be a part of this little gathering."

She snuck a glance at him, half sure he'd be scoping out the exits and plotting the most polite way to make his excuses, duck out, and never come back. But he slipped an arm around her waist, the solidness of his presence kindling a rush of affection.

"I told you I'm pretty hard to embarrass," he said with a grin.

Both Jacqui's and Julie's eyes gleamed.

"Word to the wise," Griffin said to Alec. "You might not want to say that around the Deveaux family. They'll take that as a challenge."

The exchanged glance between Julie and Wendy's mom confirmed this theory.

"C'mon," Griffin said to Alec. "Why don't we grab some beers before they start in."

Alec kissed Wendy's cheek before heading in to the kitchen with Griffin. The light dusting of stubble on his jawline scraped pleasantly against her cheek. The sensation and the realness of him with her family—grabbing beers with Griffin, joking with her mom and dad and Julie—added to the surrealness of the last few weeks. It seemed like everything had changed with her dad in the hospital. Life had shaken up everything normal and certain, like they were inside a toddler's snow globe. She didn't dare disturb anything else.

Her dad sat there at the head of the picnic table in his folding chair, bemused and watchful, taking in the scene, as if seeing his family with fresh eyes. A profound gratitude washed over Wendy that he was here and able to do that.

Alec and Griffin returned and passed Abita Ambers around.

"Your mom's right, you know." Wendy's dad looked at her, his features gone sober and pensive, like he'd spent a lot of time reflecting since his second chance at life. "When you let someone else see all of your shit—metaphorically," he cut a look at Julie, "and God knows I've got my share"—he reached over and squeezed Jacqui's hand—"and they're still willing to commit to you, put up with you and sacrifice for you whatever comes down the road, and you for them, *that's* what makes it work."

Alec slipped an arm around Wendy's waist, pulling her close, and a nervous flutter passed over her again. For the first time in her life, she let herself think it: could this be the person she could build a life with the way her dad had done with her mom?

Late afternoon gave way to the throes of twilight, and Wendy looked over at Alec, who was so at ease, even with all the oncoming commotion, holding her hand, catching her eye in that kind of intimate, silent conversation, whispering secret jokes, being her shoulder to lean on, and he seemed so... perfect. Not flawless. Not unshakeable, but the salt to her pepper, the Rory Williams to her Amy Pond.

And she knew she'd been in way over her head before she'd even realized it.

She'd always done this. Cared too much, gotten excited too much. She wasn't sure how to stop this personality flaw of hers. Especially when, far too many times, it had been to her own detriment.

So instead of pulling him closer, she looked away. She wondered if no matter how close they became, she'd always hold a little of herself back. So that there would be something intact after the fall.

Later that night, back at Alec's apartment, she slipped out of bed and into the bathroom, closing the door firmly. The memory of her mom's bathroom wisdom came back to her, and her nerves jangled. She opened it again and darted a glance at him, tangled in the covers, chest rising and falling. He was asleep, so it wasn't like he'd be checking to see what was going on. This was dumb to even worry about. She went back in and pulled the door behind her, leaving it the tiniest bit ajar. She could try to open herself up and enjoy her time with Alec. But there were some things other people just didn't need to see.

CHAPTER 24

"This *is* getting serious. You're finally meeting the elusive sister," Julie said.

While Wendy slipped into a dress, Julie rifled through Wendy's closet, trying to find something to wear to the Doris Kearns Goodwin lecture she and Griffin would attend that night. "Everything in here is black," she groused.

"Have you met me?" Wendy straightened the neckline of her dress—black, obviously—with grey and pink sugar skulls. She paced in front of her wall o' books and searched for her earrings, trying to calm her jitters.

Several months had passed since that first crawfish boil with her family. Her dad was on the mend, but still under close supervision by his doctor and, of course, every member of the Deveaux family, who wanted him around for a long time to come. It was September now, and although her nagging insecurities would likely linger long past the changing fall leaves, Wendy and Alec had become pretty much inseparable. For the first time, she had two tooth-brushes in her bathroom and a drawer somewhere other than her own place. She'd even taken up the alarming habits of waking up earlier, so they were more or less on the same schedule, and even smiling at strangers. Alec's sister had been traveling for work on and off for the past few months, so she'd avoided that big question mark. But other than that, everything felt so right. So right, in fact, that she was now constantly living with low-grade anxiety and waiting for the other proverbial shoe to drop.

"What if she's the evil twin and is plotting to kill anyone who tries to get close to her brother?" Wendy fastened an earring to her ear. "In all of her pictures on Alec's phone she's got these big sunglasses, and I've only ever seen a side view with her face hidden by her hair. What if she's hiding something?"

"You watch way too many of those B horror movies."

"Or what if she hates me?" Wendy said. She slipped on a necklace. "Or worse, acts like she likes me and then secretly hates me."

"It'll be fine." Julie shook Wendy's shoulder. "She sent you that whole care package when your dad was in the hospital. She can't be all that bad."

Wendy frowned. "Yeah. I guess."

"You're still hung up on those girls from high school, aren't you?" Julie said, finally settling on an onyx sheath dress and a spider necklace.

The sympathy on her cousin's face had her looking away. The creases between Wendy's brows deepened as anger roiled up. Why couldn't she ever get over that? It was ages ago. But no matter how much distance stretched out between then and now, it was always there in the back of her mind, reminding her that no matter how wonderful someone's intentions seemed to be, there might be disappointment lurking just around the corner.

"I highly doubt Alec's sister is a high-school mean girl," Julie said. "Plus, haven't you seen all of those twin studies? It turns out that even if twins are raised in totally different environments, nature prevails. A very high percentage of the time, they have very similar interests, values, and per-sonalities. And come on, it's Alec. If she's like him, you're good."

The doorbell rang, announcing Alec's arrival, and she took a deep breath. Yes, if she was like Alec, everything would be fine.

Alec met her at the door with a radiant smile, a bouquet of magnolia blossoms, and music playing on his phone. Not just any music, but the song by the group of angsty Canadian rockers he'd introduced her to that she'd been playing on repeat when the stress came on.

He leaned in to kiss her, and the fragrance of the magnolia blossoms mingled with the woods-in-winter scent of his cologne. She pulled him closer, letting him anchor her. A rush of affection overtook her as his lips caressed hers.

"I thought you might need a de-stress soundtrack," he said, his grin slowly spreading.

"Who says I'm stressed?" she sassed. But the guitar riff did its work, and she could already feel the tension leaving the building.

Julie's answering laugh floated from upstairs, and she trotted down to say her hellos and goodbyes before heading out.

Alec followed Wendy to the kitchen. While she searched for a vase for the waxy white blooms, he pulled open a cabinet door. "Where'd my hot sauce go?"

"Already got you covered." Wendy sang along with the music, much to Alec's amusement, and pulled from her purse the tiny bottle of sauce that he put on almost everything. "Unless Kara is a foodie purist and doesn't like her creations messed with."

Alec slipped behind her and wrapped her in his arms. He kissed her head. Letting more tension bleed out of her, she rested her head against the warmth of his chest. Angsty music played, and she reveled in the comforting press of his body against hers, the fit just right. Once again, he'd known exactly what she needed. The music to calm her nerves, the nearness. He saw her. He *knew* her. And stood here still.

"I love you," he said. Wendy's whole body stilled. The world contracted to those three words from his lips.

Her heartbeat thrummed until she was sure it was audible from across the room. Wendy shifted in his embrace until she could look up at him. "You do?"

His eyes crinkled at the corners, and the way his adoring gaze traveled her face made her lightheaded. Without a trace of hesitation, he nodded. Half in exhilaration, half in panic, emotion surged in her chest. She had to press her lips together to keep them from quivering. This was Alec, her Alec, and he loved her. He also liked to go running at six a.m. and avoided conflict like the plague, and was sometimes maddeningly agreeable, but those things she could live with. Because he was her person. The one who saw past her sometimes prickly ways and drank Red Bull so he could stay up late with her on weekends, just so they could have more time together. Those three words perched on her lips, too. But saying them aloud might be another matter.

"Me, too," she managed.

He pulled her into a kiss that sliced through all of her defenses, undoing for that moment the chains around all that she'd been holding back.

CHAPTER 25

After pressing the doorbell, Wendy tipped her head back to admire Kara's home. Set back from the street in the Garden District, it was an aging beauty of a plantation-style home. A wrap-around porch and a balcony with gorgeous ironwork lined the facade. It was much fancier than the homes anyone she knew inhabited, let alone someone in her twenties.

"She's really the only one who lives here?" she said.

Alec nodded and fiddled with the rolled-up sleeve of his blue henley.

"You're nervous, too," Wendy said, slightly taken aback. She could count on one hand the times she'd seen him ruffled.

"Well, the two most important women in my life are finally meeting tonight."

Her throat tightened. She wasn't used to being someone's most important person. "I'm sure we'll get along just fine." She rubbed his hand between both of hers and pushed to her tiptoes to kiss him.

"I love you," he said again against her lips.

Warmth melted over her once again, and her heart swelled until it was almost too full for her chest to bear. She swallowed. "I don't think I'll ever get tired of hearing you say that."

Her heart galloped as the sound of heels clacking against tile sounded from inside the house. Time to meet Alec's family—the only family he had. Smoothing her skirt, she sucked in a breath and looked at Alec again. She could feel herself falter on the words again, but she wanted to say them back. "I—"

The door swung open, and in the foyer in a turquoise dress with her blonde hair pulled up into an elegant twist stood Alec's sister.

"Alec!" she exclaimed.

Wendy did a double take, unable to process what she was seeing. In an instant, her stomach dropped to her shoes, and she went from feeling on top of the world to a laughed-at awkward teenager again. One who trusted an offer of friendship only to be a laughingstock after being stood up.

Alec wrapped his sister in a hug. "So, this is Wendy." He turned back to beam at her. "Wendy, this is my sister, Kara."

"Kara Lynn," Wendy repeated dumbly once she'd recovered her power of speech. Alec's sister was Kara Lynn Bowles, meanest of the mean girls, tormenter of outcast-kind. How had she not recognized her high school nemesis in those photos? Wendy's palms went sweaty, and she folded her arms across her chest.

Kara gave a startled laugh and exchanged a confused glance with Alec. "Nobody's called me that in years." She screwed up her features into a thinking face and examined Wendy, like Alec had never shown her any pictures, and she didn't know exactly who was coming to dinner. At least she had the sense to look mortified when realization—feigned or otherwise—dawned in those tawny eyes of hers. Though whether it was because of her past behavior or the fact that Wendy was here in the first place remained to be seen.

Alec cocked his head to the side and assessed Wendy and his sister.

Wendy gave him a tight smile.

"You two know each other?"

Wendy chose the most civil explanation she could manage. After all, she was here because she cared about Alec, and maybe Kara Lynn had changed since Wendy had seen her last. "We went to school together."

"What did we used to call you?" Kara tapped a manicured fingernail to her lips, and then her eyes lit up. "That's right! Ghost girl." She laughed, and Wendy's jaw tightened. Nope, this girl hadn't changed at all if she still found her past cruelty a load of laughs. Her stomach sank to her knees as the feeling of being taunted at Kara Lynn and Aundrea's hands came back to her with sickening clarity. She glanced back toward Alec's SUV. She didn't know if she could do this.

"Gawd, that was so long ago. Come on in. I'll get you two some drinks, and we can toast to not being awkward high schoolers anymore. I made mint juleps. Does everyone want one?"

"Yes," Wendy replied instantly. She was going to need to keep them coming if she was going to survive this night.

Alec's list of qualities he wanted in another person came back to her. Chief among them, *gets along with my sister.* Could she ever really get along with someone who had been so monstrous to her in the past? Coexist maybe. But what did this mean for them? Just when she'd finally let someone in, then this.

Kara swished off into the kitchen that was all stainless steel and granite and dark wood and as immaculately styled as she was.

Wendy's shoulders slumped, and she stepped into the dining room with Alec. She got as far as the barn door table before panic pounded at her breastbone, more intensely with every step in Kara Lynn's direction.

The warmth of Alec's hand on the small of her back brought her back to the present.

"Hey, you okay?" he said in a low voice.

"Fine." Wendy sucked in a breath and tried to school her features.

"Really? Because you don't look fine."

"Just brought up a bad memory, that's all."

"Of my sister?" At the sight of his face on the verge of being crushed by the bad news, Wendy hesitated.

"Let's just say that time in my life did not make the highlight reel." She forced herself to look at the wall adorned with decorative plates in shades of blue and tried to let her past hang-ups go. There had to be some positives here. At least Kara had good taste.

A light flashed from the kitchen. Wendy peeked over the island to see Kara adjusting three copper mugs garnished with mint in a light box and photographing them.

Wendy raised an eyebrow. "Why is she taking pictures of our drinks?"

"For my food blog." Kara strolled into the dining room and handed each of them a drink. "I'm blogging our dinner tonight."

She clinked her mug with Alec's, and for the first time, Wendy had occasion to examine them side by side. Like Alec had said, she dressed like she was always about to attend a cocktail party, the same way she had when Wendy'd known her before. Who wore heels in their own house? Kara's honey blonde hair was lighter than Alec's. They had the same narrow chin and dimple, and though their eyes were different colors, they had the same shape, especially when they smiled. It was so bizarre to see the features that she'd come to know and love on Alec reflected back on the face of her onetime tormenter.

"Yeah, Alec told me about that. I've been meaning to check it out," Wendy said, deciding to be the better person and play nice. Plus, the best revenge would be to have turned out just fine despite all of what had gone down in high school.

"Really? Do you like to cook, too?" For the first time in Kara's hopeful eyes, Wendy saw an inkling of the teenage girl who she thought might've been a kindred spirit. Before she turned out to be a jerk.

"I cook more from necessity than because I like it," she admitted.

"Oh." Kara continued to smile, but there was something dejected about it. "I guess not everyone's good at cooking."

Wendy frowned. "I didn't say I wasn't good at it."

"Oh. Well, you know what I mean." This time the smile was more plastic and condescending.

Deep breaths. Happy thoughts. I'm here for Alec.

"Anyway, I'm perfectly happy to be a guinea pig for people who do love to cook, though," Wendy said.

Alec seemed to relax a little. He'd been eyeing both Wendy and his sister with wariness since the revelation that they had a past.

"I can see that," Kara said.

Wendy's eyes widened in disbelief. She cut a glance at Alec. Even he had to have caught the rudeness of that one. "Excuse me?"

"Kara?" Alec's brows creased as he turned to his sister, but his tone was maddeningly diplomatic.

"Relax. I just mean you're not trying to starve yourself to be model-sized," Kara clarified. "That's a good thing. Most of the family friends my age are forever doing cleanses or will only eat kale and cucumbers. They won't try my food even if I tempt them with organic ethically raised chicken that had spa appointments twice a week."

Though her explanation sounded perfectly reasonable, there was still something in her tone that got Wendy's hackles up—that air of *Don't be silly. You're overreacting!* that implied Wendy was the weak and sensitive one.

Alec reached over and covered her hand with his. With a half-hearted smile, she slunk down in her chair. The way being in Kara Lynn's presence turned her back into that lonely teenager everyone picked on grated on her. She tried to remind herself how much time and life had passed since then. She was in a good place now, liked her job, her family and her volunteer gig helping kids. Plus, she had a good thing going with Alec. Most of the time, she felt pretty darn secure in who she was. No small feat considering all the teasing she'd combatted in her school days. But being here, it felt like all of her confidence and sass and peace had been slammed it into a trash compactor.

After more semi-painful conversation, Kara looked at Wendy. "You want to help me grab more drinks and get the food out?"

Fingers of dread kneaded into her shoulders, but she gave herself a mental shake. It was just a trip to the kitchen—but old habits died hard. She couldn't help but feel she was walking into a viper's nest.

"Um, sure."

Alec squeezed her hand before she followed Kara into the kitchen. Wendy fidgeted with her glass, unsure what to say. Little pots of herbs in neat cobalt pots lined the box window, letting in the evening light. "These are nice. I love the smell of mint."

"Me, too." Kara darted a glance Wendy's way. She paused and looked like she wanted to get something off of her chest. Wendy's stomach gave a nervous flutter. Was she going to apologize? *That* would be a shocking turn of events. Starting fresh would solve a lot of her problems, but being here tonight had taught her she hadn't let go of the past as much as she'd thought. Could she ever truly get over it, even if that meant fewer problems for her and Alec? But Kara's pretty face twisted up into a vexed expression, and she plucked a few mint leaves and muddled them with a mortar and pestle. She now couldn't seem to meet Wendy's eyes.

"Alec's said a lot of nice things about you," Kara said.

Wendy's eyes widened, and she waited for the rest of the backhanded compliment, but nothing followed.

"He's said a lot of nice things about you, too."

Kara's hands paused in her mint crushing, and her throat bobbed. "Really?"

She looked Wendy in the eye with such a hopeful and unsure expression that Wendy felt a pang of sadness for her.

"Sure," she said. "I know he's glad to have the chance to get to know you."

"Yeah, I'm lucky." Kara distributed the mint leaves to the cups and added crushed ice and julep mixture before tending to the stove.

"And as I'm sure you know, he's willing to forgive a lot of flaws."

Wendy grabbed the drinks and left Kara in the kitchen, trying to calm the roil of anger and resurfacing feelings that comment had kicked up. Sure, Wendy wasn't perfect, but what was that supposed to mean? Just when the queen of mean showed some humanity, she had to throw in that insult.

Before long, Kara brought out dishes of shrimp and grits with bacon crumbled over the top. It smelled delicious.

"So, your family still running that little ghost tour business?" Kara asked.

Wendy gritted her teeth at the continued condescension. "Yep. My mom has a side hustle business, too, so I've taken over a lot of what she used to do."

"What's her side business?"

"She fixes up classic cars and sells them."

Kara features contorted into a frown, like she was firmly Team Patriarchy and didn't like the idea of women getting their hands dirty. "That's... interesting, I guess."

This girl could take digs at Wendy all she wanted. She could take it, even if it made her feel like an outcast. But starting in on her family—oh, hell no.

Alec—either oblivious to his twin's disdain or trying to head it off — interjected with compliments about the Mustang Jacqui Deveaux was in the middle of working on. Wendy tried to calm her simmering anger and took a bite of shrimp and grits. Damn if the devil's cooking wasn't one of the most delicious things she'd ever tasted.

They continued to eat, and Alec steered the conversation to less contentious territory, at least for most of the meal. But Kara still got her snide comments and backhanded compliments in at every turn.

"And people really still go on ghost tours?" Kara said, folding her napkin—cloth, of course, probably something ridiculous like cashmere—next to her finished plate.

"Yes." Wendy's tone came out clipped. "A lot of them, actually. We just did a TV feature for *Alt History* a few weeks ago."

"That ghost hunter show?" Kara smirked.

"They follow myths and legends," Wendy corrected, anger still at a low boil.

"And true crime," Alec added.

"The French Quarter is full of haunts," Wendy said.

"Yeah, but you don't actually believe in the ghost part, do you?" Kara arched an eyebrow, like she was trying to get Wendy to spill the behind-the-scenes dirt, so she could twist it and use it against her. "Like, have you seen one before?"

"There are thousands of years of history in these streets, some of it scandalous, some of it bloody. Why shouldn't there be echoes of some of that?"

"Well, it just seems like a sort of snake oil thing to me," Kara said.

Hot anger flared on the sides of Wendy's neck.

"You said something about board games, Kara? Why don't we do that?" Alec said.

Wendy retreated to the living room to cool down while Alec helped his sister with the dishes. She ought to get extra karma points for biting back the nasty retorts brewing in her mind, especially when Kara Lynn seemed utterly incapable of doing the same. How did Kara do that? Dismiss everything that her family had built, and that she held dear in the course of an hour.

Wendy wandered the cozy space with deep pile carpet and throw pillows that probably cost more than Wendy's car and stopped in front of the stone fireplace. When was it ever cold enough in New Orleans for a fire? She shook her head. Placed along the mantel were photos of Kara in European villages, in a hut on the water that must have been in Bali, and wearing safari gear with a lion in the background. She picked up the lone photo of Kara with other people in the shot—a perfectly coifed older couple who Wendy guessed were her parents stood several feet away from Kara, against the railing of a yacht. Smug, aloof smiles all around. If this was going to be Alec's world, she didn't know where she'd fit into it. She felt like one of those *Bachelor* contestants bemoaning her situation from the confessional: *If that's the kind of girl he wants around, then I am the wrong girl for him.* Not that they were competing for the same spot in Alec's life, but it felt true, nonetheless.

And what if Julie was right about twins ending up with the same interests and personalities even after being separated their whole lives? She shook her head. That was silly. She knew Alec. There was nothing in their interactions to suggest that he was anything but genuine in his feelings for her. But being here tonight had her second-guessing everything she thought she knew. What if she just hadn't seen the darker side of the maple syrup yet?

Alec and Kara joined her from the kitchen with dessert plates and *Taboo.*

"Chocolate mousse?" Kara offered. "It has a dash of cinnamon and cardamom."

Wendy nodded and accepted it. Alec smiled at her from the couch where he was setting up the game. She let her gaze linger on his reassuring features—that dimple that punctuated his smile, those eyes that saw past her defenses, and those hands that held her tight when she needed him. Warmth spread through her for the first time since they'd arrived here. Surely she hadn't misjudged someone a second time.

She moved to join him on the couch, but Kara beat her to it, smoothing her skirt under her legs. Wendy took the loveseat across from them.

Wendy mustered up all the dregs of her patience and good-naturedness, for Alec's sake. Maybe a game would be nice, and get everyone, Wendy included, to loosen up.

Fifteen minutes in, though, she was already ready to bolt.

"Um, weird rainbow suits," Kara said. "Fight Godzilla-like things."

"*Power Rangers*!" Alec exclaimed.

"Yes!" The twins both dissolved into laughter. Laughter that did not seem to include Wendy.

"Wendy, your turn to give clues." Kara passed her the small box with the cards.

Wendy flipped the top, trying to push down the growing feeling of inferiority and certainty that they'd be laughing at her, not with her, very soon. *Titanic*. Okay, she could do this.

"Big water vessel," she said.

Silence.

"Oh! I survived it at the dinner theater thing." She gave Alec a knowing look.

More silence. *Seriously?* One minute ago they'd both been falling all over each other to yell out funny things.

"You can guess *something*," Wendy said.

"A phone call from your dad?" Alec said. Wendy frowned.

"Give us another clue. Or act it out," Alec said.

Wendy bit her lip and looked at the card of off-limits words. "Um, the actress who was in *American Horror Story* didn't go down with the rest."

Alec and Kara shared a frowning glance.

Wendy shot a pleading look at Alec.

"Nothing? Really?" More agonizing seconds slipped by.

"*Misery*?" Alec offered.

Wendy shook her head. Feeling like a tool, she got up and pantomimed Leo and Kate's "king of the world" bit, when they were standing at the front of the boat, "flying."

Kara's howl of laughter hit Wendy like a shot to the chest. Then Alec joined in. The sound shook loose a memory, and echoes of high school shame clawed at her insides.

"Okay, I'm done," Wendy said, the feeling still burning through her.

"Oh hey, be a good sport. It's all in fun," Kara insisted.

A flurry of memories flashed through Wendy's mind in quick succession like one of those brainwashing films they showed in movies with people's eyelids taped open. Hallways filled with cruel laughter after Aundrea and Kara Lynn had leaned a red paint can on the top of her locker and it had doused her favorite sweater and she'd trudged to the school nurse's office looking like Carrie White at the prom. The time when they'd stolen her backpack and superglued felt ghosts all over it. The time they'd ghosted her at the so-called concert. A thousand other little pranks and slights, with Kara's howl of laughter carrying over it all. And all after Wendy had mistaken their offer of friendship for the real deal. Bile rose in her throat, and heat crept up the side of her neck. The images kept coming, and she squeezed her eyes shut against the onslaught. Maybe it *was* a long time ago, and maybe she should be over it. But that toxic rage and hurt seeped back in.

Apparently growing up a little didn't erase the Pavlovian response to that laughter. Wendy's throat went dry. She needed some air. She needed to get far away from Kara Lynn Bowles.

"I'm sorry. Can we go?" She twisted her hair to the side and fumbled for her purse. "I'm feeling sick. Maybe something I ate."

Alec appeared behind her and reached for her. She flinched from his touch and couldn't bring herself to look at him. He'd been playing along with her sick games. Kara had fooled her once. Had her twin brother fooled her, too?

"If you're feeling sick, I've got a fully stocked medicine cabinet." Kara got to her feet. "I could get you something."

Wendy shook her head and headed for the exit. "You've done enough."

CHAPTER 26

"You want to tell me what that was about?" Alec said once they were safely back inside Wendy's house. His voice was still gentle, but he didn't sound pleased. The car ride had been all tense silence between them, so loud that it almost drowned out the music Wendy had switched on to clear her head.

Wendy's shoulders tensed, and she shrugged. "Which part?"

"The broody face. All of those snide remarks."

You mean from Kara? she thought but didn't say. She could feel all the shields she'd slowly dismantled over the past few months slam back into place. "That's just my personality. I'm sarcastic. I thought you knew that."

"Yeah, but I've never seen you bite back like that."

Her lips parted at the impact of that comment. Had she? If so, it was like a cat scratching in self-defense. She raised her gaze to meet his. The hurt on his face cut through her defenses, and she sighed.

"You know how I told you about those girls who used to torment me in high school?" She paced into the living room and tossed her purse on the couch.

Alec followed and nodded, his brows raised in confusion.

"The ones who invited me to the concert and stood me up and then spent the next three years calling me 'ghost girl' and pulling cruel pranks on me and trying to embarrass me?" She swallowed. "Your sister was the ringleader of that operation."

Alec's eyes widened, and he shook his head like he couldn't reconcile the fact that his twin sister had been a certified mean girl. "God, I'm sorry. That's awful." He took her hand, and a little of the poison from tonight's events left her system. See, he was here, and he was hearing her out. That was something.

"I think—I hope—she's changed a lot since then."

Wendy's jaw tightened. The way he said since then grated—like that wiped the slate clean and she should just get over it.

"I hope you're right," she said. Push it down. Figure out a way to deal.

Alec reached out to pull her closer, and the feeling she was trying to push down came out, anyway. "Did you hear the way she was condescending to me? About my 'little ghost tour business' and the horror that my mom might get grease on her nails while she was fixing cars."

"Maybe she was just nervous and didn't know what to say. It was probably awkward for her to see you, too."

Wendy's teeth ground together. Was he seriously sticking up for her behavior?

"Yeah, poor Kara has to face the girl she was a nightmare to for three years because her brother is foolish enough to date her."

Alec scoffed. "That's not what I meant."

She gave him a pointed glare and crossed her arms.

"I just meant she's obviously a better person now, and it's probably hard to be around someone she mistreated in the past."

She huffed at the "obviously a better person" comment. "Cry me a river."

"She's the only family I have left." He paced in front of the TV and raked a hand through his hair. "She might not be perfect, but she's here, and she's trying. And she's really important to me."

He turned to look at her, and all of his anguish projected straight into her heart.

"I was trying, too." But from the moment she'd stepped into Kara's perfect Southern kitchen, she'd just slipped back into the skin of that hurt fourteen-year-old girl. And didn't she have a damn good reason? But she also knew how much Kara meant to him. And knew how much he meant to her.

His expression softened. "I know you were. This couldn't have been easy for you either. This is just...complicated."

"She took me back to a dark place where I didn't like myself very much. It got into my head."

Alec let out a long breath and came to her. Wendy's anger still boiled, but she could see his side, too.

"Our first fight," Wendy said after a moment, breathing in the comforting scent of him. He gave her a half smile.

"We could go make-up now." She cut her eyes to the stairs leading up to her bedroom.

Alec's expression went unreadable. It was the face she loved, but there was an undercurrent of something else. A nervous ache began in her chest, and the relieved feeling of a moment ago fled.

"Actually, I should go. I've got an early start in the morning. And I need to clear my head."

He'd never not stayed the night before. That familiar sinking feeling of getting her hopes so invested in someone only to have the rug yanked out from under her crashed into her again. Just when she'd finally dipped her toe in trust again and had stopped pushing him away. The sick taste of bile rose in her throat as he kissed her on the cheek and walked out the door. Was she projecting, or was there a finality in the way he looked back at her one last time, and walked away? Maybe he and his sister weren't so different after all.

CHAPTER 27

The next morning Wendy'd planned to meet Julie for a run, but she cancelled. The thought of facing her cousin's excited questions about the events of the previous night caused a sinking feeling in her stomach. She wasn't ready to talk about it yet. Not when it had ended so badly.

Instead, she crawled back into bed, pulled the covers up to her chin, and tried to focus on the cheesy slasher movie streaming from her laptop. But even that reminded her of Alec, and how they'd fought.

She couldn't believe she'd done it again: put all of her stock in someone only to have him leave at the first sign of trouble. Stupid. Stupid. Stupid.

Her thoughts turned back to the beginning of the night and how Alec had wrapped her in his arms and told her he loved her. A fresh wave of pain washed over her, and she switched off the movie.

She'd let her guard down and this time even let herself tumble heart-first into something that felt so real. The pain rocked through her chest, and she stood, determined not to give in to the enormity of the fall. But then, unbidden, came the memory of Alec sitting up with her in the hospital all night and the way they lay together on the weekends, reading. Another fresh ache pulsed from her chest. She should've cut out early while she still had the chance. Avoided this heartache altogether. But she couldn't quite convince herself she'd have been better without it.

The doorbell rang. *Please be a delivery.* She didn't think she could face Julie and her onslaught of questions until she'd processed it all herself. But when she made it to the front door and looked through the peephole, her heart caught in her throat.

Alec. He stood on her porch, bags under his eyes and hair disheveled, suggesting he'd probably gotten as little sleep as she had.

One steadying breath later, she opened the door.

"Hey," he said.

She hovered in the doorway and chanced a glance up at him. "Hey."

"Can I come in?"

She nodded and stepped aside to let him in. "I wasn't sure you would want to see me again."

Alec's brows drew together, and he looked pained. "Why would you think that?"

Wendy wrapped her arms around herself and shrugged.

"Wendy, that's not how this works," he whispered. He reached out and rubbed her arm.

She hated the way she flinched away from it, like he would take it back any second.

"But I didn't get along with your sister."

"That is not ideal." Alec frowned but took a step closer. "But I think maybe if you both gave it time, that would work itself out. I hope she's a lot different than she was when she hurt you."

Wendy let her head fall onto his chest. "But you left. Last night." She finished the thought quietly, almost to herself. "I finally let myself take a risk, and you left."

He held her tight, and she clung to the sensation of his strong hands splayed on her back through her thin shirt and the steady beat of his heart against her cheek.

"That's not how I thought the night would go." He stroked her hair and let out a sigh. "In my head, I had this picture of you and my sister getting along and being friends. With what you went through, I thought maybe you'd get how she's felt about being a loner. I didn't expect what had happened between you. I overreacted, and I'm sorry. I didn't *leave* leave. I needed time to sort all of this out in my head."

She breathed in his scent and chanced a look up at him.

"And did you? Sort it out."

"Still sorting." A smile tugged at his lips. "But I want to sort it out with you."

"You sure?" Wendy frowned. "This is family. Your only family. I know this is a big deal."

"It is," he agreed. "But you're a big deal to me, too. And you had good reason to feel weird around my sister. I don't want to give up before we've even tried to make this work."

Alec cupped her face and brushed her lips with his. Wendy exhaled all the breath she'd been holding in. She tucked her arms around him and buried her face in his chest, and just sat with the feeling that this setback didn't have to mean the end. Even though in her past, it always had.

"You said before that this wasn't how this works," Wendy said. "I guess I don't really know how this works," she admitted.

"What do you mean?"

"I've had fights before. But I guess that was usually the end of things."

"Is that what you wanted with me?"

"No. Of course not. I'm just saying I've never really had anything like this before." She gestured between them. "Someone worth making up with afterward.

I'm probably going to screw up sometimes. And I'm stubborn, and I like to get my way."

"Good. Because I'm going to screw up sometimes, too. It would be pretty embarrassing if it was only me."

Her mouth tugged up at the corners.

"And we've already established that I can work with stubborn."

She pulled him closer, feeling a thousand pounds lighter.

"Do you have any plans right now?" Alec asked.

She shook her head. "I was going to go running with Julie, but I cancelled."

"Feel like doing something?"

"Can we stay in our pajamas and have beignets and watch the Doctor? All this fighting and making up has zapped all my energy."

"I think that can be arranged," Alec said. He pushed the hair out of her eyes and kissed her again, slow and lingering, and she leaned eagerly into him. "Although I'm going to have to find some pajamas."

She ducked around the corner and tossed him something from the laundry. "Fresh from the dryer."

Alec laced his fingers in hers and led them up to her bedroom. The tension of the last twelve hours ebbed with the feel of his fingers entwined with hers, with him back in her space.

"Can we just pretend last night never happened?" Wendy said.

Alec frowned.

"At least the part after we left here. I liked the part before."

Tenderness crossed his features, and he squeezed her hand. "I don't think ignoring it will do any of us any good."

"I know. But damn. Worth a try." She gave him a wry smile that morphed into something vulnerable after a moment. "I just never want us to fight like that again."

"Me neither." Alec stripped off his shirt and set his pajama pants on the dresser. "But I think there's a way forward from here."

"I hope it involves beignets," Wendy said.

"It does."

She let her gaze roam the contours of his chest, and a curl of desire warmed her all over. She hoped it involved more full body contact, too. He caught her shamelessly ogling him, and his gaze heated.

"And you know," Wendy said, "since I've never had a fight and made up before, I've never had make-up sex."

Alec stepped closer, and his fingers grazed the skin of her sides as he relieved her of her shirt. His lips brushed her neck before moving to her ear. "We should probably do something about that."

CHAPTER 28

Fall faded into winter and into early spring with live oaks budding and people flooding the French Quarter for Mardi Gras festivities. They were seasons of firsts for Wendy and Alec—first Christmas and New Year's together, first Dragon Con complete with *Firefly* cosplay, and for Wendy, the first stamp in her passport when they visited Vancouver. Not to mention her first wholly civil conversation with Kara, along with many subsequent ones. The two of them had struck up—if not a friendship—at least a mutual tolerance for each other, for Alec's sake. Sometimes Wendy even thought if she wasn't saying semi-offensive things all the time, she might actually like Alec's twin.

And for the first time, Wendy had opened her heart to someone and resisted the persistent urge to slam it shut once again and retreat into the safety of solitude.

But now it was February. Only two months before Alec's assignments in New Orleans would end. With his departure looming, the pleasant status quo they'd established would soon be shot to hell with so many unknowns.

"Ooh, what is that you're working on?" Julie approached the café table outside of Wendy's favorite lunch spot, where she was blowing off steam with some digital painting on her laptop.

"It's for Alec's birthday next month." It was a companion piece to the one at the foot of her stairs, this time with a boy who looked suspiciously like Alec and a girl with flowing red locks under the umbrella, waiting out the storm together.

Julie made a swoony face that was like the physical embodiment of a heart-eyed emoji. "I love it."

Wendy shook her head with a smile and closed her laptop. "How did the advisor meeting go?"

"You know, it's pretty fun to see all the naysayers do a complete 360 after all the stuff we uncovered about Marie and Sophia."

"I bet."

"How did it go with your dad about the app stuff?" Julie asked.

Wendy grimaced. "Let's just say it didn't take him long to pass through the life's-too-short-try-something-new phase and right on back to tried and true is best."

"He shot it down? Really? Even when you showed him the little anime ghosts?"

Wendy nodded. "Good thing Alec didn't do all the programming."

"Speaking of Alec, what's the word on you guys and his impending departure?"

Wendy shrugged and chose that moment to intently study the menu she already knew by heart. What would it be like to sleep in an empty bed again, night after night, a whole country away from him? They could still talk and make visits, but a video call seemed a poor substitute for his kiss on her forehead, his warm body to lean on, and all the little ways they'd inhabited each other's lives.

"Have you guys really not talked about this yet?" Julie folded her arms on the table.

"We still have two more months."

"That's like a blink of an eye," Julie said.

"Don't remind me."

"But what do you want to do?"

She wouldn't let this go, was she? Wendy sighed. "I don't know. Keep dating?"

"But long distance? That's hard."

Wendy's shoulders tensed, and she took a drink of her latte. She didn't want to think about it. There were so many ways they could grow apart outside of their cozy little cocoon. They couldn't even legally live or work in each other's countries without substantial headache and miles of paperwork. Eventually, wouldn't it be easier for him to find a nice Canadian girl? The thought produced a sinking feeling. "You think I haven't thought about that? I don't really want to have a long distance relationship."

"Have you thought about going with him?"

"I... I can't just leave," Wendy sputtered.

"Why not? Sure you can. You could probably do a lot of your work remotely."

Wendy opened her mouth to speak and then closed it again. She couldn't even bring herself to move out of state for college. Could she really consider moving to another country? "Would you just up and leave if Griffin's job took you away from here?"

"Yes."

"Just yes? No deliberation or agonizing? Just yes." Consternation creased Wendy's forehead.

"I'm sure there would be a lot of deliberation and agonizing, but if it were really important to him or we both decided it was necessary, then yeah. He'd do it for me, too."

"How do you know?"

"We talked about it," Julie said, with a confused frown.

Wendy brooded and set the menu aside. "So much healthy communication going on."

"You should try it. Five out of five stars, would recommend."

Wendy rolled her eyes. "Yeah, yeah. But what about Mom and Dad? You and Griffin? You just want me to leave?"

"Of course I wouldn't enjoy having you so far away. But what if it's not permanent? You guys could go there for a while and then come back here. His sister's here, after all. All the more reason to come back. I'm sure he could get a job."

"It's not so easy with the whole work visa and sponsorship thing," Wendy said.

"But not totally out of the question," Julie said, her love of arguing glowing brightly. "And you liked Vancouver, right? It could be a new adventure."

Wendy ruminated on this point, a flock of nerves taking wing in her stomach.

"It might be nice to try living somewhere new for a while... if I could come back."

"See, there's the spirit. Sometimes you have to just jump. Not think."

That prospect twisted her insides.

"I'm just saying, you guys have the special sauce. If he's as important to you as I think he is, it's at least worth considering."

Wendy clutched her mug, her stomach in tumult. "Yeah, maybe."

CHAPTER 29

*D*on't think.

Just jump.

The idea burrowed in, and Wendy couldn't get Julie's words out of her head as she went about her business that week. Especially with her dad back to his crotchety self where work was concerned, she was sorely in need of some creative freedom. Leaving scared the ever-loving shit out of her. But so did the prospect of having finally found her person, the person who got her and made her feel special and not alone, and then letting him go. Her mental list of activities that could not be done long distance reached epic proportions. They couldn't hike together. They couldn't lay in bed and watch movies, drop in on each other at work with notes or coffee. And of course, the obvious physical affection they'd have to go months without between visits.

So she talked to her parents about the possibility of working remotely. Unlike her pitch for the app, this conversation went over shockingly well. So well, in fact, that Wendy felt like the world might be in some bizarre parallel universe.

"So we haven't talked about what's going to happen when you have to go back," Wendy said one morning when Alec started the coffee brewing at her house. "Between us, I mean."

"I guess we haven't." His hands stilled on the package of coffee. "I haven't wanted to think about being away from you."

"Yeah, me neither." Wendy fiddled with the edge of the placemat on the table, the tempest in her stomach raging. Why was this so hard to say? "I was thinking. What if I came with you? Hypothetically." She wrapped her cardigan around her chest.

"Really hypothetically or hypothetically hypothetically?" Alec's eyebrows arched, and the cautious delight on his face made Wendy's stomach cartwheel.

"I'm not sure that's a thing."

"Are you sure you'd want to do that?"

"What, you don't want me to go, too?" She hated the way her voice cracked even through the bantery jab she followed it with. "You want to keep all the maple syrup and poutine all to yourself. I see how you are."

"Well, I do like my maple syrup." He gave her a wry smile, then leaned on the table next to her and slipped her hand between both of his. "I'd love nothing more than for you to come with me. But that's a big move. What about your job, your family?"

A rush of doubts came careening in—could she really give up those things?—but she shook them off. Just jump. Don't think. "Well, I talked to my parents, and there's a lot of the business stuff that I could do remotely."

Alec's eyes widened, roaming her face, a little surprise, a little wonder in them. "You've really thought about this."

She nodded. Holy shit. Was she really doing this?

"Would you want to live together?" he asked.

"Would you? I've never lived with anyone before," she said. "You might hate me after a week."

"Neither have I, but I doubt that. We practically live together now. Just in two locations."

Her stomach roiled, caught between elation and nervous spikes of moving into uncharted territory. "I guess that's true."

"I put a deposit down on a one bedroom, but I can probably switch it to two if you'd need more space, so you could work from home."

"Home," she echoed with a jolt of excitement. "Our home." Home with the two of them together, not separated by half a continent. Their eyes met, Alec's soft and luminous as his smile stretched to limit, mirroring her own.

"We're really going to do this?" he said.

She nodded. "As long as you want to."

Alec swept her out of her chair and pulled her into a long, lingering kiss that lit her from the inside. The kind they could look forward to every day now that their impending separation wouldn't be a separation after all.

CHAPTER 30

The weeks marched on, and Wendy made the arrangements for the big move: extended visa application, working out what her job would look like from afar. And despite her excitement, a growing sense of unease dogged her at every turn.

Living with Alec had seemed like such a good idea, but now she noticed every one of his annoying habits, like the way he left his socks wherever he took them off and inexplicably left wadded up paper towels on the counter after he cooked. And the other morning, he'd made a comment about how her make-up and hair potions and tools overran the bathroom counter. It was so like one of his sister's snipes that it had raised her hackles. Little things, sure, but they also made her realize that there might be even bigger landmines like this that they might not discover until they were 3000 miles away living together with no Julie to vent to as soon as she woke up in the morning.

And every time she went somewhere in the city, the Riverwalk, the bar with the skeeball machine, the sculpture garden in City Park, she wondered if this would be the last time she'd see it before she said goodbye to the city that had been her home all of her life. Even her last trip to the dry cleaner had made her weirdly sentimental.

And then there was the matter of packing. Three weeks from the move, she had done none. Though she'd amassed a great quantity of boxes, she'd only put one thing in: an old toaster she used only when Alec made grilled cheese sandwiches at her house. Every time she attempted to add a book or a trinket, she invariably retreated to the couch with a burgeoning panic attack and a bowl of mint chocolate chip ice cream to soothe herself with *Doctor Who* reruns.

Tonight though, after a visit with her mom and dad, while Alec had plans for some twin time with Kara, she surveyed the contents of her closet, determined to pack at least one full box.

Okay, what first? Winter jacket—she'd definitely need that in Canada and not at all here. She pulled it off its hanger and folded it up. Her stomach did a flip as the coat settled to the bottom. There, that wasn't so hard. Now board games. Unlikely she'd need all of them before the month was out. She ran her fingers over the faded boxes of *Jenga*, *Parcheesi*, *Scattergories*, *Balderdash*, and *Uno*, and felt a sudden rush of affection for this closet. It had been where her board games and coats had lived since she moved out on her own, and the thought of renting this place—something else she'd dragged her feet on getting done—and of other people's stuff in here tipped over the first domino of growing panic.

This was ridiculous. What was she doing getting sentimental over a closet? She grabbed *Jenga* and stuffed it in the box with her jacket. But when her hand hovered over the *Balderdash* box, she couldn't bring herself to part with it just yet.

Maybe she could take a break and start writing some instructions for Paige, who would take over most of the day-to-day operational tasks that had to be done in person. Or wrap Alec's present before his birthday dinner tomorrow night.

She'd just located some wrapping paper big enough to wrap around the canvas print of her finished painting when her phone rang.

"Hey, where are you? I miss you. Did you know I love you so much?"

Wendy smiled at that mellow happiness in Alec's voice that came out when he was sleepy or had a few drinks. From the laughter and voices in the background, she guessed the latter. Although it was ten o'clock, so it could be both.

"I do know. I'm at home. Packing. Or at least trying. Where are you?"

"At my very first surprise birthday party. Kara threw it for us. Why aren't you here?" His lovey mellow voice continued.

A coldness formed in her stomach. "Um, my invitation must have gotten lost." More like Kara had skipped, inviting her on purpose.

"Hang on," Alec said. Wendy heard muffled conversation with Kara from a distance.

"Kara, you invited Wendy, didn't you?"

Silence. She could practically hear Alec's confusion.

"I went by her little ghost shop the other day, but she wasn't there."

"But you have her phone number, right?"

A tense silence followed.

"You know she's important to me. She's going to come live with me in Vancouver, you know." His voice took on a slight slur with his buzz. "And we're probably going to get married and have very cute Canadian-American babies."

Despite the devastating adorableness of him right now, Wendy didn't know whether to laugh or cry.

"She hates me, okay?" Kara said in a tight voice. "And it's my birthday, too. Maybe I didn't want that kind of negativity at my birthday party."

"She doesn't hate you," Alec said.

Debatable, Wendy thought.

"You both just need time to get to know each other for real. Know each other now."

And just get over it. Right. This was looking more and more like Hatfield vs. McCoy-like animosity.

The rest of their conversation was too muffled for Wendy to hear.

"Hey, are you still there?" Alec said a moment later.

"Yeah, I'm here." Wendy wrapped her arms over her chest.

"So, there was a misunderstanding, but you're invited. Of course," Alec said.

"Really? Because I just overheard your conversation with Kara, and that didn't sound like an invitation to me."

"I'm inviting you. She'll get over it." He really was too optimistic about their potential not to go nuclear around each other.

Wendy sighed. Why couldn't he have a cool sister that she actually wanted to be friends with and not a Regina George doppelgänger? "It's her birthday, too. I don't want to cause any more fights between you."

"Are you sure you won't come? It'll be fun."

Fun like taking a bath in poison ivy.

He went on to suggest creative things he would like to do to her.

"All of that would probably get us both arrested in public."

"Pfft."

"Tell you what, why don't you call me when you're done, and I'll come drive you home."

CHAPTER 31

After picking Alec up and getting him set up with some water and ibuprofen, and avoiding the conversational minefield of what had happened earlier that night, Wendy fell into a fitful sleep.

In her dream, she wandered into Kara's posh living room and sat in a squashy armchair that looked way more comfortable than it actually was. She shifted in the chair under Kara's condescending scrutiny.

"Cake?" Kara held out a plate and took one for herself. Wendy took a bite, and the bitter taste of sawdust on her tongue turned her stomach.

Then everything around her seemed to get bigger. Or perhaps she got smaller. Though Kara loomed large, perched on the arm of the couch in her pink dress and crossing her perfectly sculpted legs, it was as though Wendy had picked up one of those little cakes in *Alice in Wonderland* that said "eat me" and shrunken down until the chair cushion was like an ocean.

"You don't really think he's going to stay with you, do you?" Kara said. "Just because you're following him back across the border?"

Though she should have been irritated, the sensation in Wendy's chest felt more like she was finally staring down at the truth that she'd tried to hide from herself. She folded her arms over her chest. "I... I don't know."

Kara snorted in amusement. "You're too insecure. Too needy. The fact is, you need him more than he needs you. Hasn't that always been the way of things?"

Another spike of dread hit her as the words rang true. Wendy tried to lean into the back of the chair for support, but in her current diminished form, it was much too far away.

"And you hold grudges," Kara added. "Do you think he could ever stay with you if he knew how you really felt about me? How petty you are, wishing I would just go away."

"I don't—" But she couldn't bring herself to cover it up.

"*I'm* his family. Blood. The only family he has. You know how important family is. You'd choose them over anything, wouldn't you?"

Of course she would.

"And so will he. You're just a temporary distraction." Kara sipped from a diamond-encrusted teacup. "He might not realize it now, but he will. Faster now that you'll be sharing your space." She gave a smug smile that made Wendy's insides writhe. "He'll finally see all the ugliness that you try so hard to keep from him, the things you're not proud of. And just like everyone else has, he'll find you wanting. It's just a matter of time. And who will you have by your side to pick up the pieces?"

Kara clucked her tongue. "Oh, that's right: no one. They'll all be thousands of miles away, and you'll be unwanted and alone."

"You're wrong," Wendy said in a small voice, but she felt the hitch of hesitation. "You're just trying to push him away from me."

"Oh, I think you're doing fine with that on your own. And trust me, he's more like me than you care to admit."

Wendy gasped awake to find Alec already up and in the bathroom brushing his teeth, despite the late night last night. The unease she'd felt in the dream carried over into her waking state, and she tried to shake it off and convince herself that Kara had no idea what she was talking about, even if so much of it rang true. Metal and plastic clattered to the bathroom floor. Alec muttered a few choice expletives.

"Everything okay in there?" Wendy called out.

"Yeah, just got tangled in your hair dryer and curling irons again." His normal good-naturedness sounded stretched thin. "You think you could put those under the sink or something? We won't have this much counter real estate in the new apartment. They're everywhere. I bump into them every time I come in here."

Maybe it was just the leftover feelings from the dream, but Wendy's hackles rose. "Maybe you should be more careful." She rolled over and pulled the blankets tight around herself. "I spread out. I'm messy. It's just how I am," she snapped.

Alec emerged from the bathroom, shirtless and with rumpled hair. He frowned at Wendy. "Hey, I'm just asking for a little compromise, so I can use the sink, too."

"Well, I'm not just going to change everything about myself when we move in together."

He sat on the bed and stroked her shoulder, concern creasing his brow. Her anger receded, but not all the way. "No one said you had to. I'm just talking about bathroom organization."

He leaned forward to kiss her. She willed herself to take in that salt and cedar scent of him she'd grown to love so much and to let go of this jumble of doubts and uncertainties.

But it only reminded her of that feeling she'd had the past few weeks walking through the Quarter, visiting the park: the one that made her chest ache and reminded her that each step she took, each activity she did here might be for the last time.

"This is totally normal," Julie said from the top of a ladder in the storage room at Deveauxs' Historical Haunts. She handed Wendy a box of tarot sets from the top shelf.

"Is it, though? If I have anymore dream visits from Kara Lynn Bowles, I'm going to have to resort to *Nightmare on Elm Street* measures." Wendy opened the box to see if there were enough for each member of the private tour group of tarot enthusiasts they were doing the next week. Her last week. Another pang of nostalgia hit her. She'd never been away from this shop that had been at the heart of her family's livelihood for more than three or four days. Ever. It seemed inconceivable that she would wake up in a week in a new city and not come back here until holiday time.

"Paige showed me this stress index thing the other day from her psych class." Julie descended the ladder. "It said moving to a new city is one of the most stressful items on the scale. So is cohabitating with a new partner for the first time."

"Great. Where does dealing with my boyfriend's evil twin fall on the scale?"

"I'll have to get back to you on that one." Julie's eyes glinted.

The two grabbed their supplies and headed back to the front of the store. Unexpectedly, Jacqui was standing behind the counter holding something in her hand and staring off into the distance. Her pinched expression said something weighed on her mind.

"Mom?" Wendy said.

"Oh, hey, girls." Jacqui plastered on a smile and set down the purple rabbit's foot she'd been holding.

"What's going on?" Wendy said. "You look more stressed than I do."

Jacqui flashed a half smile. "It's fine. Nothing you need to worry about. I just came by to pick up some things for your dad."

Wendy frowned and exchanged a worried glance with Julie.

"Is something wrong with Dad?"

"He'll be fine."

Wendy's stomach gave a nervous jump. She closed the distance between them and took her mom's hand.

Jacqui let out a sigh and pressed a hand to her forehead. "It's probably not a big deal."

Wendy's pulse tripped, and she felt transported to the hospital with the awful interminable waiting and not knowing all over again. "*What* isn't a big deal?"

"He's just having some chest pains again. The doctors are going to run some tests. They say it's probably going to be fine. But I can't help but think of last time..."

Wendy pulled her mom into an embrace, cradling her shaking shoulders. "Why would you not want to tell me that?"

"I didn't want to worry you and have you go change all of your plans."

She pulled back enough to meet her mom's eyes. "Let me make those decisions, okay? Do you need anything? Can I do anything?"

Her mom's head shook against her shoulder. Her mind spun with questions, and her already churning stomach went full force. Didn't the surgery fix everything? Hadn't he been eating more healthily, even if it was grudging, and been taking his cholesterol medication? She let out a breath. Like before, she knew worrying wouldn't stop anything bad from happening, but that didn't make the worrying stop.

"I've got to get ready for that midinterview with the *Ghost Hunters* website in a minute," Wendy said finally. "But call me if you need anything, okay?"

Jacqui sniffed and wiped away the tears that had not yet spilled from her eyes. "This is the one you were really excited about, right?"

Wendy nodded, glad to have another topic to focus on. "They're doing a feature on us. It might bring in a lot of traffic. And I pitched them a project we could partner on. They sounded very enthusiastic on the phone. It felt like a good note to go out on."

Later that day, after a promising interview, Wendy's worries clamored for their place in the forefront of her mind again. She sank into her office chair. What if her dad was sick again? What if this time they weren't so lucky? She couldn't really consider leaving if this might be all the time she had left with her dad, could she? And she and Alec had been bickering even more the last few days since the birthday incident, and they hadn't seen each other much. The stress of moving was affecting him, too. She put in her last day volunteering with Steve at her old high school and was walking away before the spring play sets were even halfway done. Training the new tour guide, Evie, made her feel more and more unmoored. She'd sent her life whirling in a new direction, but now it felt like she was on one of those spinning carnival rides. What had felt dizzying and delightful at first was now making her sick. And making her question why she'd ever gotten on in the first place.

Her insides tied up in knots. She needed something to ground her, something to reassure her that this was the right thing to do.

She rooted through her purse for her phone. What she really needed was to talk to Alec—though he'd been scarce this week, wrapping things up at work and trying to see Kara as much as possible—and sort out everything she was feeling. But would dumping all her insecurities and doubts onto his plate help or only make him question what they had, too?

She turned the phone over in her hands. Why did something that was supposed to be good for her to feel like this? If this was going to work, she had to take chances and rely on him. He would be there for her and understand. If he wasn't, when they were all those miles away, who would she have?

"Hey, do you have time to talk?" she asked when he picked up, in as bright a tone as she could manage. "I could really use a voice of reason."

There was a pause and a sigh on the other end, and her stomach went leaden. "Any chance this can wait? I'm about to go into a meeting with a client."

Gah. She couldn't expect him to be around all the time. But this time, she needed him.

"Can you—" She stopped and pinched the bridge of her nose. "Um, yeah. Sure."

"Everything okay? We're still going to have dinner at your place tonight, right?"

"Yeah."

"Okay. I'll see you then. I love you."

Wendy spent the rest of the afternoon co-touring with Julie to take her mind off of things and made it home just in time to whip up some pasta and open a bottle of wine before Alec arrived. T-Minus three days until his departure, and she'd be following a week later. Which you wouldn't know by looking at Wendy's still intact home decor. The inner upheaval she'd kept at bay for a few hours surged forth again. Maybe sitting down to relax, just the two of them, would ease some of the jitters. She sorely needed his arms around her and a night to reconnect after all the chaos.

With everything plated and still no Alec, she tossed some spices into an empty box, so it would at least look like she was making packing progress.

Her phone buzzed on the kitchen counter.

"Do I need to put the pasta back on the stove?" she said when she picked up the phone.

Alec let out a regretful sigh. "Would you hate me if I cancelled tonight?"

Wendy's heart sank. Her already brittle state, with all of her emotions so close to the surface, fractured even more. She tried not to let her disappointment show, but it felt like this whole thing between them was something she'd just imagined.

"Kara's having some special restaurant thing tonight and asked if I'd go. Now that we're leaving, I probably won't see her until the holidays."

Wendy rubbed her temple and brought Alec's plate back to the kitchen. It clattered on the counter where she dropped it. "No, it's fine."

"Are you sure? We already had plans. I can say no if you want me to."

Her chest tightened. Yes. Please say no and come and hold me and convince me that all these worries are in my head, she wanted to say. But that felt selfish.

"Yeah. Go. I could probably use some more packing time, anyway."

"Thanks for understanding. Want me to bring you a crème brûlée later?"

She wandered back to the table and dinner for one. "Sure."

"Oh, hey, what did you want to talk about earlier when you called?"

She swallowed and opened her mouth to spill it all out, but she retreated. "Nothing. Forget about it."

CHAPTER 32

"I can't wait to have you with me again in a week." Alec let go of his luggage handle and cupped Wendy's cheek. "In our new place."

His gaze roved her face lovingly, and he leaned forward to brush his lips against hers. The rush of travelers making their way to their gates and flight announcements over the speaker system were the only things that drowned out the blood rushing through Wendy's ears as they said their goodbyes. She held him close, memorizing the contours of his waist, the way his chest felt against hers, how tiniest bit of stubble grazing her cheek sent sparks dancing through her. She thought about the way he got her jokes and always felt safe and soothing and right at the end of a long day.

So why did this feel like an ending instead of a beginning?

Seeing him walk away toward the plane felt wrong. So did the way they never quite seemed to connect over the next week while they were in different countries. There were texts, but they never had that same spark with so much lag time. And they'd only managed one actual video call to see each other. Even that only magnified the distance between them. Good thing they hadn't decided to try the long distance thing, because this sucked with a capital S.

"Have you seen it?" Julie burst through Wendy's door the night before she would have left.

"Seen what?"

"You haven't then." Julie pursed her lips like she was now the reluctant bearer of bad tidings. "The *Ghost Hunter* article."

Wendy's nerves pummeled her. The move anxiety and the Alec anxiety had only amplified over the last week, and she didn't think she could take any more unexpected bad news.

She opened her computer and rocked back in her seat, stunned when she finished reading. "What the fuck did I just read?"

"I know, right?" Julie said.

Wendy dragged a hand through her hair. She squeezed her eyes shut against the feeling of disorientation and the uncertainty that wouldn't settle inside her. Everything in her life was shifting and changing, and she couldn't seem to get her feet under her. Her home wouldn't be her home anymore. Julie would no longer be a brief car ride away. She'd upset the balance and in the process lost all perspective on who had her best interests at heart. "I do not get this. He sounded so enthusiastic about everything we talked about during the interview," she said.

"Well, apparently he was enthusiastic about making fun of us."

"So much for going out on a positive note." She groaned. Instead, she'd invited ridicule about their company, thanks to this idiot she'd just blindly trusted to be a professional who'd do a competent report on their ghost tour operation. When had she stopped being so skeptical and trusting people right and left? Probably after Alec had been around for a while.

"Can we have him pull it, do you think?" Julie asked.

"It already has thirty thousand hits."

She flopped back on the couch and tried to recall any sign that this guy was out to make them into some kind of ghost parody. There was none that she could remember. He'd looked her in the eye with a convincing smile and then screwed her over.

"I just... I just don't get it. How did I read this so wrong?" Her stomach turned over and over.

And then a sickening thought sent her gut twisting even more: What else had she read wrong?

Two suitcases lay open at the foot of Wendy's bed, both sparsely packed. Her night with Julie had derailed her last-minute packing efforts, and her nerves jangled. She stared at her closet, emptied what she could, and then collapsed on her bed. She'd have to do the rest in the morning.

When she drifted off, she dreamed she was in the funhouse part of a carnival that came through New Orleans every year. In the dimly lit room, a trio of warped mirrors undulated along the wall, making her match-stick skinny as she passed one, bulbous in another, and with an oversized head in the last as she paced in front of them. Alec appeared between the last two, his familiar profile stretched into something unrecognizable in the reflection.

"Alec," Wendy said, her whole body flooding with relief. She threw her arms around him. "I've missed you. I know it's only been a week, but everything's been crazy. It feels like so much longer."

He smiled back at her, but something seemed off about it. "Tell me you love me."

This didn't sound like the Alec she knew, patient and kind and easy-going.

"I do. You know I do," she said.

"Then why can't you ever say it?"

Her lips parted. "I do."

"No, you say 'me too'"

Wendy protested, but it was true. It was an invisible line she hadn't crossed. A safeguard against getting close enough to get burned.

"Just say it. You can trust me," Alec said.

"Why else would I leave my home and move with you, away from my family—including my dad, who might be sick again, by the way."

Something flickered to her right, and Wendy caught sight of Alec's reflection. Only it wasn't him staring back, but Orson, the dick from the *Ghost Hunters* website, reflecting Alec's every movement. Wendy blinked, her heart jolting, and squinted at it. In a flash it was Alec again, with his resigned expression.

"So that's a no then," he said.

"No, it's not a no. I—I love you. There. I said it."

Something moved in the mirror again, and this time Kara Lynn looked back at Wendy, the funhouse mirror version of Alec, and her nemesis threw her head back and shrieked in laughter.

Wendy's stomach curdled.

"What?" Alec asked. "Wendy, what's wrong?"

"It's not you. It's her." She pointed to Kara's malevolent smile.

"What are you talking about? She *is* me. We're alike, remember? Twins." He did a little jazz hands move that the Kara reflection mimicked exactly. Then he laughed too, a cruel, unnatural sound so discordant coming from him.

Wendy recoiled and shook her head. "No. You're not her." But rising panic clawed its way up her throat. She squeezed her eyes shut against the bizarre reflection. "You're kind and you look after people. You sat up with me all night in the hospital, and you love me."

Someone—whether it was Alec or one of his doppelgangers, she wasn't sure—clucked their tongue.

"If you say so. Let's go then," Alec said. Wendy chanced a peek and the look in his eyes was once again so sincere that she reached out and took his hand.

And in the way of dreams, they stepped through the mirror. In the lush green of the park on the other side, the temperature took a nosedive. Goosebumps rose on Wendy's arms, and she shivered.

"Where are we?" she asked.

"Home."

"It's cold here."

"Hope you packed some sweaters."

The horrifying realization set in: she was completely and utterly unprepared. "I don't have any sweaters. All I packed was a toaster."

"Well, good luck with that," Alec said. "Hey, can you stand right there?" He motioned to a dais that looked like something out of an airport security line.

"Okay?" When she stepped on the dais, blue lights flashed, sweeping over her like a scanner from head to foot. "What are you doing?"

"Inspecting you."

She blanched. Alec continued to scrutinize her with a growing crease in his brow. Finally the lights stopped. Alec sighed with a dejected frown. "Should've done that before we left."

"What do you mean? What's wrong? What did you see?"

"I think you know." He held her gaze, and a sinking feeling overcame her.

"Come on. You can come back to my apartment and wait until you can get a flight back."

"Wait, don't you mean *our* apartment?"

"I don't think that's a good idea anymore."

The apartment door swung open, and Wendy followed Alec in. "Wait, isn't this what you wanted? You and me, here, together."

"I don't think that's what you wanted."

He let the thought hang between them until it hit its mark. All the air seemed to rush from Wendy's lungs. "But... but I gave up everything for you. To come here. My home, my family, being present at my business, my volunteer stuff. I left it all."

"Maybe you shouldn't have done that," Alec said with a rueful expression.

Weeks' worth of withheld tears traced down her cheeks. "But what can I do? How can I fix this?"

"I don't think there's any fixing this." He waved a hand between them. "But you can start by being honest with yourself. You never wanted to leave, no matter how much you love me. You know what you have to do."

CHAPTER 33

MOVING DAY

The next morning Wendy awoke bleary-eyed, the residue of her nightmare still clinging to her every thought. The dream had reminded her of all the unknowns, of all the pitfalls and booby traps that lay before her. All the things she'd neglected to face head-on when she'd foolishly adopted the *don't think, just jump* mentality. And it was too much. Too much. She'd finally have to open the door. And there would always be something like a ticking time bomb waiting to go off when discovered. If he rejected the version of her she let him see, that was one thing, but if she gave him all of her and he rejected that, she didn't know how she would come back from that.

A sickening feeling churned in her stomach, and with it there was a grim knowledge of what she was about to do—or rather, what she was about *not* to do.

The time when she would have done her final packing, showered, and gotten ready came and went. When the ring of the doorbell announced her parents' who planned to take her to the airport, still she lay greasy-haired and unable to move. But she needed her mom's comforting embrace more than ever, and she'd need their strength for what had to come next.

"Surprise!" Wendy's mom proclaimed when she finally opened the door to face them. Crowded on her porch were not only her parents, but also Julie, Griffin, and Aunt Angeline. "We rented a van so we could all see you off."

Wendy couldn't bring herself to move as they all piled into the house.

"Dad'll get your luggage." Her mom looked around the room. Wendy followed her gaze, and saw what she must be taking in: her laptop and last night's takeout container open on the coffee table, laundry still in a basket by the stairs, all her pictures still in their places on the walls. This did not look like a house that was about to be vacated. Julie's eyes swept the room too, and Wendy watched the dismay enter her expression.

"Honey, where is your luggage?" her mom asked. Julie grabbed Jacqui's arm and nodded in Wendy's direction. Jacqui looked again at the undisturbed room and back at her daughter, and Wendy saw the understanding dawn.

"Oh, honey." Jacqui crossed the room and cupped Wendy's cheek in her hand. She examined her daughter with a look that was pure compassion, undiluted with the judgment that should have been there. Wendy gulped in a ragged breath and sobbed into her mom's embrace, letting all the fear and sorrow out. She'd thought she could do this. Believed she was strong enough to get over the doubts that had plagued her since her teenage years. She'd thought she'd won, that she'd beaten them.

But the truth was, as much as she'd tried, she'd only been half in. She'd fooled everyone into thinking she'd changed. And she'd done such a good job that until last night, she'd even fooled herself.

"You missed your plane?" Alec asked. "Were there snakes on it?"

At the sound of his voice, so happy and easygoing, the sick feeling in Wendy's stomach intensified until everything inside her felt like it was closing in on itself. Her hand shook as she pressed the phone to her ear.

"Do you have the new flight number?" he asked.

"No." She licked her lips. "I didn't get another flight. I'm... I'm not coming." Silence.

"What do you mean?" The way his voice broke at her words was like an ice pick straight to the heart. That sense of vertigo hit her again, and she buried her face in her hand.

"I can't. I can't move to Vancouver," she got out.

"I don't understand, Wendy. Where is this coming from? Did something happen? Is your family okay?"

"Yes, everyone's okay. I don't know. I just know that I can't and I'm sorry."

He breathed out a long breath, and Wendy imagined him pushing his hair up on his forehead like he did when he was at a loss for words.

And before she could chicken out, she laid out the final blow.

"And I think trying to make this work long distance is just delaying the inevitable. We'll grow apart and need different things, so I think we should just make a clean break."

Alec muttered something under his breath. "Can we talk about this when you're not upset? I love you, and you love me. There's no reason to do this."

"I don't think so. I don't think it will change anything."

CHAPTER 34

The next afternoon, Kara Lynn Bowles stormed through the front door of Deveauxs' Historical Haunts dressed in red and spoiling for a fight. Wendy looked up at her from the front counter with nothing but numbness in her features. She felt as if all her insides had been scraped out and that this was all that remained after the anguish of the previous day's events.

"You." Kara jabbed a manicured fingernail in Wendy's face. Kara's cheeks boiled with rage. "You think *I'm* the heartless one."

Wendy lowered her eyes, hot shame coiling inside her. She deserved whatever wrath Kara had to dish out.

"Do you know what you did to him?"

Wendy swallowed and made herself meet Kara's enraged gaze. She did. She knew exactly what she did, the hurt and destruction she left in her wake, and she only wished she could have foreseen it all and saved them both from the heartache.

Kara shook her head in disgust, eyes flinty. "I may have been too insecure and cowardly to stand up for you and do the right thing in high school. But this is my twin brother. Now that I finally have a family member who gives a crap about me, I will not stand by and let you hurt him like this without knowing the damage you just did. You took one of the best human beings on the planet and treated him like some plaything you could discard at will."

She fixed Wendy with a look of such loathing that Wendy slunk back.

"You think I'm such a terrible person. At least I grew up and learned to do better."

CHAPTER 35

Wendy came back to the present with tears she didn't remember crying streaking down her cheeks. Griffin stood nearby in the dim light of her bedroom, but she wrapped her arms around her chest and rocked back and forth, watching numbly as her deepest, darkest fear played out once again.

She'd realized — too late — that her fear had pushed him away for good, and that she'd made a colossal mistake. She watched her younger self pull out her phone a month after their breakup with trembling hands and make that call to backpedal out of her missteps.

"I'm sorry, Wendy. I can't." Alec's clipped words echoed through the phone from 2,500 miles away, cementing the insurmountable distance between them. They tore open the scars from the first time she'd heard them with an icy sharpness. The pain in his voice wavered through the finality. Her heart squeezed in agony. Unlike the pain he'd suffered with his sister, this wasn't something she could soothe away. Not with a border between them. And when she'd walked away, she'd forfeited the role of the soother of his pain. She'd made a promise she couldn't keep and smashed to pieces the person and the relationship that had sustained her like no other ever had.

Kara Lynn's words replayed again in her mind and she slid down the wall to the floor of her bedroom.

You think I'm the heartless one.

You took one of the best human beings on the planet and treated him like some plaything you could discard at will.

"Am I?" When she finally spoke, Wendy's voice came out brittle around the edges. She wiped her nose and forced her red-rimmed eyes to meet Griffin's. "Heartless? A bad person?"

The kindness in his eyes only opened another crack in her all-too-fragile shell. "You are a beautiful, miserable human. Just like all the rest of us."

Wendy sank onto her bed, and Griffin followed.

"But one who's got a chance to do things differently this time around."

After a heavy silence, she spoke again. "But I tried. And you saw. I'd already hurt him too much. It was too late."

"Maybe you'd better read that." Griffin pointed to a card with a flowery typeface that hadn't been on her desk before.

She picked it up, and pain knifed through her again at the sight of Alec's familiar handwriting correcting the sappy platitude. *The only way out is through... the Popeye's chicken drive-thru.*

Something between a laugh and a sob caught in her throat.

When she looked up, Griffin had gone, but the note was still in her hand.

Somehow, inexplicably, she was back on her couch with *Doctor Who* still playing on the television, and a wave of sleepiness pulled her under again.

CHAPTER 36

Wendy awoke again with a start on her couch, wondering if that had all been a dream. But under her covers, the feel of paper between her fingers told her she still clutched the note.

"Griffin?" she called out. "You still here?"

Silence.

She blinked and found her house changed. Instead of the built-in bookcases surrounding her television, her living room opened up into a swamp. Wooden pathways ran through swaths of wetlands. Groups of trees hung entirely with moss congregated in standing water, and dragonflies buzzed about as if she were caught in some bizarre grown-up version of *Where the Wild Things Are*.

Sloughing off her blanket, she took a tentative step onto the path, into the wetlands. The low hum of a motor caught her attention, and she followed the sound. Now fully on the path, the landscape was familiar. This was Jean Lafitte

National Park and Preserve, where she and Alec had waited out a storm under a tree just before they put her dad in the hospital. The memories tumbled through her mind, stirring up the still-fresh pangs of longing and regret.

She rounded a corner, and the source of the motor sound came into view. A very, very strange source. Wendy frowned and approached the bizarre scene in the middle of the bayou.

Blocking three quarters of the pathway was a treadmill. And on that treadmill, a tree sloth with wiry brown and black fur ambled along on all fours.

"Oh, hey." The sloth looked up from its trek on the never-ending track and spoke to her like this was a normal, everyday thing to do.

Despite her freshly traumatized state, Wendy almost laughed. "Let me guess. Ghost of Midnights Present?"

The sloth raised one of its long arms and gave a two-clawed salute. It offered an expression that was almost a smile before loping on.

"Why are you on a treadmill with all of this right in front of you?"

"Eh, not really my scene."

Wendy smirked. "Really?"

"No, not really. But I could ask you the same thing."

Wendy's gaze wandered off to the swampy waters in the distance where she and Alec had waited out the storm, and a wistful ache began. The path leading back to him seemed even more fraught.

"Lots of alligators and man-eating bugs that way."

"You didn't seem to mind when you were here with him."

She winced.

"Hey, you want to give me a ride to our next stop?" The sloth pushed a button to stop the exercise equipment and held up its front paws like it wanted her to pick it up.

Wendy bent down, and the creature wrapped its long arms around her neck and nuzzled its adorable wiry-furred head into her chest.

"You might be the cutest pain in the ass I've ever met," Wendy said, hugging the creature to her.

"I get that a lot." If it was possible for a rainforest tree animal to smirk, this one did.

"Where to? Are you going to show me how dismal my life is at present?"

"I think you've probably got a pretty good handle on that already."

"Don't sugarcoat it or anything," Wendy deadpanned.

"Don't worry. I won't," the sloth said. "Ready?"

Wendy shrugged, and the heavy swamp air and greenery ribboned away and they were flying over houses miles away. Wind swept through Wendy's hair, and she looked down. The sprawling houses of the Garden District loomed below. Like two hundred feet below.

Her palms sweated where they clutched the small animal. That would be a heck of a long way to fall. And speaking of falling, they began a nosedive straight for a white plantation-style house under the cover of trees below. The fall sucked her gasp from her lungs before it could emerge. She held onto the sloth for dear life, like it could save her from plummeting to certain death.

But apparently it could. She squeezed her eyes shut, and when she opened them, she recognized the doorstep right away. From the night of her first fight with Alec. It was Kara Lynn's house.

"I'm not particularly interested in a visit here," Wendy said.

But the sloth only climbed down from its perch against Wendy's body and opened the front door, summoning her inside after it.

The same old anxiety stirring, she followed it into the kitchen. The scent of lemons and baking wafted in from the heart of Kara's home.

At one of the enormous granite slab countertops, Kara stood up to her elbows in flour and sugar and other ingredients. For once, she was only in her pajamas and a loose black t-shirt. No makeup graced her face, and she'd swept her hair up into a messy ponytail. For the first time in Wendy's experience, Kara looked like a mere mortal instead of a perfectly coifed debutante.

Next to her stood Alec in the same jeans and henley he'd worn to see Wendy earlier. Wendy's heart ached at the sight of him again as he was now. So close, yet so far away. He looked down at a recipe and back up to Kara.

"I went to see Wendy," Alec said.

Kara tensed but continued rolling her dough. "And how did that go?"

"I know you're not her biggest fan, but..."

Kara stopped and gripped the ends of her rolling pin. Her lips twisted to the side like she was wrestling with something. "I have a confession to make."

Alec raised an eyebrow and waited for her to continue.

She bit her lip and then began again. "I think I may have downplayed how I treated her in high school."

"Yeah, ya think?" Wendy said to the sloth. It nodded.

"What do you mean?" Alec asked.

"I was pretty terrible. Slime in her locker, flipping over her food, calling her names. And she probably told you about the concert thing." She dragged her forearm across her forehead and let out a sigh. "I wanted friends so badly that I followed along with the wrong people—not that it's an excuse — and I hurt her in the process. I'm not proud of it."

Kara chanced a glance at Alec. His normally serene features clouded, but there was compassion in them, too. He leaned his back against the counter.

"And when I saw her with you, I freaked out," Kara said. "I acted like it was so long ago and no big deal. But it was a big deal. I think it was just easier to act that way than to have the constant reminder of what a bad person I was." She pressed her lips together, and her voice trembled on her next words. "And might still be."

There was such a vulnerability and remorse in her expression that Wendy could hardly believe what she was witnessing. The expression was so Alec-like that Wendy couldn't help but sympathize regardless of their rocky history.

"You're not a bad person, K," Alec said, his voice gentle. He pulled her into a brotherly hug, and Kara looked utterly bewildered. Wendy felt another pang of compassion for her, so caught off guard by someone willing to love her despite her faults and missteps. Everyone needed someone like that.

"Aren't I?" Kara said, her expression still raw.

"I think the fact that you want to be better is pretty telling."

"Well, I've got a lot to make up for."

"Well, as far as I'm concerned, you can start with lemon tarts for all."

Kara pulled away and got back to her dough making. "That I can do."

After some instruction, Alec went to work zesting a lemon.

"I'm glad you broke things off with Heather." Kara pressed dough into tart pans.

"Why? What was wrong with Heather?"

"She didn't get your sense of humor." Kara shook her head in bafflement. "And you have a great sense of humor. It's just like mine."

"I know, right?" The twins shared a look and laughed. Regardless of her feelings for Kara, a lump formed in her throat. The family Alec so desperately wanted—he had it here with Kara. And she was glad.

"And she wasn't fierce when it came to you. You need someone who's fierce about you."

Alec nodded, as if taking it all in, and that poor lemon took an extra hard zesting.

"She's still in love with you, isn't she?" Kara asked after a moment.

"Who, Heather? Doubtful."

Kara shook her head. "Wendy."

Wendy stilled.

"And you're still in love with her." This was not a question.

Alec opened his mouth to reply but closed it again. Was he? Is that what his visit today had been about? Long buried dregs of hope gathered.

"Twinstinct, remember?" Kara said, the gleam back in her eye. "Now, say what you will about that girl, but she is fierce."

"It's more complicated than that."

"Does it have to be?"

Alec set his lemon aside and rubbed his chin. "Her leaving the first time hurt me. A lot." He joined his sister, pressing the dough into the tart molds. "It was that feeling, like I was tumbling into nothing and couldn't get the ground under me. Like losing my mom and dad, all over again. Except this time, she could've stayed with me, but she chose not to."

"I think I may have had something to do with that choice," Kara said in a small voice. "What if I pushed her away more than you did?"

Alec shook his head and was silent for a long moment.

"I'm sorry," Kara said. "For acting like I did with her. Maybe I could talk to her."

Alec smiled at his sister. "Even if that smoothed things over... I don't know. I've lost too many people I've loved."

"Well, you're not getting rid of me without a fight."

Alec's smile warmed, but then dimmed again. "I don't know if I could go through having her in my life and then losing her again."

He reached for a new tart pan and more dough. "Even if we could work out the cross-country logistics, how could I know that she won't spook and run again?"

Kara gave him a commiserating look, and Wendy's guilt churned like an oil slick in her stomach. That doubt—she'd put it there.

"How was it seeing her today?" Kara asked.

"Good. Hard. She seemed tired, like she's been burying herself in work." He looked up at Kara. "It was sort of like coming home and your key still fits in the lock, but you're not sure if it's still home anymore."

"And do you think it's still home—you and her?"

Alec dragged a flour-dusted forearm across his brow. "I'm afraid of my answer to that."

Kara nodded slowly. "How'd you leave it?"

"I told her where we'd be tonight. Asked her to come if she thought maybe there was still something there."

"And is she going to?"

"I guess we'll see."

Was she going? Wendy's pulse sped up. Could she brave it—putting it all on the line again when she could see there were still so many doubts in his mind? Even if she did, there was a chance he couldn't get past the constant worry that she'd take off again. He might decide it wasn't worth it. She wasn't worth it. Her gut twisted. The smart-assed sloth tugged at the hem of Wendy's tank top.

"Time to go?" Wendy asked, though things felt anything but resolved.

He nodded.

"I suppose you want a ride again."

He reached his long sloth arms to the sky, and she picked him up. Wendy cast a look back at Alec before they headed out the door. Her gaze traced over the dimple and smile that had been such a balm to her in hard times. Then to the crinkles around his eyes that came out when they made a private joke that chased away her loneliness. There was so much of him that spoke directly to her heart, and she could hardly stand the thought of walking away yet again. But if she couldn't screw up her courage tonight, this might be the last time she'd ever see him.

CHAPTER 37

The sloth brought her back to her bed, and Wendy drifted off once again, mind reeling with questions that she didn't yet have answers to, until the smell of night jasmine and air heavy with mist roused her once more. She waved a hand in front of her face and could scarcely see it with the density of the fog.

She felt her way around the bed until she found the edge and stood.

Wendy blinked, and the fog drifted away, this time leaving her in the foyer of a familiar house in the Quarter. Yellow street lamp light tinged everything.

"Come in, dear. It's getting cold."

Wendy followed the sound of the female voice, one she knew. An ancient gramophone sat to the right of the entrance, and furniture and photographs from days gone by lined the hallway. The Durocher house, Wendy thought, former home and place of business of Griffin's grandmother, Sophia. She'd been to this place so many times with her tours, but she'd been inside only once, when

Sophia had done a private showing for Steve, Alec, and herself, much to Steve's delight.

A warm glow emanated from the direction of the parlor.

"Sophia?" Wendy called.

"Yes dear. Come in here."

Wendy stepped into the parlor filled with furniture from the turn of the century that the Sophia had collected to reflect the time of the spiritualism craze. Sophia smiled up at her from behind a half-moon table. The guttering candle flame cast her silver hair and tasteful pantsuit in a dreamlike glow. She beckoned for Wendy to take the seat across from her.

"Have a cup of tea. It looks like you could use one. No sedatives, I made it myself." The wry smile in the elderly woman's green eyes reminded Wendy of an expression she'd often seen on her grandson's face. That must have been where Griffin got it.

Wendy accepted the tea, steam curling from its elegant gold-rimmed cup and saucer.

Sophia studied Wendy in a canny way that made her feel as though she could rifle through the contents of her thoughts at will. Wendy shuddered. "Quite the night," Sophia said.

"Yes, ma'am." That was the understatement of the year.

Sophia withdrew a deck of tarot cards from her desk drawer. Wendy watched in a kind of ominous fascination as the ornate illustrations on the cards flashed past in a series of light and dark with splashes of color. The cups and swords and wands and pentacles each seemed to hold a macabre portend of what was to come. How could hers turn out right from here? Wendy felt a weight in her stomach as she contemplated the thought.

"I suppose you're the Ghost of Midnight Future," Wendy said.

"I suppose I am." Sophia's eyes glinted in the candlelight, but her hands persisted in their shuffling. Why did this all feel so damned serious and futile suddenly? Getting past all this fear of hers for good seemed like a Sisyphean task.

As if knowing she needed some levity, Griffin came wandering out from another room.

"You're the Midnights Past guy. What are you doing in the future?" Wendy said, glad to have a target for her hopelessness turned ire.

"What's past is prologue." He gave her a mock sage grin.

Wendy frowned at him.

"And I just wanted to stick around to see how this part went."

She rolled her eyes, but she had to admit that his presence put her more at ease than she'd been moments ago.

"What is it you wish to know?" Sophia asked, the cards still slapping at each other and the table as her shuffling continued.

Wendy swallowed. She'd been so hopeful when she'd watched scenes from her earlier days with Alec. She'd almost believed that things might play out differently right before her eyes, even though she knew full well how they had ended. How *she'd* ended them. Now the thought that Alec might get involved with her again after all that she'd put him through seemed almost laughable. She didn't dare ask she wanted to know the most.

"I thought you were just supposed to show me. Isn't that how this works?"

Sophia made a noncommittal sound. A divot of what felt a lot like disapproval formed between her brows. "If that's the way you wish to proceed—" Sophia placed the deck in Wendy's palm. "Cut the deck. Clear your mind and let the cards speak to you. You'll feel where."

Wendy passed the stack of cards from one hand to the other. Her stomach churned. There was a good reason she'd never done a reading with Sophia before. If she were going to end up eighty years old just going through the motions at work with only a chinchilla collection for company, she wasn't sure she wanted that confirmed. But as she ran her fingers over the rough edges of the cards, her chest warmed, like she'd landed in the right place.

She hesitated a moment, and Sophia nodded at her. Wendy cut the deck where she'd felt the warmth.

Sophia lay the cards down in a cross pattern and clucked her tongue. Griffin let out a low whistle and made a face at the cards. Even with no experience reading tarot, Wendy could see the grim nature of her future landscape in the spread.

"Awesome. Swords, frostbite, jumping off a burning tower. Just the future I wanted. How did you know?" She folded her arms over her chest. Why put her through all of this just to taunt her with how epically bad her future would be?

"This is not all despair," Sophia said. Her manicured nails traced the line of the cross.

"Okay, yeah, this lady with the lion looks all right. Until the lion *eats* her."

Griffin cracked a smile, and Sophia gave her an admonishing look.

"If you stay the course, this is what your future will hold."

The scene before Wendy swirled away, and only Sophia's voice was present in the dusty vortex of blackness. Wendy scrambled for purchase as visions of blazing towers and pointed objects whizzed by. "Your source of pride will come from your work, but I fear you'll grow too focused on the day-to-day running of your business that you'll lose sight of the reasons you truly loved this in the first place. But on the upside, you will have a very cute niece and nephew to keep you company."

The dust cleared from her mind, and she was deposited near the front counter of her shop. Her future self sat slumped over a pile of paperwork. She looked up, and Wendy could see the bags under her eyes, the toll of pushing all of her creative projects to the side. Even her basket of yarn sat in the corner collecting dust. She looked... awful. Like her current self, with even more of her marrow sucked out, a brittle husk of the person she used to be. The person she could be.

But then two adorable kids streaked into the shop: a little girl with dark hair and an ice cream-streaked face, wearing a smiling skull and crossbones shirt, and a little tow-headed boy with glasses and a confident swagger even for a three-year-old. They both blew through the shop like tornadoes.

"Auntie Wendy, Auntie Wendy!"

The children tackle-hugged her, and for the first time, her future self smiled.

"Can I have the sucker with the scorpion inside?"

"Yes, Eliza. Get one for Jack, too, will you?" she said.

"Eww. I don't want to eat bugs. I want a cherry one."

"When are you going to come over and read us bedtime stories again?" Eliza asked.

Wendy's older self looked tired.

"Sometime soon, okay?"

The scene played on, and it was clear that these two and the rest of her family continued to be her only joy. It wasn't a terrible life, not at all—but it was one spent wondering what could have been.

A group of teenagers walked through the door, holding their phones and dodging shelves as if in pursuit of some invisible target.

"What are you guys doing?" Wendy asked.

"There's a poltergeist in here."

"Got it!"

They cheered. Wendy's heart sank. One of the new tour companies had set it up. Created this app that she'd wanted to build and had let languish. She hadn't acted when she'd had the chance, and one of the other companies had run with the idea. Possibly even worked with Alec to get it set up. He'd had most of the app architecture in place already. Why waste it when he could sell it to someone else who could use it?

Ghost Griffin popped his head in and joined Wendy as she watched the miserable scene. His eyes cut to the street outside the shop, and he frowned. "You should probably see this."

The dread crept up her spine and sent a wash of cold into her stomach. She had a pretty good guess of what might be waiting. "Do I have to?"

Griffin shrugged. "I think it might make a difference."

She walked numbly out onto St. Peter in time to catch Alec walking away. On one side of him, his sister chattered away, and on the other...

Wendy swallowed and tried to drag her eyes from the scene in front of her, but she couldn't. She couldn't take her eyes off of this man that she had loved, that she still loved even after everything, even as he held the hand of another woman. The pretty blond threaded her fingers through his and leaned against his shoulder. Their forms were getting farther away now, but Wendy thought she saw a glint of light off a ring on the woman's left hand. He leaned over to kiss the woman. His fiancée. His *love*? Curiosity about this woman ate at her like acid from the inside. Of course he would've moved on and found someone else to love him and be the person he needed. Of course. After the way Wendy had treated him, why wouldn't he? But did she appreciate his sense of humor the way Wendy did? Did they share jokes and leave little notes for one another? Did he know when she was sad, even when she tried to hide it? And in turn, did she see when he needed space and when he needed to be held? Were their weekends filled with hikes and kisses while they waited out the rain? Did they curl into each other in the middle of the night, breathing in each other's scents and saying nothing at all?

Wendy looked at their joined hands again. At the look on his Alec's face. Did she fill the void he carried inside him and become the family he so desperately wanted for himself? Maybe none of that mattered if this woman could give him the one thing Wendy had not: the assurance that she would always stay.

Leaden guilt and rage and sadness sat heavy in her gut as she watched him walk away, out of her life for good. Her heart seemed to implode and crash in on itself in a great heap.

Back inside the shop, the scene seemed to focus in on future Wendy as she stayed rooted to her spot at the desk while everything else moved on around her at breakneck speed, like a time-lapse video. People came and went. Julie and Griffin and Eliza and Jack, her mom and dad, yet she stayed, hair going grey, skin turning soft with age. The scene jumped to her house, where she sat petting a chinchilla in her lap. And then back to the store again, surrounded by people and somehow still alone. Alone. Alone.

Sophia and Griffin came back into focus in the dusty parlor. Wendy rubbed her arms against the chill that ran much deeper than her skin. "So that's it, then. That's my lot." She sat miserable, unable to speak any further.

"On the upside, your cousin and I make very cute kids, am I right?" Griffin said.

"Why even put me through all this if I just end up back in the same miserable place?" Wendy scowled at him, but even her heart wasn't in that. He was trying to lighten the mood for her sake, and she needed somewhere to direct her sadness.

"You asked me to show you what *was*. If you continue on your current path taking no risks to change the parts you are unhappy with, then yes," Sophia said.

"But that's *not* the final word? I can change it?"

"I sense there is another way. But only if you're willing to confront your fears." Sophia swept up the cards from the first spread and began shuffling again. After a moment, she handed them to Wendy. "Shall we?"

Wendy took the cards and held them to her chest. There was a chance of evading the gloom and doom she'd seen lain out before her. If only she could get past this. If only she could make peace with the possibility of rejection.

"Set your intention as you hold the cards this time. Be your most courageous self."

Wendy closed her eyes and tried to envision herself living without the defense mechanisms she'd used to safeguard herself from pain for most of her life. They'd served her well, but they'd also kept a solid wall of brick and barbed wire between her and the genuine connection that had fed her soul more than any other. She'd tear them down in a second if she could be sure of the outcome. But that was the trouble. There were no guarantees.

"Channel your inner Gryffindor," Griffin whispered. Wendy shook her head with a smirk.

Feeling the edges of the cards again, she tried to let go. She cut the cards and handed them back to Sophia.

The older woman flipped the cards, each one landing on the table with a satisfying *swick*.

Nine of Cups: fulfillment of wishes, happiness, comfort, satisfaction, according to Sophia. Then Temperance: steadying the scales, a sense of purpose, and then the Empress and the Emperor, who seemed to balance each other out.

"I already like these a lot better," Wendy said.

"This path is harder won," Sophia said.

"Can I see what this looks like, like I did with the other one?" Wendy closed her eyes and willed the wispy fog to come and take her away again to some other place where she could repair the past and go after her chance at a happy ending. But the curls of fog only circled her ankles. She focused harder. Maybe seeing it with certainty, with rock-solid clarity, could convince her to take that ultimate step, to help her make the leap that she needed.

But only brief flashes surfaced, she and Alec hiking together, taking their niece and nephew to a petting zoo. There was work, but the fulfilling kind along with the mundane, and she saw herself energized, smiling. But there were only fits and starts. She wanted more than this to stake her hopes on.

"I'm afraid further glimpses of this future don't yet exist. You're so far down the other path. If this is the one you want, you'll have to take that leap and forge it on your own."

CHAPTER 38

Another wave of vertigo enveloped Wendy and stole the ground out from under her. As the spirits hurtled her away, Sophia, Griffin, and the parlor receded into the distance. Her thoughts thrashed through all the scenes she'd relived tonight. Everything replayed, from being stood up by Kara Lynn and Aundrea, to that dismal future of the status quo, being a supporting character in the lives of everyone she loved, but never fully taking center stage of her own.

And then there was the middle. Her heart ached for that part more than any of it. It was a beautiful messy middle, a time when she'd put some of her fears and doubts aside and take a chance on her creative endeavors at work. A time when she'd taken a chance on a sweet Canadian who loved cheesy movies and playing dress up and showed up for her when she never expected him to. He was there when she needed him the most, without her having to ask. He'd loved her, and she'd had so much trouble believing it was real that she'd cut herself off from it. She'd let the ugliness of fear, uncertainty, and insecurity rule her. She'd pushed away the only person outside of her family who made her feel like she wasn't the odd person out in the world. The person who never let her down.

It was a middle that shouldn't have ended so soon. Like one of those perfect cult TV shows, it got canceled prematurely and had a rushed, clumsy ending instead of the full satisfying run it deserved.

Wendy took a shuddering breath in this liminal floating space she inhabited. Even some of those cancelled shows got picked up later by a streaming service. Why she was thinking of television at a time like this, she wasn't sure. The subconscious was a weird place.

She clenched her fists and gathered up all her courage to face the question: Which of these futures did she want?

Did she want to go on with barbed wire around her heart, content with just getting by?

Or did she want more of the messy part? The part with someone who reminded her that there was more to life than just work and to take a break every once in a while and pursue the parts that mattered to her? She pictured more mornings with Alec, with him waking her up too early so they could have coffee together before work. Having *her person* again, who she could turn to even when Julie and Griffin and her mom and dad were busy, someone who was there just for her. Having him to laugh with again and curl up next to. The yearning for a life she looked forward to everyday, instead of one where she was just going through the motions, nearly hollowed her out.

But a new swarm of nerves buzzed in her chest. The outcomes in this future were untested. There might come a day when she was too much, when he might not want her anymore and her heart might crash and burn. But wasn't his coming to see her today proof that there was at least a chance?

The nothingness she floated in seemed to eat at her. She'd already walked down the path of safety and deprivation for nine long months, a path where she could control the outcome. And that had yielded only unnecessary loneliness and a sloth on a treadmill. However, she'd been in control. She'd decided the outcome before the pain could come out of nowhere and ambush her. It had been a comfort to know she was the one in charge of the outcome.

His words from this morning came back to her: You were it for me Wendy. I thought you felt the same. Was I so wrong?

She blew out a breath. Love was never a question. She loved him with a fierceness that could crush legions and wanted nothing more in the world than for him to have what he needed to be happy. It was that tight hold on control she'd have to give up for her to be with Alec again. She'd have to learn to live with the uncertainty. She'd messed up once, chosen the wrong path. But wasn't he—wasn't what they had, what they shared—worth giving up that stranglehold?

She just had to be brave enough to risk losing what mattered to her most.

Wendy's mouth went dry. All thought turned hazy and her consciousness drifted.

The next thing she knew, she was back on her couch, the TV still playing softly in the background.

She scrambled through her purse for her phone. 10:45 p.m. Shit.

Heart thumping with more fear than she'd ever allowed it to hold before, Wendy sprang up and called for a ride share. She'd be cutting it close anyway, and there was no way she was going to find a place to park near the French Quarter on New Year's Eve.

She pulled on clothes in a hurry, and as she stood before the bathroom mirror brushing her teeth, for the first time in her life, there was no hesitation. She knew with absolute certainty what she needed to do.

CHAPTER 39

"Can't you go any faster?" Wendy gripped the edge of her seat in the Corolla that had picked her up at her curb minutes before. Moss-draped trees and small restaurants on Tchoupitoulas Street crept by at the agonizing speed of a school zone.

"It's New Year's Eve," the driver said. His unhurried smile matched his rumpled t-shirt and surfer-dude hair. "If you wanted to be somewhere by midnight, you should've called hours ago." His genial tone—totally devoid of all accusation or ill will, only irritated Wendy even more.

"Do you want a tip or not, dude? If I wanted a lecture, I would've had my cousin drive me. Geez."

The driver—Luke, according to her app—held up his hands in surrender, and Wendy thought about how the bitter, acerbic tone of her voice sounded like the version of herself she was ready to leave behind. She blew out a breath and tried again.

"Sorry." She forced her hands off of the seat and placed them in her lap. "It's just really important."

Luke's face softened into an irritatingly understanding smile. "Hot date?"

Wendy frowned at the sea of red brake lights standing in between her and where she needed to be. It seemed impossible that she would make it. She slumped back in her seat and hissed out a breath.

"Not exactly. More like a last chance to make things right."

She pulled out her phone and typed a message with shaky fingers. She could sacrifice a splashy entrance in the name of actually seeing him.

Alec, are you still at the restaurant? Please don't leave. I'm coming.

She flexed and balled her fingers. At least that would buy her some time if traffic kept up, and she didn't make it by midnight.

Her phone buzzed and her mouth went dry.

Message not sent.

"Shit. Shit. Shit. Shit."

She dialed instead, but had no luck that way either.

"What is it?" Luke asked.

Wendy tried to clear her mind and claw at some kind of solution.

"You think I could use your phone?"

"Sure, but I've got shoddy service tonight." He handed it over.

"Looks like I do, too."

She had just as much luck with Luke's phone. She even tried calling Kara, but no dice.

She handed it back with a strangled sigh. All this lead-up and she wouldn't even make it to him after all. It seemed like the universe's cruel joke.

"You want to talk about it? Might help pass the time," Luke said and shot her a friendly smile in the rearview mirror.

She was not in the habit of sharing details of her personal life with strangers. What did this guy care if she got to Alec and poured her heart out before he hopped on a plane again? But she eyed his open, genial face again.

"What the hell. We're stuck here anyway, right?"

Luke's eyes lit up. "Lay it on me."

He listened like a friend getting into a juicy soap opera plot as she poured out the complete story from beginning to end.

"And Alec said he's leaving at midnight?" Luke asked once she'd gotten to the part about today.

Wendy nodded.

"But you can't reach him to tell him you'll be late?"

"Right."

"This might call for some drastic measures. Let's go get your man."

Luke swerved and cut off another car. Wendy's heart swooped in time with the honking horns.

The clock on the dashboard clicked over to 11:25. Wendy brought her forehead to the back of the headrest. Her chances of getting there in time seemed less and less possible, even with all the good intentions in the world.

"We're never going to make it, are we?" she said.

"We're almost to the Quarter," Luke said.

"Yeah, but the restaurant's a thirty-minute walk from any edge. Especially with all the streets blocked off."

Luke turned down a side street, in the opposite direction of their destination.

"Hey, where are you going?"

"I have an idea. I have some friends that live right up here."

Wendy arched a skeptical eyebrow. "Do they have a helicopter? Because—"

"Do you want to get to your man or not?"

Wendy squirmed. "Yes. Yes, I do."

"Good. How do you feel about two-wheeled transportation?"

Five minutes later, Wendy climbed aboard a tandem bicycle decked out with gold, green, and purple ribbons and a horn the size of a baby's head.

"How am I going to keep this safe and bring it back to your friends? I don't know if there will be anywhere to lock it down, and there are crazies out tonight."

Luke shrugged. "I'll go with you and drop you off."

Wendy's eyes bugged out.

"Am I your driver or what?" He motioned for her to take the back seat.

"Why would you do that? Aren't you missing out on prime income-earning time?"

"Isn't this a once in a lifetime thing for you?"

Wendy swallowed and nodded.

"Then it's more important than a few extra bucks. Plus, I'll have a great story to tell my friends."

Wendy changed seats, not sure what to do with this overwhelming feeling of gratitude in her chest. She had done nothing to earn this guy's going out of his way to help her, and it ate at her, but she sat with the discomfort on the tandem bike seat and whispered, "Thank you."

"Coming through! Gotta make a love connection by midnight!" Luke honked his way through the steady stream of revelers.

Wendy rolled her eyes, but like the Grinch, she felt her heart grow several sizes as people on Bourbon and Canal Street lifted their drinks and herded their friends back to create a bike path.

They arrived at the restaurant with eight minutes to spare. For the second time today, someone had shown Wendy that the people you roll the dice on don't always let you down.

Dismounting from the bike, Wendy wrapped her driver in an uncharacteristically exuberant hug.

"Thanks for all of this."

Luke nodded and doffed an imaginary cap. "Go get 'em!"

Wendy hurried through the front door and was immediately hit by a brick wall of people raising drinks and dancing to pop music. She smoothed her dress and pushed to her tiptoes to scan the crowd. There must have been two hundred people stuffed into every inch of the first floor, not to mention the rest, who were laughing and dancing on the terrace upstairs. And didn't this place also have a back patio? None of the faces she saw belonged to Alec or Kara or any of his friends. How was she supposed to find him in this crowd in eight minutes? She looked at her phone again. Shit. Make that seven.

Wendy's chest tightened with panic as she moved through the crowd, methodically scanning faces, but she forced herself to breathe. She was here. She could find him. Not finding him was not an option. She just had to think.

Whenever they went out together, he always found the quietest spots so they could hear each other talk. Though any pocket of quiet was less likely to exist in a packed bar on New Year's Eve, Wendy hoofed it through throngs of people with beads and Happy New Year's hats toward the small fountain with bar seating around it.

Not a single familiar face. Her chest constricted, and hopelessness tried to rain on her New Year's miracle, but she shook it away. She had to do everything she could to find him. Then her gaze landed on the loudest part of the room. The DJ booth. And she had a new idea.

It took some elbow-throwing and sweet-talking, but before too long she had a microphone in her hand, and the music went silent.

She cleared her throat and stepped up onto the platform next to the DJ.

"Alec? Alec, are you still here?"

Hundreds of sets of eyes swiveled in her direction. The chatter settled to a dull murmur. Her throat went dry. But she willed herself to keep talking.

"You would not believe what I had to go through to get here to you. Both physically and metaphorically, I guess." Her voice trailed off into nervous laughter. "I'm sorry it took me so long to get here. But I'm here."

Wendy met each set of eyes in turn, frantically searching for the one pair she wanted to see, sea glass green, so full of intelligence and warmth and a weird sense of humor to match her own. The silence drew out until her heart was as taut as a bowstring.

Each false positive sent her heart fumbling. Beside her, the DJ shifted her weight.

Then it hit her—why hadn't she even considered this, so hopped up on adrenaline and fear of missing out as she was? What if he already left? No. At the prospect, her heart tumbled down three flights of stairs. Unless...

Unless he'd gotten tired of waiting, gotten tired of being the one waiting only to be disappointed and played for a fool.

Wendy's heart seized up. "Alec, please be here," she whispered into the mic.

With one last sweep of the room, she handed the mic back to the DJ and thanked her. Wendy's shoulders slumped, and she debated drinking her weight in margaritas before doing a walk of shame back home. She made it halfway across the floor before she spotted a familiar face, though not the one she was hoping for. Griffin leaned against a high table, wearing a New Year's crown and a crisp white shirt.

Caught between her inner struggle to sink into a well of despair or punch something, she punched Griffin in the arm.

"Ow." He rubbed his bicep.

"Are you ghost Griffin or real Griffin?"

He raised an eyebrow. "How many New Year's libations have you had?"

Wendy scowled.

"Easy, fiery one. I thought we were on friendly terms."

The gathered crowd counted down to midnight. "Ten, nine, eight..."

She blew out a breath and dragged her hands through her hair. She'd never been much for teary confessions, except maybe with Julie, but she glanced up at her cousin-in-law to be. The look on his face was not one of mocking that said *well, that was embarrassing*, so much as it said *this sucks and I get it*. Taking that in broke apart something deep inside, and the anger went out of her.

"Three, two, one. Happy New Year!" Shouts and confetti kisses rained down all around them.

"I was too late. When it mattered, I was too late."

She shook her head and let the idea sink in. In a room full of drunk, celebrating people, she felt like crying.

Griffin squeezed her shoulder. "If I hug you, will you promise not to hit me again?"

"Don't count on it." Wendy managed a weak smile, but appreciated the gesture. "What are you doing here, anyway? I thought you guys were going to the heavy metal mariachi place."

"Julie wanted to catch up with you. I think she was also hoping to see a little history in the making."

Wendy felt the blow of the statement. "Yeah, well, it doesn't look like history's getting made tonight."

Griffin's gaze locked onto something over Wendy's shoulder, and his eyes took on a mischievous twinkle.

"I wouldn't be too sure about that."

Wendy followed Griffin's gaze, and her heart did a flip. Emerging from the patio were Julie, Alec, and Kara.

Alec looked up, and their gazes locked.

He was here. He hadn't left. He was *here*.

CHAPTER 40

He wore a fresh shirt, charcoal grey this time, and she wondered if he still smelled like dough and lemons, with that salt and cedar scent that was all his own underneath. Her heart pounded like it was starting its own percussion section in her chest. His smile spread as he approached, and his face, his presence was so familiar, yet all together new, like past and present and future had gotten all tangled up in this moment. Every pore in her body tingled with anticipation.

Julie gave her a low-key thumbs up, and Wendy answered with a shaky smile.

"Hi," she said to Alec as he approached and then turned to his sister. "Hey, Kara. Happy New Year."

"Happy New Year." Kara's manicured eyebrows scrunched together in assessment, and then she gave Wendy what looked like a commiserating smile. "I'm going to go get a glass of water."

Fear crept up on Wendy again until her whole body felt electrified with it. Griffin gave her a nudge. She took another step toward Alec, and Julie tugged Griffin away.

Alec stood with his hands in his pockets, and Wendy twisted hers together.

"So, I guess you heard that," Wendy said, hooking a thumb at the DJ stand.

Alec nodded. "I caught most of it, anyway. Kara filled me in on the beginning."

A couple extending their midnight kiss knocked into Alec, jostling him closer to Wendy. She shot out a hand to steady him and froze, hand gripping his bicep. The heat from his chest radiated toward hers, only inches away. She didn't want to pull away, but she removed it awkwardly and smoothed her dress. Party poppers sounded, and confetti flew and landed in their hair. They shared an amused look, and he picked an orange streak out of her hair. Their gazes locked again, and she couldn't stop drinking him in, the wonder of him standing here with her after all this time. She gathered up all of her courage.

"What do you think?" she said. Her heart swooped. "Do you think you could ever give this another chance?"

His expression went unreadable, and her smile faltered.

"What happened between this afternoon and now to bring all this on?"

"I did a lot of thinking since you came by earlier. Probably an entire year's worth of thinking. Not getting on that plane and making it work with you was the biggest mistake of my life. You were right. I was scared. And because of that, I sabotaged everything. I let it get in the way of what I needed. What I still need. You."

Alec raked a hand through his hair, and she watched the struggle to believe her play out on his face.

Wendy's voice shook. "I love you, Alec. I never stopped loving you."

Alec's gaze softened. "I never stopped loving you either."

"Even while you dated that other girl?" Wendy smirked.

He smiled. "I did *try* to stop."

"Do you remember that movie we watched with the goblin that gave that girl his magic goblin fruit? It was all perfect and irresistible, and after she tasted it, she couldn't eat normal food anymore because everything tasted like sawdust after the goblin fruit?"

Alec grinned. "Yeah, that one was awful."

"Awesomely awful," she agreed. "But I think you're like that for me: my goblin fruit."

His smile spread and the way he looked at her felt so like the way he'd looked at her before that her heart swelled. "So, in this scenario, I'm the devious creature trying to roofie you with my delicious fruit, so you'll never eat mac and cheese for all eternity? I'm not sure if my feminist sensibilities are on board with that." His eyes twinkled with amusement.

"No, silly, you're the fruit."

"Can I be the feminist goblin fruit that consults with said girl on all important decisions and wants all parties involved to make their own choices?"

Wendy rolled her eyes and laughed. "Yes, you can be my feminist goblin fruit."

"Also, I'm not sure how I feel about being eaten."

She smirked. "Devoured then." She gave an exaggerated eyebrow pump.

They both laughed and then fell into silence, the party raging on behind them.

"I have to leave to catch my flight soon," he said.

Reality came crashing back in, and Wendy's mood darkened. The pained expression came back to Alec's face. "Wendy, as much as I love hearing you say all this, there's still a lot to work through," he said. "Even if we can get past what happened before, there's still the fact that you're here and don't want to leave, and I'm a Canadian citizen. I would love to live here, but there's still the matter of being able to work here with no sponsorship or visa. It would probably be long distance for a while and would probably be hard on both of us." He looked up at her with sorrow in his eyes. "But most of all, I've lost too many important people. I don't know if I could go through having you back in my life and losing you again."

She swallowed, an icy dread washing over her, but she would not shrink away and let fear beat her this time. "You're right. The logistics would be hard, and..." She steadied herself. "And I know it's going to take time for you to trust me again. I know how much I hurt you, and I'm so so sorry." She swallowed around the lump in her throat. "But I'd like a chance to make amends."

He closed his eyes, and she could see the tug-of-war there again when he opened them. He wanted to believe her, but he'd need more to go on. She'd have to show him. And she could stick it out, no matter how long it would take. And the outcome might not be what she'd hoped for, but at least she wouldn't have chickened out this time. If she was going to get her heart stomped on this time, she'd do it knowing she'd laid it all out there—imperfect and unsure, but knowing with absolute certainty that she'd tried everything in her power to give this a go. To have by her side that one person who knew her better than anyone and pushed her to be the person she wanted to be.

"I'm only asking if we can keep talking. See if we can find a way."

"Yeah." Alec nodded finally. "Yeah, let's keep talking."

CHAPTER 41

The next morning, Wendy knew two things: 1. Maybe her cold, dead heart wasn't so cold or so dead after all. 2. Now that she had a tiny sliver of a chance to work things out with Alec, she didn't want to wait another moment.

So she did what Wendy Deveaux did best: she went to work. She had to do something that would show him she was in this for the long haul, and after some research, she printed some forms and called her parents. "Can you guys meet me at the shop? I might need your signature on a few things." She explained her idea, her chest tightening and bracing for impact as though she'd already made the leap and laid it all out for Alec. The line went quiet for a moment, and her dad said, "I'm proud of you, kiddo. Let's do this."

After getting everything sorted with her parents, it was on to part two. Wendy rang the doorbell and stood on the front stoop of Kara's house, bouncing on her toes. Kara answered the door with a quizzical look.

Wendy greeted her former enemy with a sheepish look.

"Can I come in?" Wendy asked. "I could really use your help."

Several hours later, Wendy had survived a flight with many hungover but very polite people, and practically vibrated with nerves as she made her way through customs in Vancouver. This was it. She wasn't holding back anymore.

And finally, there she stood on Alec's doorstep. She had the driver wait, just in case. A swarm of butterflies battered at her ribcage, but she rang the bell. A moment later, Alec looked back at her wide-eyed, caught between shock and something else she hoped was happiness to see her.

"I come bearing Timbits and all five *Sharknadoes* on DVD," Wendy said with a nervous laugh.

Alec blinked at her.

"How are you here? How did you know where to find me?"

Wendy swallowed. "Kara helped. A lot, actually."

"You went to see my sister?"

Wendy nodded. *Desperate times*, she thought. But actually after their visit today, she thought it might not take such desperate times to bring them together.

"Can I come in?"

He stepped aside to let her pass. Her gaze swept around the small but cozy apartment. She took a deep breath to steady her nerves. The place smelled like him, woodsy and crisp, and her chest tightened at the comforting scent. The sliding glass doors beyond the living room looked out over the beautiful denuded winter trees of his Vancouver neighborhood. "Not a bad view you've got here," she said.

He smiled, a puzzled look still present on his features. "Not that I'm complaining, but what are you doing here?"

Wendy blew out a breath and set her bag of donuts and movies on his kitchen table. "I thought it would be easier to keep talking in person. And I was due some vacation time. A lot of vacation time, actually. If you've got other plans, I can just hang out at the hotel or see the city."

He shook his head.

"Donuts?" She offered him the bag of donut holes, and he settled into the chair next to her and took one. "So, what are you up to?"

Alec raised an eyebrow. "You're doing small talk now?"

Her cheeks heated. "When the occasion warrants."

He smiled. "Just unpacking. And thinking."

"About what?"

"Last night. The last year."

"Auld lang syne?" Wendy said with a gleam in her eyes.

"Yeah, I guess." His gaze warmed, and his knee grazed hers under the table. He turned to the hallway, and Wendy caught sight of the digital painting she'd made for his last birthday, with the two of them huddled under the umbrella, safe from the storm. Seeing that brought a tightness to her chest.

"I took it down, you know, *after*." His brows creased. "But a few weeks ago, I got it out again."

Her thrill of hope was quickly tamped down. The severity of what she'd done to him by leaving fell heavy over her, and the misgivings gnawed at her resolve. How could he take her back after that? She cut a glance at the door, but then steeled herself and sat with the shaky feeling in her chest. If he was going to reject her, she'd deal with that, but she wouldn't cut and run before he even had the chance.

"I think I'll hang it up again."

A swell of emotion caught in Wendy's throat. "I'm sorry, Alec. For what I did before. So sorry."

He looked at the painting, and then back at her, remnants of the pain in the tightness around his eyes. But there was also a tentative olive branch in his expression. Once again, she marveled at how close he let his emotions run to the surface, the pain, the joy, all the messy things that made up the fabric of his life. "You said that last night."

"I know, but I think it bears repeating."

"I made mistakes, too." Alec rubbed his chin.

"But not as royally awful as mine." She gave him a half smile.

"I was tense and distant before the move. And when you tried to make things right, I wasn't ready to hear it. I'm sorry, too."

She bit her lip. He squeezed her knee, and the brief contact gave her hope again. They talked some more about regrets and hopes and all the things they'd left unsaid, and Wendy felt her shields crack open and fall, once and for all as she and Alec fell back into easier, teasing conversation.

"So we need to set some times when we're both available, so we can video chat once you go home," Alec said. "You're three hours ahead, so maybe—"

Wendy finished her powdered donut, and her insides trilled with nerves. "Were you serious before about wanting to move back to New Orleans?"

"Yeah, but it will take some legwork. Job hunting. But I could come see you when I go out for interviews." He tapped his leg against hers and leaned closer.

She took a deep breath and snuck a glance at him. "I have a proposal for you," she said. She rummaged through her purse and passed him the folder she'd prepared.

"What's this?"

Wendy wet her dry lips and tried to steady her voice. Her heart beat so loudly in her ears that it nearly blotted out everything else. This was a risk. One he might flatly reject, but as she looked into those eyes that she'd missed so much, she didn't care. She could live with the outcome, even if it was bad, to have a chance at the good.

"A job offer. To finish work on our app and some of the other tech projects I've been thinking about doing. More creative stuff. The salary is negotiable, of course."

"You really want me to work with you?"

"You don't have to decide right now, but I just wanted to put the option out there." She bit her lip, nerves still flaring.

"And your dad even went for this?"

"You'll see all three Deveauxs signatures on the offer letter there." She tapped the bottom of the letter, grazing his fingers with hers. "He said as long as it meant you came back, he could handle some unnecessary technology."

Alec's grin widened.

"And it doesn't have to be permanent. You can find a different job after but this would let you be there legally while you looked. Or, until down the road if we decided to, you know, apply for a different type of visa."

A touch of awe registered in Alec's eyes, and his lips curved into that slow smile she loved. "And what kind of visa is that?"

She swallowed. Had she really said that part out loud?

Alec gave her a teasing grin with mock innocence. "L1, TN1?"

He was going to make her say it, wasn't he? "*No*, the other kind."

"Are you proposing to me, Wendy Deveaux?"

Her cheeks heated. "I... I'm just talking about possibilities. For our future."

His expression softened at her last words, and he ran a hand down her arm. Chills raced along her skin at the return of his touch after such a long, foolish absence.

"Last time I gave up too easily because I was scared. You were right."

"And now?"

"I'm still scared," she admitted. "But you're worth facing that fear. If you want me to go and forget about all this visa talk, I'll go. But if you let me work to earn your trust again, I'll do that as long as you'll let me."

Alec's eyes crinkled at the corners, and he leaned closer.

"And I'll even watch that *Making a Murderer* show with you. And put some of my hair tools under the sink in the bathroom so you have more room. You know, if we're in each other's spaces again."

Alec took her hand and stood, drawing her up with him until there were only inches between them. Having him so close once more sent sparks igniting all along her skin with the anticipation of his touch. Did this mean—?

He lowered his gaze to settle on hers, those sea glass eyes filled with tenderness and humor—and dare she even hope?—something more.

Yes. Yes, she did hope. No more tamping it down so she wouldn't end up disappointed. And she wanted this man in front of her more than anything else. There was something liberating in finally giving herself over to that. Her pulse thrilled.

"You've got some powdered sugar right here." His gaze heated as he dragged his thumb across her lower lip.

Her whole body trembled. His eyes moved to her mouth and back to her eyes again. Wendy swallowed around the lump in her throat. She leaned forward the tiniest fraction. Alec brushed the hair from her face and threaded his fingers through it until he cupped the back of her neck and pulled her to him with agonizing slowness. He kissed the corner of her mouth and then the other, her nerve endings lighting up at the exquisite touch that felt like home. Her breath came heavy as his mouth lingered bare centimeters from hers. She wanted more, so much more, but she'd wait until he was ready. Luckily, she didn't have to wait long.

He pressed his lips to hers, and emotion overcame her as he kissed her senseless, the world dissolving into nothing but the press of their bodies, which still remembered their way around each other even after all this time. Their breaths mingled and limbs tangled as they clutched each other so tight in the dance of you are mine and I am yours and this time I'll never let you go.

After a long moment, Alec leaned his forehead against hers. "I always want us to be in each other's space."

"I love you," Wendy said.

"Me, too," Alec said with a glint of mischief in his eyes.

Wendy whacked him on the arm and he nuzzled closer, chest shaking with laughter. He kissed her on the soft, sensitive spot below her ear, and she let out a sigh.

"I love you, too. I guess you're not the only stubborn one."

"Good thing." Her heart swelled with a flood of emotion: happiness, relief, a risk taken with a happy ending.

"Now about these movies you promised me," Alec said, the gleam still in his eyes.

"Really? You want to watch a movie. Right now?" Wendy trailed kisses up his neck and along the line of his jaw. She loved the groan this elicited.

"On second thought, that can wait. Maybe a long, long time."

EPILOGUE

Nine Months Later

"You ready to do this, kiddo?" Rob Deveaux said, looking rather dashing in his tuxedo. He offered his arm and beamed down at his only daughter.

Wendy nodded and linked her arm through his, and she smoothed her long ivory dress. Her chest fluttering, she cast a glance at the scene in front of them. The sun had just dipped below the horizon, casting the park and all of their gathered guests in a riot of sunset colors that reminded Wendy of the painting that now hung above the bed in the house she shared with Alec. Cicadas buzzed, and a light breeze cut through the September heat.

Her mom, escorted by Griffin, rounded the end of the petal-strewn aisle. When they took their seats, Alec was finally fully visible before her.

Below the tree where they'd shared their first kiss, Alec cut an impressive figure in his tux and bow tie—and suspenders he'd surprised her with. When he laid eyes on Wendy, his lips parted. His blue-green eyes glistened in the evening light as they met hers. A tug of connection warmed her from the inside out.

The brass band began that traditional song with New Orleans flair.

"I think that's our cue." Rob patted Wendy's arm.

Grass and rose petals crunched beneath her feet as they walked past their handful of gathered guests. On two seats in the front row sat a hiking backpack, a treasured possession of Alec's dad's, and a highlight reel of his mom's movie collection. Wendy had put them there herself, so Alec could feel the presence of his parents on this day, but at the moment, she hardly noticed them. Her unwavering gaze locked on Alec's.

Alec: The one who got her. The one who got away. And the one who was worth working through her fears for. It was hard to believe they'd made it this far, but her heart swelled with gratitude when her dad gave her away and she joined hands with Alec in front of the people who mattered most to both of them.

The preacher began the ceremony and ended with vows spoken through glistening eyes on both of their parts.

"You are my light and my family," Alec finished. "And I promise never to give up on us, and to never let you give up on yourself. You are worth weathering all the storms. I would even brave an alligator-nado for you."

Wendy squeezed his hand, and wanted to kiss him now, though it wasn't time yet. Instead, she looked him in the eyes and said the words she'd written for him. "I promise to always keep you supplied in hot sauce and make your family mine and mine yours. You are my best friend." Her voice broke. "I know I'm not always perfect. I have a temper and too many hair products and I'm stubborn and I sometimes leave laundry in the dryer for a whole week, but I promise whenever we disagree or whatever problems we come up against, I'm not going anywhere. We'll face it together."

In her peripheral vision, Wendy caught sight of Julie with tears running down her cheeks in her spot as maid of honor. Wendy and Alec looked at each other while the ring bearer searched for the rings, and then out at her mom and dad and Griffin and Aunt Angeline, Steve, the crew from the tour company, and a few friends. Alec's eyes tightened and flashed a momentary sadness as they rested on the two empty seats where his parents should have been. Wendy squeezed his hand, and he looked back at her, so full of love.

They slipped rings onto each other's fingers and joined their fates together. There would still be uncertainties in their lives. There might be loss and sorrow and disappointment, but there would also be love and private jokes—and whatever came at them, they would not have to do it alone.

"Who's ready for some ghost hunting?"

Wendy and Alec held up their phones, screens glowing with the landing page of their new app as the wedding party gathered around the limos that would take them to the reception at one of Kara's family's restaurants.

"Everybody downloaded and ready to go?" Alec asked. A chorus of cheers rang out. Their ghost-catching game app had finally been through beta testing. This would be the first preview before the official rollout after their honeymoon on Prince Edward Island.

"Okay first stop: Yo Mama's. Whoever catches the most ghosts on the way to the reception gets an open bar tab," Alec said.

"And whoever catches the least gets to clean our house before we get back from our honeymoon," Wendy said with a smirk. "Kidding. Kind of."

"Ready, go!" Alec said.

Everyone scrambled to their limos. As Wendy and Alec led the procession down the streets of the French Quarter, they clinked champagne glasses and stood to hang out the sunroof. The wind caught their hair in the lamp-lit evening.

Alec slipped an arm around her waist and pulled her into a soft, sweet kiss. The forward motion and wind on her cheeks and press of his body against hers was dizzying.

"This definitely doesn't suck," she said, smiling against his lips. Their car pulled to a stop.

"No, it doesn't." He trailed a hand up her back. His eyes crinkled at the corners in the way that she loved. Riding that warm, melty feeling, she kissed him again.

The other two limos parked behind them, spilling out the Deveauxs followed by Kara and her date and Steve, along with the rest of the tour crew. Laughter trailed behind their family as they jostled for position, ghost hunting down the street.

"Got one!" Griffin shouted.

"No fair, you already know where they all are!" someone else shouted with a shriek of laughter.

Wendy held Alec's gaze. Both of their smiles stretched to bursting.

Alec tipped his head toward their family and friends. "Shall we, my wife?"

Another surge of happiness consumed her. "I think so, my husband."

He ducked out the door and offered her his hand. "Come on. Let's go catch some ghosts."

THE END

Thank you for reading! For news on new releases, including my new Ghosted paranormal cozy mystery series, set in the same world as Ghosts of Midnights Past, visit www.jessicaarden.com and sign up for my newsletter.

Read on for an exceprt of the first book in the series:

Once Ghosted, Twice Shy.

Professor Pickett in the cafe with the Mardi Gras beads?

New Orleans ghost tour gift shop manager, Paige Harrington, makes a wish for her twenty-fifth birthday: to find the one thing she can be as passionate about as her cancer-curing scientist parents.

She doesn't, however, expect her calling to come in the form of a mysterious app on her phone that matches her up with the ghost of a cute bartender who wants her to solve his murder. Nor for her pet hedgehog, Auguste, to start talking to her with a French accent.

When her favorite professor turned cafe owner, Liz Pickett, is framed for the murder, Paige can't sit by and let all of this happen. Even if uncovering the truth means tangling with the Enclave, a secret society with the power and connections to make someone like her asking too many questions disappear without a trace.

With the Enclave and their dark secrets dogging at her heels, Paige will have to step up her sleuthing skills and unmask the real killer before she ends up their next victim.

EXCERPT OF ONCE GHOSTED, TWICE SHY

"Sometimes when opportunity knocks, it's with a polite hello. Other times, it's a sledgehammer through a wall leading to a secret passageway." -Matilda Mayhew, girl detective in *The Mystery of the Nine Hedgehogs*

"You *sure* this is for me?" I scrunched my eyebrows at the massive cardboard box on the delivery guy's hand truck.

He glanced at the manifest. "If you're Paige Harrington." His New Orleans accent was as thick as the bald cypress trunks in the bayou.

"That's me," I said. Paige Magnolia Harrington. Ghost tour gift shop manager, devoted friend, newly 25, and still with no idea what I wanted to do with my life.

"I actually have specific instructions that you're the only one who can sign for it," he said.

My eyebrow rose, and I sized up the enormous box currently blocking the main aisle of the Deveauxs' Historical Haunts gift shop. I briefly entertained the idea that my parents had sent a present — something to atone for the last-minute cancellation of their trip to visit me this weekend—but quickly discarded it. Their newest scientific breakthrough at work had come up unexpectedly. They'd hardly have planned ahead for an apology gift.

Not to mention that whatever the package contained was big enough to be a refrigerator or an arcade game. Anything like that they would've sent to my house.

"Hmmm," I said. I tried to shake it, then leaned my ear against the box. Heavy. Solid. No chirping. Phew.

The delivery guy adjusted his hat and looked at me like I was a few specters short of a ghost tour.

"The last unexpected package I accepted was a bulk delivery of live crickets," I explained. "It was supposed to go to a reptile exhibition in town. Only when I was calling to have it picked up, my co-worker peeked inside and accidentally unleashed a plague of biblical proportions on our little shop here." I wasn't exactly eager to repeat that experience.

Norman, ghost tour operator, friend, and unleasher of the aforementioned cricket plague leaped from the next aisle. His top hat slanted over his flop of wavy brown hair and pale face. "Don't accept it! It's a Trojan horse."

A smile tugged at my lips. Norman was an odd bird with a penchant for conspiracy theories and vampire novels, but a good sort otherwise. "I'm pretty sure we're safe from invading armies."

Norman lowered his voice melodramatically. "Or are we?"

The delivery guy looked at us like dealing with us was above his pay grade. "Nothing live in here or it'd have a special sticker. Where do you want it?"

"Storeroom, I guess." It was the only place in the shop big enough to hold whatever this was.

Once I'd signed for the package, I pulled off the tape, but struggled with the flaps of the awkward box. Norman appeared a few minutes later, slapped a box cutter into my hand and saluted. "I'll watch the shop while you uncover the secrets." He disappeared back into the shop with something that sounded like, "Godspeed."

After wrestling the cardboard off and removing the foam pieces packed around it, I regarded the hulking thing with even more questions than answers.

A large carnival-style fortune telling machine stared back at me. But instead of Zoltar inside the glass, wearing a chintzy wrap and looking crafty, this fortune teller resembled Madame Sophia, the famous NOLA psychic wrongly accused of murder and recently exonerated.

I got on the phone with Julie, one of my bosses, who also happened to be Sophia's granddaughter-in-law. "Hey, did you guys order a fortune telling machine for the shop with Madame Sophia inside?"

"No. Why?"

"Because there's one sitting here, and it came addressed to me, of all people."

"That's odd. Maybe it's from one of your admirers," Julie teased.

I snorted. "This is a pretty unusual gift to come from a stranger. Should I take her to dinner or buy her a fortune telling machine?" I balanced my hands like scales. "Fortune telling machine."

"Really makes a statement, I'll give it that."

"Maybe we can put it out front to attract more walk-by traffic."

"Sure. Hey, I gotta run. Text me a picture of it and let me know if you find out any more about the mysterious origins."

"Oh. My. Stars." Norman peeked in again and took in the fortune teller in all of her purple, gauzy glory. He covered his mouth. "Have you tried it yet?"

"Already abandoned your Trojan horse theory?"

Apparently so, because he was unwinding the cord from the back of the machine. The bare bulbs around the glass casing flashed to life, and an envelope fluttered to the ground.

I had to admit, the odd wonder of it all gave me a little thrill. There is nothing I loved more in the world than a mystery. Besides, I could use something to focus on other than my traffic jam of a life.

I lunged for the fallen envelope. Maybe it would hold the answers I sought.

On the outside, in vaguely familiar handwriting I couldn't place, someone had scrawled *Paige Magnolia Harrington*. Hmmm. Whoever had gifted this to me knew my middle name. Not that it wasn't public record somewhere.

Probably. Inside, a thick cream paper merely said *welcome*. I squinted at the tiny cartoon drawing of a ghost at the bottom of the paper.

"Welcome to what?" Norman read over my shoulder.

I frowned. "That's the question, isn't it?"

Mannequin Sophia's heavily glittered eyelids blinked, and her plastic jaw opened and closed. "Pull the lever and make a wish," a mystical voice said.

Another thrill zipped down my spine. Something about this felt oddly inevitable. And right, somehow.

I pulled the lever.

A ball rolled through a metal maze behind Sophia.

OK, Paige Magnolia, make your wish. I sucked in a breath and thought of the way I'd felt growing up with parents who were passionate, so young, and were currently literally working on a cure for cancer. About how my friend Ines lit up at anything that involved planning or hacking into complex systems. About seeing how so many of my sorority sisters had found their "it" thing in life when I'd attended our alumnae luncheon last month.

And then there was me. Twenty-five, working in a ghost tour gift shop, and going home to my hedgehog for company. Granted, I had a lot of treasured friendships and positive things going for me. And I was *good* at managing the gift shop. My meticulous eye for details most people missed came in handy here. But it wasn't that thing that lit me up, not how my parents had their research. It ached sometimes, that hole inside of me where my phantom calling, a way I could help change the world for the better, should go.

Mannequin Sophia's arm swept across the space, and lights chased each other around the cabinet. Just a silly machine. Not a real fortune teller with the power to grant me a calling, I reminded myself.

A card dropped into the slot at the bottom of the machine. My fingers trembled when I snatched it up.

Chapter 2

Instead of a fortune, the machine spit out a tarot card. I retrieved it from the slot and squinted at the dismal-looking illustration. The Tower, this one read. Lightning flashed across the card. The requisite tower loomed in the background, flames gouting from its windows. In the foreground, people fell from the sky to their demise.

I shuddered. "Well, aren't you the worst fortune telling machine that ever was?"

Despite carrying the cards and other sorts of divination items in the shop, I was no expert on their meanings. However, it didn't take a genius to see this wasn't a warm and fuzzy portent. If the card's scenario foretold "my thing," that was a firm "no, thank you" from me.

I sighed. Maybe I'd just double down on being the best darn gift shop manager ever.

I handed Norman the card. "Know anything about tarot?"

He shook his head. "Dude, whatever you wished for, I don't think you're going to get it."

I mulled over where the mysterious machine could've come from for the remaining fifteen minutes of my shift. Wendy Deveaux, one of the owners of Deveauxs' Historical Haunts, blustered in with a flurry of long red hair and stompy boots.

"All ready for your awards gala this weekend?" I asked.

Wendy groaned. "Don't remind me. I'm only going to that ceremony to humor Alec." They were both being honored at the Crescent City Forty Under Forty gala for an app she and her husband had developed together. It was sort of like *Pokemon Go* for French Quarter ghosts.

Wendy could be grumpy and snarky at times, but was also competent and would do absolutely anything for her family and long-time staff, which now included me. She'd seemed perpetually annoyed with me for the first three months I'd worked here, but I had a hunch from the start there was a squishy marshmallow center inside her cactus exterior. Turns out I was right.

Her, "What the hell is this monstrosity?" from the back room told me she wasn't behind the delivery either.

Could it be a prank? A custom-made machine like this made for a pretty expensive prank.

"I wouldn't try that thing unless you like your forecast cloudy with a chance of apocalypse," I said.

Wendy pushed the lever anyway, but nothing happened. She shrugged. "Guess it only gives fortunes if there's bad news. You heading out?"

"Yeah, I'm meeting my old professor, Liz, at Crumbles around 5:30."

Liz was my favorite professor from college and had become my mentor and something like my cool aunt. We had a standing puzzle night every other week at the cafe she opened a few years back with her late sister.

After poking and prodding at the wooden cabinet for any hidden compartments or more clues to its origin, I went to text Liz I was on my way.

A notification I didn't recognize popped up.

You have a match, it said next to an icon of a ghost.

I cocked my head and clicked the notification. My screen flashed purple, and an icon of a cartoon ghost wearing a Sherlock Holmes hat and sporting a magnifying glass for a mouth appeared.

Weird. Did one of my old apps get rebranded? With the "matched" language, I wondered if this was a revamped dating app for people on New Orleans ghost tours. That was actually not a bad idea.

Clicking on the waiting matches notification took me to a screen with two buttons to choose from: *Fresh* and *Cold.*

My nose wrinkled. *I'll take my dates fresh, please.*

Swipe up to accept. Swipe down to reject, the directions said.

The screen populated with tiny pictures, some in black and white and others in color. I squinted. In one photo I recognized the cute, if a little too surfer dude-esque guy who worked at the daiquiri bar down the street. He always waved to me as I walked by. Sometimes we exchanged flirtatious banter, but we'd never formally introduced ourselves.

I clicked on his picture, which had a purple star in the top right corner. The bartender looked back at me with his floppy sun-kissed hair, tan-bronzed white skin, and lazy grin. Austin Des Jardins, the caption read. Occupation: bartender.

That was it. No profile about how he loved baby sharks and fast cars and wanted someone who wouldn't play games.

Wait, one more thing remained when I scrolled down further: DOD: yesterday. What the heck was DOD in this context? Duke of Daiquiris? Director of Denial? Date of Death?

I laughed a little at that, but shifted in my chair to fight the unease that accompanied the thought.

After a second, a message bubble popped up with a heart and a ghost emoji.

You and Austin are a match! Austin would like to communicate with you. Swipe up to accept.

Without thinking it through, I swiped up. Any caution I'd retained from my southern upbringing had long been thwarted by years at boarding school, being left to my own devices and following my curiosity, sometimes to unpleasant ends.

Aww, son of a stroopwafel, had I just downloaded the mother of all malware on my phone?

Three dots bounced on the screen. Anticipation pinged around my insides like the balls in the vampire pin-ball machine next door.

Austin: *Hey*

I rolled my eyes. Really?

The three dots bounced again.

Austin: *Sorry. New at this. Hit send before I finished my message. It's nice to see a familiar face on here.*

I had no idea u did this sort of thing. But then again, you work at a ghost tour place, so maybe I should have suspected.

What was *that* supposed to mean?

Austin: *So, anyway. You're the only one on here who doesn't look intimidating and might be friendly enough to give me a chance. Plus, I've always thought you seemed tough. I like that.*

Tough. Huh. That was a new one. I sat up straighter. Most people took one look at me: white, blonde-haired, blue eyed with brightly colored clothes and wrote me off as sweet, compliant, and harmless. At least until they knew me better.

Austin: *What do you say, want to team up?*

Okay, clearly I was missing something here. This was light years from Austin's smooth flirty charms. He sounded hesitant, almost backed into a corner to find someone. I highly doubted he was hurting for dates.

But before I could give it further thought, a scream pierced the air.

Chapter 3

I fumbled the phone, my thumb swiping up the screen, and ran outside after Wendy to see about the commotion.

Norman lay sprawled in the street, one of his legs bent at an odd angle.

I crouched next to him, jostling his fallen top hat adorned with ribbon and skeleton hands. A few feet away, the wheels of an upside-down skateboard still spun.

"Are you okay? What the heck happened?" My gaze swept over him, landing on—oh no, was that bone?—peeking out from a tear in his black jeans. I swallowed and looked away to keep from losing my lunch all over him.

Dozens of bystanders on our heart-of-the-French-Quarter street waiting for their tour to start looked on under the street lamps, murmuring and chattering to each other.

"Someone lent me their skateboard. Wiped out warming up the crowd."

Wendy already had the paramedics on the phone.

"Next time, maybe just stick to the vampire jokes," I said.

He grinned and tried to stand. I caught his leg before he pushed too far and caused even more damage. "Easy."

"Speaking of next time, think you could take over my tour for tonight?"

And that's how I ended up leading a ghost tour down Chartres St. that Friday night. Even though I'd hardly dressed for the occasion. Most of my coworkers rocked a sort of goth chic look, lots of black lace, top hats, and skull accessories. And here I was in my cheery pink sundress and strappy heels. I pinned a black lace fascinator with a pink skull in my hair to look a bit more the part.

I'd lament the heels part of filling in for Norman after our mile and a half trek through the Quarter, though.

Still, I carried on, until we arrived across from the old Ursuline convent with its white French-colonial facade. In the early evening light, the shadows played on the gray shutters and manicured hedges.

We stopped across the street under the purple and cream awning of Crumbles bakery where I should've been having coffee with Liz right now. I peeked into the window and waved to her. She delivered coffees to a table full of customers and tucked a lock of her shiny black hair with its single streak of gray behind her ear. She wiped her hands on her apron and gave me a warm smile and wave. I felt bad all over again for bailing on her tonight. Since her sister had passed away earlier this year, she'd tucked into herself and did little besides work.

But as much as I'd like to be in there having puzzle night, I turned back to my tour group.

"So, the Ursuline convent that you see across the street is one of the oldest buildings in New Orleans. And one filled with the most secrets." I paused for dramatic effect. I could be a performer too if the occasion called for it. "If you're into vampire lore, you may already know the story of the Casket Girls."

I told the story of the young women who'd arrived from Quebec in 1728 with nothing but coffin-shaped caskets of belongings, set to stay with the nuns in the Ursuline convent until they were married off and were later rumored to be vampires.

"But there are legends of even more secrets buried under the oldest standing building in the city," I said. I mentally rubbed my hands together, getting to my favorite part. "Has anyone ever heard of the Enclave?"

"That's the secret society, right?" A mustached gentleman who looked distinctly like a math teacher asked.

"A splinter of the Illuminati or something," said another tourist.

"That's right. There have been whispers about the Enclave running the power structure in New Orleans for hundreds of years. Secret underground meetings. A deal with the devil. Ritual sacrifices in exchange for power and riches beyond their wildest imaginings."

"Where do I sign up?" a guy in a Red Sox jersey asked, drawing laughter from the rest of the group.

"You don't go to the Enclave. The Enclave comes to you," I said. "Rumors abound of secret invitations, lavish vetting parties, and for the chosen few who prove worthy of initiation, the granting of their deepest wish."

"You just have to sell your soul, right?" Red Sox guy joked.

"So the stories go," I said.

I'd long wondered how much truth lay behind the shrouds of mystery. Growing up on my great grandmother's mystery novels, I'd been obsessed with the idea of the secret passages under the French Quarter and had spent more than a few nights in college searching for signs of them after a few cocktails.

Just as I was about to get into the fabled network of secret tunnels underfoot and the ghosts of the Enclave that haunted them, something heavy crashed from the balcony to the awning above my head.

I flung my arms out and stepped back to protect my group. Something large thudded at my feet.

No, not something, some*one.*

A person falling from the sky. Or rather, from the upstairs balcony. The similarity to the creepy Tower card wasn't lost on me.

Heart hammering, and breath hitching all over the place, I knelt to check for a pulse and see how much damage had been done.

All my thoughts jumbled, and weird disjointed bits of observation hit my senses before I could process it all. Nice dark washed jeans and a blue button-up shirt. The smell of garlic and cherries overpowering the street smells of red beans and rice. Shrieks from behind me. I was afraid to look at his face. I maneuvered his shoulder, so he lay flat on his back.

I held two fingers to his neck to check for a pulse. Icy cold seeped into my fingers at the touch. Bruising and puffing mottled the surrounding skin like a macabre necklace. I waited and waited, willing his heart to beat, but nothing came.

That's when I finally allowed my attention to shift to his face.

I did a double take. One of his cheeks pressed to the dirty street; the other faced upward. Prickles of dread raised the hairs on my neck as I pushed the hair off of his forehead.

No. No. No.

His left eye had swollen shut. He was missing the flirtatious smile, but this was definitely Austin Des Jardins. The same guy from the daiquiri bar that I'd been mysteriously "matched" with on that Ghosted app.

"Austin?" My voice came out with a squeak, halfway between a statement and a question. He was so young, barely older than me, if I had to guess, with so much life ahead of him. I wondered if he'd had a chance at a calling of his own before his untimely death.

"Hey Paige." Austin's familiar voice answered with a somber note.

I jolted.

My palm flew to my heart, then I held it out in front of his mouth, waiting for breath. Maybe I'd made a mistake before. But none came.

A cool breeze floated over my neck and shoulders, lifting the hair from my nape. A cool that was out of place in the sweltering Louisiana summer.

That's when I realized the voice had actually come from behind me. Goosebumps paraded up my arms again.

Sirens wailed in the distance. Good. Hopefully, someone called 911.

I spun around, standing in the process. Hovering just above me was a perfect copy of the now-dead body on the street. Only this one was bleached of color, and I could see right through him to the tables and cases of muffins and pies in the cafe.

Ghost Austin gave me a sheepish smile and tucked his hands into his incorporeal pockets. "So, thanks for taking my case."

My knees wobbled, and my vision swayed. I pitched backward. The world went black.

To read on, get Once Ghosted, Twice Shy here: https://jessi-caarden.com/books/cozymystery/onceghostedtwiceshy/

ACKNOWLEDGEME

Thank you so much to everyone who helped bring this book into being. First, to my beta reader extraordinaires: Jennie Booth, G.G. Andrew, Amanda Gale, Lindsay Wright, Sandra Hume, and Jeanna Bini, thanks for your thoughtful comments, helping me streamline Wendy and Alec's story and pointing out the actual rules of Uno (thanks, Jennie!). Thank you also to Amanda Gale for the fabulous job copy editing.

In addition, huge thanks to all of the ladies of Binderhaüs 2017 for all of your ideas and laughter during our hot tub plot tub party and making sure this book had some actual conflict. You guys complete me.

I'm also grateful to all of my writing communities both online and in person, particularly BFoRW and LVRWA and my writing partner in crime, Sheryl Greenblatt, all of whom continually fill my well and make me stronger.

A huge shoutout also goes to all of you reading. Kayla, Jinhee, Abby, Becca, Katrina, Lai, Nate, Jenny, Jenny, Jennie, Laure, Vicki, Debbie, Binder friends, and so many more, thank you for sharing and/or reviewing my books and being such a source of support during this writing journey.

Thanks to everyone who helped with research for Ghosts of Midnights Past. Deborah Wilde was a tremendous source of help on all things Canadian and Vancouver-related to help with Alec's background. My husband Paul helped with City Park New Orleans background and was game for a trip to the beautiful city of Vancouver for our anniversary and also to do some fact checking. My brother-in-law Michael helped with medical questions relating to Wendy's dad's heart condition. (Note: I still took some heart-attack timeline liberties for plot reasons; all mistakes are my own on that front.) My dad Jon, picked out all of the classic cars that Wendy's mom fixes up in the book. And Danita Britton from my newsletter group is responsible for the name of Wendy's favorite band, Rougarou.

And last but not least, the biggest of thank yous to my family: my parents, in-laws, siblings, grandparents, aunts, uncles, cousins, and my husband and boys. You've all been unfailingly supportive and willing to make sacrifices for me. Thanks for giving me the gift of time to nurture my need to write. I love you all.

ALSO BY

Also by Jessica Arden

Cozy Mystery

The Ghosted Cozy Mystery Series

Once Ghosted, Twice Shy (Book 1)

Romance

The Skeptics' Guide to Love Duet

The Skeptics' Guide to the Mysteries of the Universe (Book 1)

Ghosts of Midnights Past (Book 2)

Vegas Strong Collection

Collide

About the Author

About the Author

Jessica Arden writes cozy mysteries, and quirky contemporary romance, usually with a supernatural twist. She's stomped grapes in her native California, hiked 350 miles on an ancient pilgrimage route in Spain, had breakfast with a coatimundi in Costa Rica, and spent the night in a monastery. But no matter where life takes her, her true north will always be with her husband and two energetic boys.

Jessica's short fiction has appeared in *Woman's World* and various anthologies.

When she's not writing, you can find Jessica teaching, dabbling in design projects, crafting, collecting tarot cards, burrowing down a new research rabbit hole, and of course, finding and hanging out with her community of kindred spirits.